Sophie Fournier is the first woman drafted into the North American Hockey League. Playing hockey is something she's done all her life, but she faces new challenges as she finds her place on the struggling Concord Condors. She has to prove herself better than her rival-turned-teammate, Michael Hayes, and her rival-turned-friend, Dmitri Ivanov, and she has to do it all with a smile.

If she's successful then she opens the door to other women being drafted. She can't afford to think about what happens if she fails. All she knows is this: if she's not the best then she doesn't get to play.

No pressure, though.

BREAKING THE ICE

Sophie Fournier, Book One

K.R. Collins

A NineStar Press Publication

Published by NineStar Press
P.O. Box 91792,
Albuquerque, New Mexico, 87199 USA.
www.ninestarpress.com

Breaking the Ice

Printed in the USA
First Edition
March, 2019

Print ISBN: 978-1-950412-34-1

Also available in eBook, ISBN: 978-1-950412-21-1

Chapter One

TODAY, SHE MAKES history.

As Sophie Fournier takes her seat among the other prospects and their families in the Denver, Colorado stadium, soft boos reach her ears. A glance at the large screen behind the stage shows the cameras are trained on her.

She keeps her expression neutral. Many of the athletes here blame her for the lockout that ground last season to a halt. The North American Hockey League had other things to discuss than whether or not women should be permitted to play, but she makes an easy target.

The boos grow louder, and Sophie squares her shoulders to absorb the abuse. This time, however, the cameras are directed at the Commissioner as he steps up to the podium at center stage.

Someone they hate more than me, she thinks as the Commissioner approaches the microphone. He's a stout man whose face is shiny under the bright lights. His hair is greased and styled like a hockey player but that's as close as he's ever come to being one. He spends his days behind a desk and tells the players how they should act, how much they're allowed to be paid, how many years they're allowed to sign for and then demands they be grateful for his interference.

It's no wonder he isn't popular.

Her only crime is daring to be good at hockey. There were other paths she could've taken—the burgeoning NAWHL, one of the European leagues which already accepts women—but she wants the NAHL.

And she's too talented for them to keep her out.

If it weren't for the stupid rules, she could be drafted first overall today. As it is, the Concord Condors are the only team eligible to draft women. As a concession to team owners who thought the Commissioner stretched the limits of his authority by granting women access to the League, teams had to apply for co-ed status.

And because hockey isn't known for its risk-taking, only Concord applied for that status. The consensus is they don't have anything to lose. Everyone's attention will be on Concord this season and the Sophie Fournier Experiment. If it goes well, then other teams in the League will draft women.

If it doesn't, then Sophie will have the dubious honor of being the first, and only, woman drafted into the NAHL.

Seattle's management files on stage to make the first selection of the 2011 draft, and she's forced to listen as they select Eldon Carruthers. He's a center, same as her, selected by a team in desperate need of a franchise player.

It could've been me, she thinks as Carruthers pulls on the blue and green jersey of the Seattle Seafarers. *It* should've *been me*. But another woman will have the honor of being drafted first overall. All Sophie can be is the first.

As Seattle files off the stage, Sophie sits up straighter in her seat, because Concord has the second overall pick at the draft. They're a team in need of someone to step in and turn them around. She's been a difference maker all her life. They'll select her, give her a chance at her dreams, and in return she'll bring them the Maple Cup for the first time in franchise history.

Martin Pauling, the owner of the Condors, leads the procession onto the stage. When he steps up to the podium, Sophie's breath catches in her throat. This is what years of hard work have come to. This is the moment which makes every bag skate, every bruise, and every nasty hit worth it.

"With the second pick of the draft, we proudly select, from the Weston School, Michael Hayes."

Sophie's expression freezes.

Hayes?

They've been rivals for the past four years while she played for Chilton Academy, and she's beaten him every year in the scoring race and in the playoffs. She's better than him.

And Concord picked him instead of her.

Next to her Colby, her brother, nudges her knee, reminding her to breathe. She claps politely in case there are any cameras on her and reminds herself the day is far from over. Concord has a pick in the second round and two picks in the third. There's still time.

Concord doesn't select her in the second round.

They don't select her with their first third round pick.

They don't select her with their second one either.

The first day of the draft ends without her making history. *There's still tomorrow*, she tells herself. *It should've been today*. Doubt creeps in, insidious and poisoning her thoughts. What if she isn't drafted at all?

What if the production made of this draft has been part of an elaborate setup? What if all the media attention and hype focused on her has been to make an example out of her? Don't hope. Don't dream. Women aren't allowed.

"Hotel," her dad says, gruff, once the draft is officially over for the day.

Tomorrow, rounds four through seven will take place for a total of two hundred twenty-four prospects selected. She's no longer sure she'll be one of them.

"I'll meet you there," Sophie says. She stands and smooths imaginary wrinkles out of her suit. As much as she wants to wash off her makeup and mess up her hair and hide out in her hotel room, her responsibilities aren't over. There are cameras to smile for and reporters to talk to even if the conversation they're about to have is far from the one she was hoping for this evening.

She hugs her parents and then her older brother, clinging to him for an extra moment. Colby is the reason she started playing hockey in the first place. He's a goalie and, like any older sibling, drafted her into helping him be better. He was the one who taught her to skate, shoving her feet into a pair of his old skates when she could barely walk. A couple of years later, he taught her to shoot then made her practice on him over and over.

She's improved more than he has over the years, but he never resented her for it. He's always been there for her, and he's here for her now, steady and strong, lending her the support she needs to make it through the next hour.

"We could sneak you out," Colby offers. "Just like old times, eh?"

More times than she can count, Sophie has put on a fake jersey and jammed a baseball cap over her French braid to avoid people after a game; the other team, pissed they'd lost, parents angry their sons were beaten by a girl, sometimes even parents of her own teammates who thought she was stealing the spotlight from their sons.

Sophie laughs and squeezes her brother's shoulders as she steps back. "I thought we said no more of that."

"Text me when you get back to your room, and we can watch shitty TV."

It's a sign of how rattled her mom is by the draft that she doesn't scold Colby for his language. Sophie leaves her family to make their way back to the hotel before she takes them up on their offer to sneak her out.

She heads out to the concourse. During the season, this area will be full of fans looking to see the Denver Boulders play. Right now, it's packed just as full but with prospects in suits and their parents and reporters being trailed by their cameramen and women.

The National Sports Network is the first to spot her. A man whose press credentials hang from a "NAHL DRAFT 2011" lanyard thrusts his microphone in her face. "Are you worried you won't be drafted? In all the buildup, people forgot there's no requirement for co-ed teams to have a girl on them."

Sophie's fingers hook in the pockets of her suit. She wants to shove them all the way in, to hide in whatever small way she can, but her mom's voice echoes in her ears. *Don't slouch, sweetie. Stand tall and proud. You never back down on the ice, don't back down off it either.* And her mom is right. Sophie has faced guys trying to end her career with a big hit or a vicious slash to her wrists. A man with a microphone isn't someone to cower from.

"I've presented my résumé to the NAHL. They've seen my video, my stats, and, like the other top prospects, I went to the Combine. There's nothing for me to do but wait and see."

"How do you feel about the Condors selecting your long-time rival Michael Hayes in the first round instead of you?"

"Hayes is a two-way forward who's strong on the puck. He can contribute on the power play and the penalty kill." Sophie leaves out how he always had an extra check or slash for her when they played each other. She doesn't say she outscored him in all four years they competed against each other or that she won three Werner Cups to his zero while she played for Chilton Academy.

She doesn't say how much it stings to see him picked ahead of her. She has the numbers to prove she's the better player and she was still passed over. What more does she have to do to be taken seriously?

Carol Rogers from *After the Whistle* sees Sophie and hurries over, her cameraman in tow. *After the Whistle* is on following every Canadian broadcast to break down the game. Sophie grew up watching Carol interview players and dissect their games and point out how they could be better. She watched and she learned, adjusting her own game based on some of the things Carol saw.

And now Carol Rogers stands in front of her and asks, "Is it true Concord is exploiting how they're the only co-ed team to draft you later than you were projected?"

Sophie, normally unfazed by the media, is caught off guard by the question. She flounders long enough that four other reporters flock to her, sensing a headline if not an entire story.

"I'm sorry, what?" Sophie asks.

Carol pushes closer, battling for space. "No other team is allowed to draft you. Can you comment on the speculation that Concord will use it to their advantage?"

Could they? Of course they could. Hockey is a business. Sophie's thoughts threaten to spin away from her. She wants to cling to the hope being offered—they're biding their time, she *will* be drafted even if wasn't today—and she wants to stomp her feet at how unfair it is.

Instead, she smiles, bland and practiced, the expression giving nothing away. "I can't comment on that. I'm not privy to the decisions made by Concord's management."

"You haven't been assured of your place on the team?" another reporter asks. "It would be anti-climactic for the first draft with a woman to end without the first woman being drafted."

"There are no guarantees in hockey. If you'll excuse me, I need to head back to the hotel now. Enjoy the rest of your evening."

AS SOON AS she's safely in her hotel room, she turns the deadbolt and hooks the door chain. Only then does she allow her shoulders to slump. She wrestles her suit jacket off and tosses it on her bed. She kicks her shoes against the wall and feels a small spark of satisfaction when they hit. But it's only a spark and it doesn't catch, instead, fizzling and leaving her exhausted.

This isn't how she's supposed to feel after the first day of the draft.

She's supposed to be elated, high off finally realizing her dream. She's wanted to play in the NAHL since she was a girl watching the Montreal Mammoths play while visiting her *mémé* and *pépé*. As a special treat, she would be allowed to stay up late enough to watch a whole game. Sometimes, she would fall asleep during second intermission, but her *mémé* would always wake her up for the third period so she didn't miss any of the action.

The players seemed larger than life on the small TV. They delivered booming hits and clutch goals. Her *mémé* talked about the players as if they were part of the family. *Oh, Bobby? He had a good game last night, but he looks tired tonight. Someone needs to feed the boy better.* Or, *If Gabriel doesn't score in this period, then I will call up his coach and have him benched for the third. Don't think I won't.*

Her *pépé* passed away a couple years ago, but she bets her *mémé* watched the draft tonight. Is she as disappointed as Sophie is? Did she shake her fist at the TV and threaten to send Concord's management to their rooms?

She opens the mini-fridge and surveys its contents. There are tiny bottles of alcohol and an assortment of candy bars. Snickers are her favorite and there are even two of them, but she closes the fridge without taking either one out. There are too many reporters here this weekend. Someone will get their hands on the bill for her room, and she doesn't need an article written on how the Condors passed on her because she doesn't have the diet of an elite athlete.

The collar of her shirt presses against her throat as if it's trying to choke her. She undoes the top few buttons, but it doesn't make it any easier to breathe.

Two seasons ago, Chilton beat The Weston School in a five game playoff series 3-2. The series started nasty and grew nastier with each game. The next season, their first game was against The Weston School, and they picked up where they left off, playing as if it was Game Six of last year's series.

Hayes crunched Sophie into the boards behind the goal less than three minutes into the game, and she fell to the ice and struggled to breathe as the away crowd cheered and hoped she wouldn't get back to her feet.

She feels the same way now, knocked off balance and gasping for air while everyone around her hopes she stays down.

She hangs her suit up in the small closet next to her second suit, the one she brought in case she spilled something on this one.

Now, she'll need it for tomorrow.

She closes the closet door so she doesn't have to look at the suit. She digs her Chilton sweatpants out of the dresser drawer. They're from her first year on the team, almost worn through at the knees after so many years of wearing them. They're tight across her ass, because she got them when she was fourteen, and she's spent the past four years putting on the muscle she'd need to succeed in a professional hockey league.

They're comfortable, though, and she pairs them with a tank top and a shirt with sleeves so long she can pull them over her hands. She flops down on her bed with her phone and, against her better judgement, checks the NAHL Twitter.

A picture of Carruthers, Hayes, and Almonte pops up. They're in their new jerseys, Seattle, Concord, and Boston, and they're all wearing giant smiles. And they should be. They're the top three draft picks for this year.

She should've been one of them.

A knock at her door makes her turn her head, but she doesn't move from her bed.

A moment later, her phone buzzes.

COLBY: *Open your door.*

She rolls out of bed and undoes all the locks to let her brother in. He's changed into sweats too, green with large white letters that say UND. He's been a steady goalie for North Dakota, but he's entering his senior year of college and there's been no professional interest. In all likelihood, his hockey career will end after this season.

A wave of guilt hits her as she realizes she's been wallowing because she wasn't drafted on the first day when her brother was never even invited.

"Stop that," Colby says, because all goalies have freaky mind-reading abilities. He ducks under her arm to slip into the room. "Dad wanted to come, but I figured you didn't want him here right now."

"I don't."

It's a betrayal of the worst kind, because Dad's the one who has believed in her this whole time. He's the one who relentlessly campaigned for her to play with the boys. He's the one who worked overtime to make sure she had the hockey equipment she needed to be successful, then stayed up late to put her through drill after drill so she'd be able to play at any level she wanted.

But he's also the one who doesn't like it when she cries, because hockey players are supposed to be tough.

She sits down next to her brother on her bed and pulls her knees up to her chest. Tears well up in her eyes, but she doesn't fight them. "I don't understand. I'm *good*, Colb."

"You're the best," he tells her.

If you're not the best, then you don't get to play. She was five the first time her dad told her that. It was as true then as it is now. She has had to battle every step of the way as she carved out a play for herself in this sport. It's bullshit that being a woman is what kept her from being drafted first. And it's bullshit that it's kept her from being drafted so far. If she was a man, then she'd be a Seafarer right now. She wants to scream or maybe punch something.

Instead, she leans against her brother. "I wish Concord believed it."

"Maybe they do. I heard they might be using the rules to their advantage. No one else can draft you so there's no pressure on them and hockey—"

"Is a business," she finishes with him. She sighs.

Colby pulls a Snickers out of his pocket. "I figured you weren't going to touch anything in your room."

"*You're* the best," she says as she takes the chocolate bar from him.

"And don't you forget it." He takes the piece she offers him. "They're going to draft you, and you're going to tear up this fucking League."

Chapter Two

THE BREAKFAST ROOM is half-full of sleepy athletes clutching mugs of coffee when Sophie takes a plate and goes through the buffet line. There were cameras who watched her work out this morning in the hotel's small fitness center, and there are even more here now, watching as she puts together a balanced plate: a premade omelet, two sausage patties, two pieces of toast with peanut butter, a bowl of fresh fruit, and a plain yogurt.

"Yo, Sophie!" Travis Mollett, one of her Chilton teammates, stands up and waves his arms above his head to catch her attention. He was one of her wingers, and he's sitting with Shawn Wedin, a defenseman, and the only other Chilton player at this year's draft.

The last time she saw them both, their hair was peroxide blond for their Werner Cup run. She refused to go completely blonde, dip dyeing the tip of her ponytail instead, another inch for each round of the playoffs they reached. She's long since cut her hair, and they're both back to their natural colors, but she still sees them and thinks *team* and *winning*.

"Big day today," she says as she joins them at their table. Neither of them was drafted yesterday, but it would've been a surprise if they had. They're both solid players, but not the kind who would go in the top three rounds.

They aren't franchise players the way Sophie's supposed to be. She's been tasked with the same thing on every team she's played for: lead them to a championship. She's never resented the responsibility or buckled under the expectations. Concord, an expansion team that hasn't even made the playoffs in their sixteen-year history, is desperate for a difference maker.

She'll be that difference maker; they just have to draft her.

"Yeah," Travis says. He has a mound of eggs on one plate and an even bigger pile of bacon on a second. His gaze darts about the room, and his narrow shoulders are pulled up close to his ears.

"You're a good player. Plenty of teams will see."

"Thanks, Cap."

"I'm not your captain anymore." She was for three years, and he was even one of her alternates their senior year. "But I will be the one clapping the loudest when they call your name."

"Louder than my mom?" He laughs. "You always have to be the best at everything."

If you're not the best, then you don't get to play.

Travis misses the way her smile slips. He takes a big gulp of his orange juice. "I can't believe you're with us this morning." He winces as soon as his brain catches up to his mouth. "I'm sorry. That was—"

Sophie waves off his apology. "I get it." She didn't expect to be with them this morning either, but she can't say that. She can't come off as cocky or ungrateful. As the first woman in the draft she has to be gracious, approachable, and apparently stand silently as she's undervalued. *One day, there will be enough women in the NAHL that we can speak out. We'll have a firecracker of a forward and a hard-hitting defensewoman.* That isn't Sophie's role. Being the first means she clears the path for those who follow behind her. They can push the envelope in ways she can't.

"At least you have the NAWHL if you aren't drafted," Shawn says. "It must be nice to have a backup plan."

Sophie dips her cantaloupe in her yogurt and chews slowly so she doesn't have to talk. The North American Women's Hockey League isn't a backup. It's a professional league in its own right, but she's decided if she can't be the first woman in the NAHL, then she'll play overseas. Ever since last year's lockout when she realized there might not be a NAHL to be drafted into, let alone that one would accept her, she told her agent to put out feelers to the European leagues. Most of them have been co-ed for years. The Swedish Hockey League is her first choice if she can't play here.

She doesn't say that. Instead she tells Shawn, "You'll be drafted."

She talks up the strengths of his game and it almost feels like they're in the locker room before a championship game. That's when she'd go stall to stall, giving her teammates what they needed. For some it was a clasp to the shoulder or a friendly facewash. Others needed to hear the game plan one last time. Shawn always needed a reminder that he deserved to be on the ice with them.

It's a role she embraced, but sometimes she wishes there was someone to give *her* a pep talk.

"I think *TNSN* is creeping on us," Travis says. "Do you want to give them a show?"

Before Sophie can say, "Absolutely not," Travis shoves four strips of bacon into his mouth and chews so obnoxiously not a single camera lingers on their table. Sophie can't help her laugh. She covers her mouth, but it's obvious the way her shoulders shake.

Travis grins, spraying bits of bacon everywhere, and gives her a thumbs-up.

SOPHIE SITS BETWEEN her mom and dad again, last night's panic behind her. Concord has five picks left in the draft. She'll be one of them.

None of their picks are in the fourth round, but Milwaukee picks up Travis and Edmonton selects Shawn, and Sophie's happy for them both even if she can't shut down the voice that says *I should've gone before them.*

The fifth round passes without her name being called.

Then the sixth.

There's still time. Concord has two picks in the seventh round. They'll choose me. They have to.

Concord opens the seventh round of the draft by selecting Karl Ekberg.

They only have one pick left.

She takes a deep breath and folds her hands in her lap so she can squeeze her fingers.

The two hundred and twentieth selection is made.

Then the two hundred and twenty-first.

Two twenty-two.

Two twenty-three.

There's one pick left.

Martin Pauling steps up the podium and taps the mic once then a second time, even though the microphone has worked all afternoon. Anticipation prickles at the back of her neck.

"For the final selection of the 2011 Draft, the Concord Condors select, from Chilton Academy, Sophie Fournier."

She doesn't react at first, too focused on keeping her expression neutral. It isn't until her dad nudges her that she realizes her name was called. She's been *drafted.* She stands, her family standing with her, and hugs her dad first.

"Thank you," she murmurs, holding him tight. He claps her shoulder, a familiar *good game* gesture.

She hugs her mom next, then her brother.

"Fucking finally," Colby mutters, and she laughs as she makes her way to the aisle so she can walk down to the stage.

Her heart beats a desperate, erratic rhythm. Her blood thrums and her thoughts are a litany of *I did it* and *it happened* and *holy shit*. She doesn't let any of it show on her face.

When she reaches the stage, Martin Pauling hands her a red jersey with black and white accents. There's a condor, its wings spread wide, on the front. Her name, FOURNIER, is stamped across the back. Even bigger are the numbers beneath it, 93.

She pulls the jersey over her head then takes pictures with the management team. First woman drafted into the NAHL. In a few months, she'll be wearing this jersey in *games*. Maybe it'll be enough to tempt her *mémé*'s loyalty away from Montreal. She can compete for the *Maple Cup*. Maybe one day she'll even lift it.

She forgets about her media training and her carefully constructed persona. She beams for the pictures, then lights up even more when her family joins them for another round of pictures. She hugs her brother again and lets her mom thumb away the few tears leaking out.

It's the draft. She's allowed to be emotional.

Once the cameras retreat, Mr. Pauling says, "Sophie, could you come with us? We have some things to discuss."

She leaves her family behind as she follows the cluster of men who hold her hockey future in their hands. She's intimidated and a little angry but mostly still struggling to process that come fall she'll be a NAHL player. One day, there might be a little girl on the carpet in her grandparents' living room who watches Sophie play the same way she grew up watching Bobby Brindle and Gabriel Ducasse. And she'll think *if she can do it then I can do it*.

Mr. Pauling opens the door to Room 423 and gestures for Sophie to enter first. She steps through and hooks her fingers through her pockets so she doesn't fidget. *Why did you pick me so low?* she wants to demand. *Did you pick me for the publicity or will you let me play? All I need is one game, and I'll prove to you why I deserve more.*

Room 423 is a suite. The living room has a large TV mounted on one wall and a weird hotel picture on the other. It's some kind of landscape, which she supposes is better than the pastel flowers they usually go with. She hovers by one of the couches as the men file in.

She recognizes some of them. Mr. Pauling, obviously. Ronald Wilcox, an older man who is only just beginning to go gray, the general manager of the Condors, is here. So is Coach Butler, a severe looking man who has served as the Condors' coach for the past three seasons. A couple of the assistant coaches are here as well.

It's a lot of fanfare for the two hundred and twenty-fourth pick of the draft. Hope stirs in her chest. Maybe Carol Rogers was onto something. Maybe it's simply a business decision. It still stings.

She locks down all her feelings and offers the men in the room a polite smile. She won't give them any reason to send her to Manchester, the minor league team. She's here to play for Concord and make an impact right away.

A knock at the door interrupts the building silence. At Mr. Pauling's nod, Coach Butler opens the door.

A woman in a smart business suit strides in. Her black hair is twisted into a high bun, showing off her Condors earrings. She tucks her phone into her suit pocket and glances around the room, the smallest of frowns furrowing her brow. "I hope you didn't start without me." Before anyone can say anything, she holds a hand out to Sophie. "Mary Beth Doyle. I'm the Condors' PR manager."

"Sophie Fournier." She shakes her hand. "It's a pleasure to meet you."

Mr. Pauling takes over the introductions. Sophie attaches names and importance to each man, but before they can finish, Mr. Wilcox interrupts. "We don't have a lot of time before the press conference, and there are things we need to cover."

"The press conference should be happening now," Ms. Doyle says. "It looks like we're prepping her."

"Because we are prepping her. We need to talk about the draft and living arrangements. Everything else can be 'no comment' until we have more time."

Ms. Doyle makes an irritated sound in the back of her throat but doesn't say anything. Sophie's gaze flits from person to person. She wonders who she's supposed to take her cues from.

"Ronnie and his wife have offered to let you stay with them this year," Mr. Pauling tells Sophie. "Most players live with an older teammate or sometimes the rookies will rent an apartment together, but we think, given your situation, neither of those would be a good option."

"I understand." Sophie always had her own hotel rooms when she traveled with Chilton. She had teammates who resented it because they were two, sometimes even three or four to a room and she had a room, and a bed, all to herself. It figures that the NAHL would be more of the same even if she doesn't want to stand out more than she already does.

Of course... "If I make the team," she's compelled to add.

"What?"

Everyone's looking at her, and she pulls her hands out of her pockets and stands tall. "During training camp and preseason, I should stay in a hotel like the other players. The optics wouldn't be good if I stayed with Mr. Wilcox right away." She glances at Ms. Doyle for backup.

"She's right. We don't want it to look like preseason is a formality. We can say there are plans in place for if Sophie makes the team, but they shouldn't be implemented until it happens."

"Everyone knows she'll make the team," Coach Vorgen, one of the assistant coaches, says.

Sophie shoves down her bubble of relief. Out loud, she says, "I was drafted last. That means something."

"We know you were the best player in the draft," Mr. Pauling tells her. "Just like we knew no one else could touch you."

So, it was a business decision. Concord picked her last because they could. She should be glad her new team was able to get two first round prospects with only one first round pick, because it will make them a better team. She isn't, though. She should've gone before Hayes. She should've gone second overall.

A tiny seed of resentment settles deep inside her chest. If left unchecked, she'll grow bitter and unhappy until she hates her team. Since she wants a long career in the NAHL, she can't let that happen. She takes a deep breath, then slowly releases it.

She'll be Rookie of the Year and win the Clayton Trophy and prove to the entire League and her management she's the best. Game in and game out, she'll do what she excels at, playing hockey.

"I should take over the prep for the press conference," Ms. Doyle says.

"Of course," Mr. Pauling says. "Welcome to the Condors, Sophie. You'll be a star for this organization."

"Thank you."

Ms. Doyle leads Sophie to a simpler hotel room. This one, like Sophie's, isn't a suite. There's only two rooms: the bedroom with a king-size bed, and a small bathroom.

"We don't have much time, but you can sit if you like," Ms. Doyle says. "Relax, save some of your posture for later. If you're comfortable with it, I'd like you to call me Mary Beth." She offers Sophie a warm smile as she sits in the desk chair. "I'm here to help you manage the pressure and attention you'll receive for being the first woman in the NAHL."

Sophie takes a seat in the armchair.

"Let's start, then. Why is playing in the NAHL important to you?"

Sophie doesn't roll her eyes but it's a near thing. She takes a deep breath, but Mary Beth shakes her head. "Not that answer. The real one."

Sophie hesitates.

"There can't be any lies between us. We have to trust each other. We might get...creative with the answers we give outside these conversations, but when it's only the two of us then I want to know what you're thinking."

She's only known this woman for five minutes. She isn't willing to promise the truth all the time, but this is an easy answer to give. "I want to wake up every morning and be paid to do what I love. I want hockey to be my job and what I do for fun and in my downtime."

The NAWHL was never more than a brief consideration for her, because while the league is gaining traction, most players still have to hold down at least a part-time job in order to play. Some people suggested she put her skill and talent toward growing the women's game, but she won't for the same reason she never thought seriously about college. She won't split her attention between hockey and school, and she won't split it between hockey and work either.

"I love hockey," Sophie finishes. She flushes because she knows it sounds stupid and young, but Mary Beth asked for the truth.

"I want you to remember that. There will be a lot of highs and a lot of lows this season. As prepared as you are, there will be days where you feel like it's more than you can handle. On those days, remember why you play."

Sophie nods.

"All right. Now, let's do a bit of prep before I throw you to your first NAHL press conference."

SOPHIE WEARS HER Condors jersey and a Condors baseball cap to her presser. She can feel her nameplate against her shoulders, stiff because it's a new jersey, but it's a reminder of where she is and what she's done today. And even if they didn't do it right away, Concord did pick her. She has an entire hockey future ahead of her and nothing anyone can say will bring her down.

She sits behind a table with a name card in case anyone here doesn't know who she is. She folds her hands on the table so everyone can see she doesn't fidget. This is like press conferences back at Chilton except there are more cameras and this is being broadcast to all the United States and Canada. But no big deal, right?

"How do you feel about being drafted last?" Carol Rogers asks. "Do you think you should've gone higher?"

Wasted question, Sophie thinks. *You and I both know you won't get a good answer.* "I'm honored the Concord Condors chose me to be a part of their organization. There are a lot of athletes who work hard and aren't selected."

A man from *The Denver Post* asks the next question. "Is this a publicity stunt? If you were selected last, then what chance do you have at making the team?"

"Being drafted means I have an opportunity to show Concord what I can do for their team. I have the rest of the summer to practice and improve so when training camp comes, I can showcase my best skills."

"What do you say to the rumors Concord took advantage of the system to get you?" a reporter from *TNSN* asks.

I bet more teams will apply to be co-ed now. "I don't listen to rumors but as a member of the Condors organization, I want Concord to be the best team it can be. I think they made steps toward that today."

"Because they gamed the system," the reporter presses. "There was no competition to force them to draft you high."

Next year it will be different. Women will be drafted higher, the way they deserve. "This isn't my area of expertise."

A man from *The Concord Courier* stands up. His suit is too big in the shoulders as if he bought it a size too large, expecting to grow into it. He pulls a pad of paper out of his pocket and studies it before clearing his throat. "Concord drafted your high school rival Michael Hayes second overall. Do you think you'll play together? Rivals to linemates?"

Concord drafted him ahead of me, and I'm sure it went straight to his head. Four years of showing him I was better and now he has the draft to hang over me. But if, at the end of the year, anyone thinks he's the better player, then I didn't do my job.

"That's a decision for the coaching staff to make," Sophie answers.

"Who has to give up their number?" someone shouts out.

Like Sophie, Hayes wears 93, because it's the year they were born, but she's never lost to him when it mattered, and she doesn't intend to begin with her number. It'll be exactly the statement she needs. She'll make the team, claim her number, then make her case for the Clayton Trophy.

"Right now, I'm focused on making the team," Sophie says. "Choosing a number doesn't happen until the hard work has paid off."

"So you think you'll make the team?" It's the guy from *The Concord Courier*.

"I have the rest of the summer to make myself the best player I can be, and that's all I can do—train so I'm at my best when it matters the most. This fall, I'll find out if my best is good enough."

A woman from *Representation Matters* stands up to ask, "What does it mean that the first woman in the NAHL was drafted last?"

"It means the NAHL has drafted its first female player, and I'm going to do everything I can this season to show there should be more of us."

Chapter Three

IN SOME WAYS, the summer passes in a normal fashion. She trains, running her favorite hill in her neighborhood, pulling weighted sleds at the local soccer field, and blowing through speed ladders until she can beat her own times. In other ways, the summer is completely different. There are phone interviews and sit-down interviews and she flies to New York City, because a couple of late-night talk show hosts want to ask her what it means to be the first woman drafted into the NAHL.

Despite the packed schedule, the summer seems to drag. She can practice her backhand and work on her stickhandling and lift weights all she wants, but it isn't *hockey*. She itches to be on the ice so she can show every doubter she's a good player.

Two weeks after doing her late-night circuit, she flies back to New York City to record some NAHL promos. After a season of no hockey, the NAHL knows they need to draw their viewers back into the fold. Sophie is perfect for that. Fans of the game's progress will turn the TV on to watch her and fans who hate her are equally likely to turn the TV on to shout at her.

Normally, hockey avoids controversy. It's a sport as bland as her media smile, but a little bit of controversy is exactly what they need. She's been promised a costar which makes sense. She might be the newest, shiniest tool in the NAHL's belt, but she's far from the only one.

Did they bring in Gabriel Ducasse? He's a Montreal Mammoth and Captain Canada, and he led the men to a gold medal at the Stuttgart Winter Games. He's one of the darlings of the NAHL, a solid two-way center who plays in a big Canadian market. He would be the perfect appeal to the conservatives who want to see her tossed out of the League before the season has even begun.

But what if they bring in Mikhail Figuli? His name is synonymous with the NAHL, coming into his twenty-second year in the League. He's the old to her new, having played longer than she's been alive. His poster was right next to Ducasse's on her wall growing up.

Mary Beth picks her up from the airport, her hair in what Sophie is beginning to suspect is her customary bun. She's dressed more casually than the last time Sophie saw her, but she still has her phone in hand. As a PR manager, it's probably as much a staple as Sophie's hockey stick is for her.

There's a black car with tinted windows waiting for them outside the airport. Sophie slides into the backseat first. Mary Beth follows her in.

"You'll be working with Dmitri Ivanov for the next few days," Mary Beth tells her.

Born in Yaroslavl, Russia, he played professional hockey for his hometown before he was drafted first overall by Boston in the 2010 draft. He spent the lockout playing for Yaroslavl, but he'll be in the NAHL for this season.

As much as she was hoping to work with one of the veteran players of the League, Ivanov makes more sense. Boston was the first American team added to what was then the Canadian Hockey League. Concord wasn't added until the League's seventy-fifth anniversary season when the NAHL execs figured Boston could draw Massachusetts fans and Concord could draw from the rest of New England and they'd have ready-made rivals in a growing market.

Instead, the Boston-Concord rivalry has been more like big brother against much littler brother.

But here's a chance to ignite the rivalry, and the storyline practically writes itself. She's Canadian, he's Russian; she was drafted by Concord, he to Boston; she was drafted last, he was drafted first.

He's a skilled player and even though he plays wing rather than forward, she can use him as a measuring stick. If she's better than him, the first pick of the 2010 draft, and better than Carruthers, the first pick of the 2011 draft, then she can prove she should've been drafted first round. Ivanov is the caliber of player she wants to be discussed with and if this promo is what she needs to link their names together then she'll do it.

SOPHIE SLIDES HER room key through the card reader and the red light twinkles at her for the second time. She glares at the card then the reader as the door next to her opens. A head of messy black hair pokes out, followed by the rest of a body. The guy's in denim, distressed to the point where she's afraid it will dissolve, a T-shirt with the Russian eagle on the front, and a Red Sox cap. The look is completed by a pair of gold-sequined high tops.

It's like staring into the sun, blinding and a little painful.

The guy smiles at her, crooked, as if he's taken a couple of pucks, or maybe fists, to the face. "I had problem too," he says in accented English before he bounds forward to pluck her keycard out of her hands. He flips it around, swipes it, and the light flashes green this time.

"Thank you," she says. She carries her bags into her room, and he takes it as an invitation to follow her. Her shoulders draw up, because this is obviously Dmitri Ivanov and maybe he wants to jump-start their rivalry. Of course, he just helped her figure out how to get into her hotel room so maybe he's a nice guy? She rolls her eyes at the thought. "Maybe don't tell anyone about the assist with the door. It might ruin the narrative that we're rivals."

"Maybe I trip you." Ivanov sprawls across her bed, making himself at home. "Or spill juice at breakfast."

"I'd rather you didn't."

She takes her toiletry bag out of her duffel, and when she looks up, Ivanov is watching her, a curious expression on his face. He's so *open* as if he doesn't have years of PR training under his belt already.

"Was joke," he says. "Ha ha?"

"Ha ha?" she echoes. She sets up in the bathroom, her toothbrush and toothpaste on the left side of the bathroom sink and her shampoo and conditioner on the other. She feels sometimes as if she's spent more time in hotel rooms than she has at home. Unpacking is a small way to make the unfamiliar more familiar.

When she returns to the main room, Ivanov's still stretched out across the bed. *Rude*, she thinks, uncharitably.

"Food?" he asks.

She shrugs but picks up the room service menu and scans it as he calls in his order. By the time he hands the phone to her, she knows what she wants. She hangs up the phone once she's done and can't help but wonder what the hotel staff thinks of them. Do they know they're hockey players? Do they think they're international travelers? Do they think they're on a honeymoon?

Sophie wrinkles her nose. The optics of being alone in a hotel room with a guy only a year older than her isn't good. She knows nothing will happen, she's uninterested, and he's studying her more like one would one of the big cats at the zoo than as someone he wants to have sex with. Still, it doesn't look good, and for her, more so than anyone else in the League, image is important.

The alternative, of course, is eating alone.

"Early start tomorrow," Sophie says.

Ivanov shrugs. "Coffee."

They lapse into silence again.

She returns to unpacking, making use of the dresser drawers. By the time she's done, Ivanov has one arm under his neck and the other draped across his stomach. His eyes are half-lidded as if he's a breath or two from falling asleep.

She flicks one of his socked feet.

"Mean," he says. He kicks at her.

"You're not sleeping in my bed."

"Little nap," he bargains. "Until dinner."

She flicks his foot again.

He grumbles but forces himself to sit up. He pulls out his phone and amuses himself until their food shows up.

Sophie answers the door, glad that Ivanov stays on the bed and out of sight. She sets the tray on the desk and pulls the armchair over so there are two seats. When Ivanov doesn't move, Sophie says, "You're not eating on my bed."

Ivanov huffs but gets up and joins her at the table. "So many rules about bed."

She glares at him, ready to toss him out of her room if he says anything else. But he plops down next to her and uncovers his fish. He coos at it before cutting it into messy pieces and mixing it in with his rice and vegetables.

Sophie cuts off a piece of her own fish and spears a broccoli floret to complete the bite.

"Fussy," he says.

"Messy," she retorts.

He grins, delighted with her admittedly pretty immature chirping. After that, dinner is quiet, both of them too focused on eating to try to talk. When their plates are cleared and Ivanov makes no move to return to his own room, Sophie turns the TV on so she doesn't have to think of something to say.

They end up watching *The Big Bang Theory* reruns and laughing when the fake audience prompts them to because neither of them understand what's happening.

It's...weird. She isn't used to other hockey players wanting to hang out with her more than they have to. Is this like the time her bantam teammates spent a whole week being nice to her because they heard some players from the Winnipeg Porcupines were coming to see her play and they wanted a chance to meet them? Or maybe it's like the time her Chilton teammates invited her to a highlighter party then dumped a bucket of water on her head so her white T-shirt clung to her?

There's always a punchline. She just doesn't know what direction it'll come from.

SHE EATS BREAKFAST on her own and doesn't even see Ivanov before she has to report for hair and makeup. Today's shoot is taking place in one of the hotel's conference rooms, and Sophie skirts the lighting tests and the rack of props and outfits as she makes her way to the small vanity.

Two women are waiting for her, one armed with a curling iron, the other brandishing a mascara brush. Sophie only wears makeup when she can't escape it. She wore it to the draft, but she doesn't understand why she needs it here.

It isn't like Ivanov is being poked and prodded and criticized.

"You should really tweeze your eyebrows," one of the women says.

"Or get them threaded," the other adds.

"You want a smaller line."

"It'll open up your eyes more."

Sophie cares how many points she puts up in a season. She cares if her defensive game is as strong as her offensive one. She cares about her team's place in the standings. She does *not* care what her eyebrows look like. That doesn't help her win hockey games.

The two women use enough hairspray that Sophie chokes on it and when she pats her curls, they're *crunchy*.

One of the women smacks her hand. "Don't touch."

She folds her hands in her lap and carefully keeps the scowl off her face. She doesn't need to be labeled as difficult before the season even begins. Still, she can't help her resentment. She feels more like a doll than a hockey player right now. She knew things would be different as a woman playing in the League, but this is ridiculous.

When Ivanov comes in, rubbing his eyes and holding what's probably his third cup of coffee, he spots her right away. She squirms, embarrassed, as he heads over. This is where the other shoe will drop. He'll mock her for being a *girl* or tweet out pictures of them side by side and—

"What's this?" Ivanov asks. "Special treatment?" He picks up the foundation they used earlier and turns it over in his hands. "How much to make my face pretty?"

"You don't need that," one of the women says, snatching it away.

Ivanov pats his cheeks. "Pretty already." He snags the mascara next. "For eyes, yes?" He bats his eyelashes, and Sophie can't quite stifle her giggle.

Ivanov winks at her and the last few minutes of makeup pass quickly.

SOPHIE WEARS JEANS and a Condors jersey and Ivanov wears jeans and a Barons jersey, and they lean on their hockey sticks as the photoshoot director, his assistant, the photographer, and the head of NAHL advertising argue over the concept for the first shots.

"The chair is tradition," the advertising director says.

"It's time for something new." The photoshoot director glances over at where Sophie and Ivanov wait. "If we use the chair, then we have two choices. She sits with him above her, his hand on her shoulder, or him sitting with her standing above him. Neither will go over well."

"You know pictures, I know my market," the advertising director says. "Fournier, sit."

Sophie sits down on the folding chair, her stick balanced across her lap. Ivanov stands behind her, his stick held in one hand, his other hand heavy on her shoulder. She twitches at the initial touch, but she doesn't shrug it off.

It's worth a couple stupid pictures to be able to play in the NAHL.

"Smile," the photographer says.

Her shoulders tense for a moment before she smiles.

"That's a grimace. Give me something softer. Like you actually want to be here."

When they switch positions, Ivanov's allowed to hold his stick in his hand, the butt of it planted on the ground as if he's a moment away from springing to his feet. She's told to bend her knees so she doesn't loom as tall over him.

There are more pictures after that and it's past dinner time by the time they're released. All Sophie wants is to wash away the hairspray and the makeup, then scream into her pillow for at least half an hour. She slips out of the room and takes the stairs because she needs to *move*. Maybe she'll go for a run. She wishes there was a fully outfitted weight room here so she could slam weights around. There's nothing like a good deadlift to exorcise her frustration.

She jams her keycard into the reader and pounds her fist on her door when the red light flashes at her.

"Forget already?" Ivanov appears out of nowhere and tries to take her card.

She snatches it out of reach because she can open a damn door on her own. She flips the card, then yanks it through the reader. As soon as the green light flashes, she shoves her door open, but it does little to settle the restlessness humming under her skin. If she was back at Chilton, she'd grab Travis and wrestle with him until she was too exhausted to move. But the only person here is Ivanov, and she won't ask him for that.

"Dinner?" he asks, hovering in her doorway.

She wants to snap at him, but he doesn't deserve her temper. He's been kind to her today when he didn't need to be, making her smile during makeup and in between shoots. It isn't his fault the NAHL is a backwards League. She tries to run her hand through her hand but her fingers catch on all the hairspray.

"I need a shower."

"I order then. Meet in my room." He pulls the keycard envelope out of his back pocket and hands one of the cards over.

She stares at it as if he's offering her a live octopus. "You can't give me that."

"It's for room."

She knows what a keycard is for. But it's for *his* room. Doesn't he see the problem with that? Of course he doesn't. He hasn't grown up hearing about optics and image as much as advice on faceoffs and backchecking.

He presses the card into her hand. "Shower, then my room for dinner."

She tries to give him the card back but he won't take it. "We're rivals," she reminds him "You can't just—" *be nice to me.* "I'm the reason you didn't play last year."

"Bullshit. NAHL wants rivals. I say fuck them. Friends."

That isn't how it works. Their teams don't like each other. The NAHL doesn't want them to like each other. The media's drawn up their narrative, and Sophie has spent her career conforming to narratives. She stands out in so many ways that in all those she can, she blends in. She can't—they can't—

"Shower," Ivanov tells her gently as if he's afraid he's spooked her. "Then dinner."

He turns to leave but Sophie touches his shoulder. "Fuck them?"

He nods, looking serious for the first time since they've met. "My story. Not theirs."

"Then I want steak."

A smile breaks out across his face. "Yes. Big steaks. NAHL pay."

This time, when he leaves, Sophie doesn't stop him. She looks at the keycard in her hand for a full minute before she starts the water for her shower.

Her story.

THEY SPEND THE second day doing everything they did the first day only with hockey pads on under their jerseys. At least tomorrow they're scheduled at an ice rink. They plan for dinner in Ivanov's room again, and she uses his card instead of knocking like she did last night.

He'd laughed at her and said, "Key is invite."

She cracks the door open so he can call out a warning if he's changing. When he doesn't, she comes all the way inside. He hasn't even showered yet, sprawled across his bed with his phone to his ear as he talks in rapid-fire Russian. His voice is softer than she's ever heard it. He waves to her before returning to his conversation.

She hovers by the armchair, unsure whether she's interrupting. It's not like she can understand anything he's saying, but maybe it's a private conversation. She's edging toward the door when he hangs up.

"Mama," he explains, unprompted. His voice is rough around the edges, and he's missing the spark in his eyes that led to him making faces at her during her solo shots today. "She say, *Dimulya, you are superstar but spend too much time away from home.*"

"Dim—what did she call you?"

"Dimulya. Is name for Mama, not you. Ah! You call me Dima. Friend name."

"Or I call you Ivanov." She ignores his answering pout. There's a difference between them bonding over sticking it to the NAHL and being the kind of friends who have nicknames. "Isn't it early in Russia?"

Ivanov's smile dims again. "Yes, but very important day so Mama call." Her confusion must show because he adds, "Birthday."

She knows how many points he had last season, more goals than assists, because he's what hockey analysts like to call a pure goal scorer. She knows his average ice time per game and his go-to moves during the shootout and *everyone* knows his favorite place to shoot from on the power play, but she didn't know his birthday.

She should've warned him she isn't any good at friends.

"Happy birthday," she says, but it seems lacking. He shouldn't be stuck in a hotel room in a strange country with someone he doesn't know on his birthday. He should be in Russia with his mom or partying with his real friends. But there is *something* she can do. "Shower. Dinner's in my room tonight."

He raises his arm so he can sniff at his armpit. "Can wait for tomorrow."

She rolls her eyes. "Shower," she says again, then leaves before he can argue.

Back in her room, she calls down for dinner. She places their order then adds a piece of chocolate cake with a single candle. She doesn't think the slices of cake are large enough to fit nineteen candles and, even if they were, it's probably a fire hazard.

Ivanov arrives at the same time as their dinner, and he carries it to the desk. He eyes the small covered plate with interest, but she pulls it close to her.

"Terrible at share," he tells her.

She's about to argue that *her* assist totals are higher than his, but he's smiling, teasing her again, so she lets it go. When they're done with their dinner, it's her turn to smile as she pushes the plate toward him.

He lifts the top off, wary, but his entire face lights up when he sees the cake. He plucks the candle out and licks the bottom.

"Happy birthday," she tells him. "I don't think they gave us any matches. I'm sorry."

"It's okay." He turns a sly smile on her. "Sing?"

"Don't push your luck."

He laughs and hands her the fork the cake came with.

"It's your cake," she protests.

"I'm good at share."

"I gave you the cake!" she squawks. "And I've seen your footage. You had sixty-one goals in a goal-stingy league. No one else on the power play even pretends they'll shoot the puck."

"You watch me play?"

"I watch everyone play, but yeah. We're rivals, remember?"

"Friends," he corrects. "But a real friend would sing."

"Guess we're just fake friends, then, *Ivanov*."

He clutches his chest and gasps dramatically. She kicks his shins then steals the best bite of cake, the one with the most frosting. He ruins her victory by turning the cake so she can have the frosting side.

Maybe this friends thing will work out after all.

FILMING A COMMERCIAL means speaking, and she knows from watching NAHL commercials that the players always sound stupid, but she doesn't care because they're filming at a rink. They break for lunch, and, without having to say anything, she and Ivanov both rush through their sandwiches so they can skate before they have to film again.

She's the first one to find a puck, juggling it on her stick before catching it in her bare hand.

"My turn," Ivanov says, slapping his stick on the ice. "Share, yes?"

She skips the puck over to him. He does everything she just did except he catches the puck behind him.

"Show off," she says.

"Jealous," he counters.

He juggles the puck again, and she swoops in to steal it. Skating backwards, she holds the puck out to him, a taunt and a dare rolled into one. He skates after her and knocks her gently into the boards to try to take it back.

"No visible bruises!" the commercial director shouts.

"No sweating!" one of the assistants calls.

They ignore the assistant, battling hard for the puck as their competitive natures take over. She'd feel guilty for elbowing him in the gut to steal the puck, but he hooks her just a couple minutes later.

She has to have her makeup redone before they shoot again, but it's worth it for the sweat trickling down her spine and the flush on her cheeks and the opportunity to play hockey even if it was only for fifteen minutes.

When they're finally done with the day, Sophie turns her stick over in her hands. The producer says it's hers to keep, because it's the brand and style she prefers. She borrows a Sharpie from one of the assistants and signs it *Sophie Fournier 93* before she holds it out to Ivanov.

"Switch?" she asks.

He grins as he takes her Sharpie to scrawl his own name on his stick. They trade sticks then, pushing his luck, Ivanov convinces her they should exchange phone numbers too.

They're hustled out of the rink after that, because they both have planes to catch. They take a cab to JFK and stick together through security. They even grab a quick dinner before they part ways.

She hasn't been sitting for even five minutes before Colby texts her.

COLBY: *want me to punch Ivanov for you?*

He's attached a link to an article from *The Sin Bin*, an online hockey blog which is more tabloid than actual news.

Sophie Fournier Gets Her Hand on Dmitri Ivanov's Stick the headline proclaims.

There's a picture to go along with it, her and Ivanov standing together, both smiling, and the picture is cut off at the waist, hinting that anything might be happening beneath.

Sophie hits the *read more.*

...His Hockey Stick that is, the headline finishes.

There's a full picture now too and it shows the two of them exchanging hockey sticks.

She texts her brother back to tell him her honor doesn't need defending, then she texts Mary Beth with a link to the article and an apology. She rubs her temples. This is why she doesn't do friends.

Chapter Four

THE HYPE AND expectations have been building since the moment Martin Pauling drafted her to the Concord Condors. And now, after a summer that felt as if it would never end, training camp is here.

This is her first opportunity to show that while maybe it was a good business decision to pick her last, it'll be an even better hockey decision to put her on the opening day roster. On the morning of the first day of training camp, she catches a glimpse of herself in the hotel mirror. Strong quads, equally strong glutes, a solid torso. Her body is compact and designed for hockey. She isn't pretty, even with all the makeup they keep layering on her face. She's plain, her eyes a washed out blue and her eyebrows apparently too thick.

But her hands are big, made for gripping a hockey stick, and her shoulders are packed with muscle. She doesn't have the hardest shot in the world, but she's accurate with it. She's even better with her passes.

She's ready for this.

She touches her hip where two crossed hockey sticks have been tattooed onto her skin. One of the blades has her number, 93, etched into it. The second is blank, waiting for something. It was supposed to be her draft number, but she doesn't want that reminder on her skin for the rest of her life. She'll have to save the space for something special.

She rubs her thumb over the simple black ink. Hockey is who she is and what she does. There will be players at camp who are older than her and taller than her and bigger than her and far more experienced than she is. But she'll carve out a place for herself on this team the same way she has at every single level she's played at before.

There's a reason she left Chilton Academy with the most points scored in the school's history. There's a reason she was chosen to represent Canada at the Stuttgart Games, the youngest hockey player to ever play, let alone win gold.

She's an elite player, and she'll make sure everyone knows it.

She shows up to practice far too early, but she takes advantage of the opportunity to walk around. The locker room carpet is black except for the white circle which surrounds the condor they're named after. The bird's wings are spread wide and there's a hockey stick clutched in its talons.

All the walls are lined with stalls, and she trails her fingers over them. They each have a piece of tape stuck to them with everyone's names in alphabetical order. *Delacroix, Benoit* with *Faulkner, Kevin* next to him. Further down *Rodriguez, José* then *Smith, Theodore. Mathers, Daniel* and *McArthur, Jeffrey* are side by side. Each stall has practice clothes hanging in them.

Well, all of them but one.

She steps closer to the empty stall, her stomach sinking when she sees *Fournier, Sophie* written on the tape. Has someone already pulled the first prank of the season? The locker next to her reads *Garfield, Luke* and she pulls Garfield's shirt from it. It's a plain gray T-shirt with a condor on the front. On the back GARFIELD is stamped across the shoulders. Lower down it reads:

Practice Hard
Play Hard

#CondorsCamp

She puts it back where it belongs.

The doors open, and she spins around, wondering who else is here too early. The man who walks through is middle-aged and wearing a Condors polo. He's too old to be one of her teammates.

"You're early," the man says. "I wasn't expecting you for at least another hour."

"I wanted a look around before things got too busy."

"I'm Ben Granlund, your equipment manager. My kids have been talking about you nonstop since the draft. Welcome to Concord, Sophie."

"Thank you. I, uh—" Her gaze flicks toward her empty stall.

"You have your own room, League recommendation. I can show you where it is."

Her relief that someone hasn't already tampered with her clothes is quickly eroded by the walk down the hall to what looks like a converted supply closet. There's enough space for her to have a stall, and there's a single curtain with a showerhead behind it. She supposes it's better than Chilton where Coach had to clear out the locker room so she could shower, but she doesn't like being separated from the team. How's she supposed to be a part of them when she's banished to this little room?

"I'll let you take everything in," Granlund tells her. "If you need anything equipment-wise, I'm your guy. I'm excited to see what you'll do here."

"Thank you," Sophie says. She gives him a genuine smile, because it isn't his fault she's been set up in here.

Once he's gone, she takes another look around the room. It's bigger than she initially thought. There's space for another stall next to hers. Maybe next year, Sophie won't be the only woman in the NAHL. She might not even be the only woman on the Condors.

She'd better get to work, then.

THE TEAM IS given an official tour of their practice facility, shuffled from one place to another, before they're sent outside to the parking lot. There's a lot of them, far too many people for them all to make the preseason roster let alone the opening day roster. She looks around, sizing up the other players. She has to be better than every single one of them here.

"This is when the real tour begins," Daniel Mathers says, a grin on his face that Sophie knows better than to trust.

Mathers has been the captain of the Condors for the past four years, ever since he was traded from the Olympians. He'd been a good player for New Orleans, and he's now the first-line center for Concord. She saw him in passing at the Winter Games last year, but they didn't talk because she had a maple leaf on her jersey and he had an American flag.

Like with Ivanov, she could easily write a player profile on him, but she doesn't know anything about Mathers the person. Is he a good captain? Does he resent the attention she's drawn this summer?

He leads them out of the parking lot, breaking into a slow jog. They're running through the city? Her teammates fall into pairs to create a long, winding column behind their captain. Hayes bumps her shoulder as he passes her and mutters, too quiet for anyone but her to hear, "You go last, remember?"

Part of her wants to charge in front of him, but everyone up there already has a partner so there's no place for her. She ends up hanging back until a guy with a scraggly, copper-colored beard falls into stride with her.

"You must be one of the new kids."

She stares at him, incredulous.

"I'm sorry," he says as his brown eyes dance with mischief. "Am I supposed to know you?"

"I'm Sophie Fournier."

"You know, that name does ring a bell. I think I might've heard it mentioned once or twice this summer."

Surprised, she laughs and gently knocks her shoulder into his. "You're Jeffrey McArthur." He's a right winger with the most accurate shot on the team. Right now, the other teams are all over him once he has the puck, cutting off his space and, therefore, his effectiveness. If he had even an extra second he'd be lethal. She could give him that second.

It seems too much to say in their first meeting, but it leaves the conversation dangling. Fortunately, he picks it back up. "Matty's really into the city. Like *really* into it. He'll probably stop outside the State House to give us a lecture. Can you believe I used to think running couldn't be more boring than treadmill workouts? Give me a treadmill and *TNSN* over lectures on Ebenezer Eastman any day."

"Ebenezer?"

"You'll learn," McArthur says, the warning almost ominous.

AFTER THEIR RUN, there's a tall stack of red yoga mats waiting for them in the parking lot. In the scramble to get a mat, she loses track of McArthur and ends up between two guys who dwarf her even though she isn't small at six feet and almost two hundred pounds.

"Theodore Smith," the guy on her left says. He's the bigger of the two with a full beard even though it's been a hot summer. Maybe it's to make up for the thinning hair on the top of his head.

"Sophie Fournier," she says.

He laughs, showing off two missing teeth. "I don't think you need to introduce yourself."

"Americans are heathens," the guy on Sophie's right says. "I'm Kevin Faulkner and this idiot here is my d-partner." Faulkner is dark-skinned and he has a friendly smile. He isn't quite as large as Smith, but he still looks plenty strong, his biceps straining against his T-shirt.

"I'm the idiot?" Smith demands.

"We switch off every month," Faulkner tells Sophie.

Before she has to worry about some kind of answer, Mathers yells at everyone to quit gossiping and start their push-ups. He puts them through a whole circuit of exercises then makes them do it twice more. By the end of it, Sophie wants to know who thought gray T-shirts were a good idea. Everywhere she looks, people have dark patches of sweat on their backs and under their arms.

"We're finishing with a plank-off," Mathers announces.

Next to Sophie, Smith groans. "I hate planks. They hurt my back."

Sophie obediently rolls onto her stomach. "You're probably not doing them right, then."

She flushes, because coming across as a know-it-all on day one won't make her any friends. Faulkner laughs, though, and teases Smith as Mathers tells them to begin.

She pushes up into the required position. Her trainer told her planks are 80 percent mental and 20 percent physical, and she's never met anyone who can beat her in a mental exercise. She holds her body in a tight, straight line and focuses on her breathing.

It's not long before Smith drops to the ground with a grunt, but she doesn't look over. Sweat beads along her forehead and drips down onto her mat. More sweat pools at the small of her back. Her body begins to tremble, a plea from her muscles to give up.

She holds her position.

The background noise grows louder as more and more people drop out. She's almost startled out of her plank when McArthur pops into her periphery. "You're doing great, kid," he tells hers.

Not a kid, she thinks with a glare.

"Matty's the only one left besides you, but he's shaking pretty badly. You look like you could do this for hours. You're sweating up a storm, though. That's not very ladylike."

She glances at Mathers to confirm he's struggling. His knuckles are white and there's a dip in his back, a sign he won't last much longer. She carefully shifts into a one-armed plank and uses her free hand to flip McArthur off. Then she falls back into her two-armed plank.

"That was *definitely* not ladylike," McArthur says.

"Impressive, though," Smith says. "Is this what you do for fun?"

"This is painful, not fun."

"You're just lazy."

"Me?" McArthur squawks. "You were the first out!"

"I have more weight to keep off the ground which means I worked harder than you did."

"Did not!"

It's hard to plank while she's laughing so Sophie closes her eyes and blocks out everything happening around her. She isn't allowed to relax until she's won. If training camp is about proving herself, then this is the first test.

Someone pokes her shoulder.

She slits her eyes open and glares.

McArthur, about to poke her again, realizes he has her attention and draws his hand back. "Uh, Matty's out."

She glances up. Sure enough, Mathers is face down on his mat. Everyone else is sitting or lying down which means she's won. She slowly lowers herself to her mat.

"Nice job," McArthur says. He holds his hand out for a fist bump.

Once she gives him one, Smith holds his fist out, then Faulkner. When Mathers approaches her, the side conversations die down, everyone waiting to see how he'll react. Sophie stands to meet her new captain, hiding her nerves behind a neutral expression. She'll never hold back to appease male egos, especially not now when so much is on the line, but she never knows how a guy will react the first time she beats him at something.

And Mathers isn't just some guy on her team. He's her captain and yes, this was only a plank competition, but she's been given a rough time over less. Smith and Faulkner stay at her sides, and she appreciates the show of solidarity.

"Good work," Mathers tells her. "Next time, I'll set up next to you. Maybe you'll push me to be better." He clasps her shoulder, then addresses the entire team. "Roll up your mats and bring them inside. We have two hours to shower and eat before our second session. If you all behave yourselves today, tomorrow we can hit the ice."

Everyone cheers, Sophie among them.

SOPHIE ARRIVES EARLY, but not quite as early, for day two. She makes it as far as the parking lot, but she doesn't leave her rental car. The front entrance is swarming with people. There are adults with little kids and teenagers with their cell phones and people holding professional cameras.

She hides in the safety of her car as she wonders where she's supposed to park let alone how to get past all those people unnoticed.

Her phone buzzes with an alert from the team advising everyone to use the back entrance today. She pulls her car around back before heading inside. From their tour yesterday, she knows where Mary Beth's office is, and she isn't surprised to see the woman already there.

"Good morning," she says without looking up from the spread of papers in front of her.

"Big crowd," Sophie says. It's arrogant to assume they're here for her, but she's never heard of Concord drawing this kind of attention before. "Do you want me to change and say hi?"

"You don't need to get ready?"

She's here an hour and a half before she needs to warm up for practice. Instead of saying that and admitting to her nerves, she shrugs and says, "I have some time."

Mary Beth smiles as if she heard the truth anyway. "Get changed and we'll do an impromptu meet and greet. Don't go without me, I want to make sure security is on site in case people get pushy."

Like yesterday, Sophie's practice clothes hang in her stall and, like yesterday, she smiles when she sees them. She hopes she feels the same rush of excitement and anticipation and hope every time she sees the condor with its wings spread wide. It's silly, not to mention dangerous, to think too far ahead, especially when she's still only at her second day of training camp, but she can't help but hope she's a Condor for life.

Before Chilton, she bounced from league to league, always trying to play up a level or an age group, always switching teams before she could wear out her welcome entirely. Chilton was the first place she stayed for more than just one or two seasons, and it wasn't always easy, but she found herself a home with the team.

She wants the same thing here. She wants management to look at her and see their future, someone who will play hard for them year in and year out. They have depth and experience in Mathers, Delacroix, and Lindholm, and she wants to be a part of the next wave of talent.

But being a part of a franchise is different than being a part of a team. She doesn't just have to fit in on the ice but off it too. Hence going out and meeting fans. She changes into her shorts and T-shirt, braids her hair, and she's preparing to leave when she spies something sticking out of her gear bag.

It's a package of Sharpies in a variety of colors. The back of the package has the initials *BG* in the corner. She'll have to ask Mr. Granlund how many kids he has so she can sign something for them.

"Good call on the markers," Mary Beth says when Sophie meets up with her. They head toward the front entrance. "You won't be able to talk to every person and sign every picture or jersey or stick. There's too many people and you don't have the time."

Sophie isn't new to having people show up at her games, but she's never seen a turnout this high. There has to be over a hundred people, maybe even more, crammed outside the rink. When they see her, they surge forward, everyone trying to reach her at once.

Sophie smiles as dozens of phones are lifted in the air to try to catch a picture of her.

"Good morning," she greets. "I guess I'm not the only one excited for hockey to be back."

After one of the security guys nods at her, she approaches the first fan, a teenage girl in a Boston Barons T-shirt and a Condors hat. The brim of the hat is stiff as if it's brand new.

"Boston's always been more fun to watch," the girl says as she hands her hat over, "but now that you're here, I'm going to watch both teams."

"I hope we can make a true convert of you by the end of the season," Sophie says as she loops her signature across the red brim.

The girl disappears into the crowd with her prize and a man in slacks and a dress shirt takes her place. "My son's at school right now. Could you sign this for him?"

It's a picture of his son in his hockey gear, the kind of photo Sophie's mom has dozens of by now. The kid grins, bright and wide, missing teeth because he's young enough to be losing them and not because he's old enough for them to be knocked out.

"What position does he play?" Sophie asks.

"Defense."

Protecting your goalie is the most important job there is, she writes on the back of the picture. *Good luck this season*. On the front, she signs her name followed by her number. She hands the picture back and is shuffled to the next person in line.

She talks to parents of hockey players and former hockey players and teenagers who skipped school for a chance to meet her. There are only a handful of girls here who play hockey, and Sophie pays a little extra bit of attention to them. *This* is why it's been important for her to make it to this level. She wants to show all these girls that if

Sophie can do it, then they can do it too. She wants to show them there's a future for women who play hockey. It isn't play up through college then graduate and have a family or find a career.

Hockey can be a career and team can be family.

She signs things until Mary Beth clears her throat and says, "It's time for you to go inside if you don't want to be late."

There's a groan from the crowd, and Sophie's turning to leave when she spots a little girl on the verge of tears. She glances at Mary Beth. "One more?"

"One," Mary Beth answers, firm.

Sophie kneels in front of the girl so they're closer in height. "Thank you for coming to see me today."

"I'm Marcie. I don't have anything to sign, I just wanted to say hi."

Sophie smiles. "Hi."

"Are you nervous? I was nervous for my first day of school but then I got there and I made lots of friends. Joey's my *best* friend. He shared his snack even though we're not supposed to do that. Do you think you're going to make a lot of friends?"

"I hope I'll be as lucky as you. What grade are you in?"

"First." Marcie puffs her chest out, proud. "I get to go to *real* school now, but I'm late."

Next to Marcie, her father looks vaguely embarrassed.

"Do you want me to sign your shirt before I have to go inside?"

Marcie thinks about it for a moment before she turns around so Sophie can sign across her right shoulder.

CONCORD DOESN'T GIVE out numbers for training camp. They have to earn them by making it onto the opening day roster, and it makes the back of her practice jersey seem too open, as if it's missing something. But even if there's no familiar 93, her nameplate is there, ironed across the shoulders, and she traces her fingers over the letters before she pulls her jersey on.

Soon, she'll have a number. Preseason numbers are random, no preference given to the veterans, let alone the new players. Once she officially makes the team, she'll have 93 on the back and arms of her sweater again. Baby steps, though. She'll use training camp to earn herself a place on the preseason roster, then she makes her case for a permanent place.

The 1C spot is Mathers's, he's the captain, and while she firmly believes she was the top prospect at the draft, she knows there are players in the League who are better than her right now. The 2C position can be hers. Concord is weak down the middle which is why they drafted Petrov at the 2010 draft then herself and Hayes at the 2011 one. They need skill anchoring their lines, and she's up for the challenge.

She'll prove herself better than Hayes and Petrov and keep her eyes open to see what other center prospects she needs to be better than.

Once she's geared up, she waddles down the hallway to the main locker room. Coach Butler is outside it in a Condors tracksuit, black with red accents. His whistle hangs around his neck, and he has a clipboard tucked under his arm.

He came off as a severe man when she met him at the draft, and his face hasn't gained any warmth since. That's okay. She's used to stringent rules and strict routines and the comforting bark of her coach's orders.

Coach Butler looks at her, assessing, but his face doesn't give away any of the conclusions he's drawn. He opens the door to the locker room and shouts, "Everyone better be dressed in the next two minutes or you don't join us on the ice!" He stays there, door cracked open until, presumably, everyone is dressed. Then he opens the door to Sophie.

Yesterday, the locker room seemed huge when she was in it. With guys crammed together in front of the stalls, elbows and knees knocking into each other as they buckle their pads or lace up their skates, it doesn't seem big enough.

Sophie squeezes into the empty space between Faulkner and Garfield, then ducks so she isn't elbowed when Garfield pulls his jersey over his head. Today, they're all in black. They'll have red ones and white ones introduced for scrimmages and when the coaching staff wants to break them out into smaller groups. But right now, they're all in the same, subdued color, because it isn't their jerseys that are supposed to make them stand out but their play.

"I left you in the tender care of your captain yesterday," Coach Butler says. He stands in the doorway so he can look around the room. His lips curl into a smile as some people can't hold his gaze. "If you're sore, then I have tough news for you. You aren't ready for the big league."

There's nervous laughter, some players unsure of whether he's joking or not.

"We hit the ice for the first time today, and I hope none of you have performance anxiety, because we have a whole team of coaches to assess every single thing you do on the ice and, as I've been told, quite the crowd in the stands. If there's rust on your blades, then get it off quickly because as harsh as the coaching staff will be, the fans will be worse."

The locker room's attention shifts from Coach Butler to her, but Sophie keeps her gaze on him. It's been a long time since she had a new team, the Winter Games don't count, and she'd almost forgotten what it was like to stand out this obviously.

"Yes, you've found the one person in the locker room who doesn't look like the others," Coach Butler drawls. "Congratulations, you all grew up with *Sesame Street*. We're the first team in the NAHL to draft a woman. Mary Beth, our PR manager, would like me to remind you Fournier is just that, a *woman*. She isn't a girl." His brow furrows as if he doesn't understand why he has to make the distinction. "*I* would like to remind you Fournier is your competition."

Many of the looks turn decidedly less friendly at the reminder that she's here to outplay them. It'll only grow worse once she does. Whoever thinks she was a pity pick or PR move is in for a rude awakening as soon as she's on the ice.

"Training camp is about working hard," Coach continues. "It's about proving why you're the better fit for our team than the guy next to you. Or gi—woman. I don't care if you've never played with these people before. I don't care if you're asked to play in new positions. You have to push through everything and show your best or you won't make the team." He checks his watch. "On the ice in five minutes."

As soon as he leaves, Mathers stands up, his helmet tucked under his arm. His hair is already matted with sweat, and he seems larger than life, up on his skates while the rest of them are sitting down. He looks around the room, his smile far more welcoming than Coach's had been. "You heard him, boys." His gaze darts to Sophie before he forges ahead. "There's a shit-ton of people out there excited for us. Let's show them what we've got."

The locker room cheers and the slowpokes rush to finish getting ready. Sophie follows Faulkner out of the locker room. Mathers joins them a moment later, and Faulkner smoothly steps away to ask McArthur a question.

"Boys is fine," Sophie says, anticipating his question. "So is guys. Your speech would've lost some gravitas if you said *you heard him, boys and girls.*"

"Boys and *woman*," Mathers corrects, adopting his best Coach Butler voice.

She smiles, brief and fleeting, before she tugs at her jersey. "I'm one of you. That's what this means, right?"

There's a beat of silence, and Sophie's stomach twists and turns until Mathers nods and says, "Yeah."

"Then you can lump me in with the rest."

They head up the tunnel together, and the sounds of the crowd grow louder, the closer they get. Mathers's smile returns. "They've never been this excited in all my years here. They're here for you."

"They're here for the team," Sophie says.

When they emerge from the tunnel, she takes a moment to look around. It's the practice arena so it's smaller than where they'll play their games. It's also seen better days, the seats hard plastic and the walls exposed cement blocks. But the glass is lined with fans wearing red or black Condors jerseys. Some of them already have 93s on their sleeves even though Sophie hasn't made the team yet. When they spot her, they bang on the glass and wave signs and shout to try to grab her attention.

"They're here for you," Mathers says again but he doesn't sound upset that a fresh-faced rookie is getting the attention he deserves.

She hangs back so he can take the ice first, his right as the captain. She feels a spark of envy as his blades cut into the fresh sheet of ice. This has always been her favorite part of the season and for the past three years, this right was hers. There's nothing better than a smooth surface waiting for her to carve her season into it.

Mathers turns, skating backwards so he can make a *hurry up* gesture at her.

She grins and buckles her helmet on. Then she takes the ice for the first time in a Condors jersey. It's a practice jersey, sure, but it has her name on the back, and the crowd grows even louder as she takes her first strides.

This could be home, she thinks as she races after her captain.

SHE'S SKATED IN dozens of rinks at this point in her life; in Canada, the United States, Germany, Italy, Switzerland, all over the world, and the one constant is how good it feels to be on the ice. The crowd is amped up, the players are flying, it's a building full of people excited about *hockey*.

She feels as if she could skate for the entire day without getting tired. Coach could blow his whistle and bag skate them for the rest of practice, and she'd do the brutal repetitions happily, because she's here at Condors training camp and—

"I didn't know you could smile like that," McArthur says.

They're taking a drink break, and Sophie's leaning against the boards, looking out at the ice. Immediately, her smile dims, a reminder that even if her thoughts take her different places, she's still here, and there are always people watching.

"It's not a bad thing," McArthur says.

She plucks the water bottle out of his hands and arches her eyebrows when he tries to snatch it back. "Are you scared of cooties? Our mouths don't even touch." She sprays a stream of water into her mouth before handing the bottle back.

"There was one right there," he says, pointing to the bottle by her elbow.

"More fun to take yours." She hasn't seen anyone drink out of the one next to her and while "team" is supposed to mean bonds of brotherhood and all that, she knows "brotherhood" doesn't exactly apply to her. She pushes away from the bench. "Wanna play keep away? I bet you protect the puck worse than your water bottle."

She uses her stick to corral a loose puck, and she skates backwards away from him, daring him to come after her. He charges forward, and she tosses the puck through his legs then catches it on the other side. He spins, shouldering her off the puck and snatching it for as long as it takes her to recover.

They battle back-and-forth until Coach Butler blows his whistle, ending their break. They sneak another drink while Coach details the next drill, a basic three-on-two to get an idea of forward chemistry and defensive instincts. This time, McArthur tosses her his water bottle when he's done, no theft necessary.

Coach Richelieu takes the goalies to the far side of the rink to do their own thing. Coach Vorgen takes the defensemen to explain their side of the drill which leaves the forwards with Coach Butler. The drill is simple. There are three lines, right wing, center, and left wing, and they rotate through the lines, playing in different positions with different players.

Sophie is most comfortable at center, but if the coaches want to see her on a wing then she'll play wing. She ends up the third person back in the left-wing line and McArthur claims the same spot in the center line.

"I've gotta raise my profile," he tells her with a smile.

It's possible he's joking, but it wouldn't be the first time teammates have used her to make themselves look better. At least he's up front about it. She smiles back and turns her attention to Mathers as he takes the ice with the first set of the forwards.

The d-men position themselves in the passing lanes, their sticks on the ice, but they're turned toward Mathers, ready to react if he drives to the net. His first pass doesn't connect cleanly, but Garfield tracks it down, reaching it before Faulkner can. Another two passes and Garfield shoots, but the puck deflects off Smith's stick and out of play.

When it's Sophie's turn, McArthur starts with the puck. She cuts toward the net, taking Rodriguez with her before turning sharply and pushing back to her original spot. She taps her stick on the ice, demanding the puck, and McArthur delivers. She skates around Rodriguez, then slows down so he'll crowd her behind the net. Then, after a glance over her shoulder, she makes a back pass to McArthur, who is wide open.

He snipes the puck into the unguarded net.

They meet each other halfway, exchanging high fives before they turn to their third. Hayes scowls at them both but skates to the end of the lines with them.

"You need to be more vocal out there," McArthur says, sounding like an experienced veteran now instead of the fun guy she's grown used to. "Get open then make some noise like Fournier."

Hayes turns a sharp glare on Sophie who meets his expression head on. *That's right. If you want to be better, then you have to be more like me.* She allows her lips to curl into a smile, nothing friendly or team-like about it.

The next time she's in the drill, she centers Mathers and Nelson. She streaks toward the net, drawing both defenders to her, then makes an easy pass to Nelson who slides the puck across the ice to Mathers. Mathers nets it with a flick of his wrist.

The crowd in the stands cheer as if this is an actual game and not a drill that doesn't even have a goalie to guard the net.

"That's the easiest goal you'll score all year!" Lindholm, last year's starting goaltender, calls out from the other end of the ice.

Mathers grins as he yells back. "Nah, I'm saving that one for when you're in net."

There's some good-natured laughter from the players and the onlookers before Coach Butler blows his whistle. "If you can joke, then you're not working hard enough. Increase the tempo."

Ten minutes into the drill, Sophie's on a wing with Hayes centering her. She knows his style of play, because in years past she wanted to shut him down. Now, she uses that knowledge to try to play on a line with him. They've had their battles over the years, and they'll never be friends, but for the sake of the Condors, they need to at least manage teammates.

Knowing he'll plant himself in front of the net for a tip in, she drifts closer to center ice as he takes the puck to the net. He passes to Garfield even though Sophie's open, and Garfield has to use some fancy footwork to break free from Faulkner before he can pass to her.

Hayes isn't in position yet, but Delacroix is closing the gap on her so she makes a split-second decision and shoots. The puck rings off the crossbar and flies up into the netting. The crowd groans. *Same*, she thinks. She collects the puck and hands it to Coach Butler before skating to the back of the line again.

Hayes grabs a fistful of her jersey before she reaches it. "Quit making me look bad."

Boys and their *egos*. She doesn't roll her eyes, but it's a near thing. "I didn't miss on purpose." She has even more riding on training camp than he does. She doesn't have very long to make a good first impression and, unlike Hayes, she won't have the opportunity for a second or third if this one doesn't go well.

"Yeah but they don't expect anything out of the last pick." He brushes past her, and she only keeps the anger off her face because of years of practice.

Maybe even treating her like a teammate is too much to expect from him. She'll just do her best to keep out of his way and play her game. Maybe he'll start the season in Manchester, and she won't have to look at him every day.

TRAINING CAMP IS all about evaluating options. Coach Butler blends the lines every practice, even within each drill. It means they only have a small window to work on their chemistry before he mixes things up again.

Sophie isn't always able to play her preferred position, but today he's consistently had her at center. For this particular scrimmage, she centers Garfield and Zhang. They put each other offside a few times before they find their rhythm.

Sophie carries the puck up the ice and when Hayes challenges her, she slides the puck over to Zhang. She slows up enough for him to cross the blue line first, and Garfield cheers, quiet and a little sarcastic as they manage to stay onside.

Zhang shoots the puck and it hits Berklund's goalie pads. Garfield swoops in to knock the puck home. They exchange helmet taps, congratulating themselves on a good play.

"Manage that another ten times and I might be impressed," Coach Butler says.

Sophie shoulders the challenge to be better, her mind already turning over ways they can improve. Zhang is speedy, something they can use to their advantage, and Garfield knows how to bang pucks in. They can use Zhang to confuse the defense and then Garfield as a screen. They can score their next time out. She's sure of it.

They skate to the bench so the lines can switch out.

"If Coach keeps us together, then we can be the Diversity Line," Zhang says.

Hockey loves its nicknames. There's the Letter Line when the captain and two alternates play on the same line. Last decade, the Legend Line was born at the All-Star Game when Stucki centered Figuli and Cousineau. There was the Flapper Line when all three forwards had numbers in the twenties.

The Diversity Line would be a new one. It would probably cause another lockout. Most hockey players look like Thurman, brown hair, brown eyes and white as Wonder Bread. *A good Canadian boy* as Lenny Dernier would say. Sophie isn't a good Canadian boy. Neither is Zhang. And, apparently, Garfield isn't either.

"I'm from Browning, Montana," Garfield says. Sophie nods as if that means something to her. He laughs a little. "It's the headquarters for the Blackfeet Indian Reservation." He nudges Zhang. "Where are you from again?"

"Taiwan."

McArthur leans over to join their conversation. "I love Thai food."

Garfield punches him. "Fucking idiot. Thai food is from *Thailand.* Quit making us Americans look bad."

Sophie laughs as McArthur rubs his arm. "Where in Taiwan?"

"Taipei," Zhang answers. "We hosted the U-Tourneys when I was a kid, and I fell in love with hockey. I had to move halfway across the fucking world to play but it's worth it."

"Damn right," Garfield agrees.

Chapter Five

AFTER TRAINING CAMP ends, Concord makes its first big round of cuts. Sophie's one of the players invited to stay for the preseason. Hayes is another. Coach Butler packs the trimmed roster on a bus, and they spend the weekend on a team building adventure. When they return, tired and sore, but closer as a group, everyone is desperate to go home and shower.

Petrov, forever to be known as Marinara Man after he fell asleep in his spaghetti and meatballs last night, stumbles off the bus, rubbing his eyes. McArthur talks up the aloe gel waiting for him at home, because his shoulders are sunburned. Smith and Faulkner playfully shove each other as they argue over who gets the master shower, because they're sticky with sweat and sunscreen.

Sophie thinks longingly of her own shower and quiet hotel room. Those hopes vanish as soon as she sees Mary Beth waiting for her. She has a folder tucked under one arm and her ever present phone in her hand.

"Sofe!" Smith calls out as she breaks away from the group. "Are you coming over for takeout and movies tonight?"

Mary Beth checks her phone and gives Sophie the tiniest shake of her head. Fighting off her disappointment, Sophie says, "Another time? My evening's already booked."

"*TNSN* will be on the phone in twenty minutes," Mary Beth says. "If you want to shower, then we need to head inside."

She takes a quick shower in the locker room, the first half of it too cold as the water warms up and the second half too hot, but she doesn't have the time to fuss with temperature settings. She washes the weekend off her skin and even has enough time to braid her hair before Mary Beth knocks on the door, then comes in with an outfit.

Sophie has two suits, three dress shirts, and three interview casual outfits hanging in Mary Beth's office in case of emergency. She tugs her jeans up over her thighs, then scowls at the bra sitting harmlessly on top of her blouse. She covers a yawn with her hand and spares a second to wish that she was burrowing under her blankets right now or hanging out with her teammates.

She finishes dressing and joins Mary Beth in her office. She leans back in the chair and rests her eyes until the phone rings. Mary Beth puts the phone on speaker as Sophie sits up straighter.

"Good evening," Sophie greets.

"Good evening. This is Alex Cercy from *The National Sports Network*. Congratulations on surviving the first roster cut. A lot of people are saying that Concord took a chance on you at the draft, but you must've shown them something they liked during training camp."

Concord didn't take a chance on her. They used the last pick of the draft to take her which is the opposite of taking a chance. If she doesn't work out, Concord didn't waste a pick and if she does, they'll be seen as making a brilliant hockey move. There's no risk in it for them.

"I must have," Sophie answers.

"Preseason is next. You'll play in your first NAHL-level hockey game. Are you prepared for it?"

"I've spent all summer and all training camp preparing for the jump. The real test will be that first game, but I'm ready for it."

"You certainly like a challenge," Cercy says with a chuckle. "Forgive the common question, but what's it like being the first woman in the NAHL?"

"I've been the first woman in several leagues now. There are always challenges but it's worth it to be able to play hockey and know that I'm carving out a path for other women to follow."

Cercy's laugh, when it comes again, is a touch mocking. "Already planning an invasion of women? Let's see how you manage in the League first."

"Of course."

She answers Cercy's questions until Mary Beth cuts him off. After she hangs up, she says, "You have half an hour before the in-person interviews. You should eat something but do *not* spill."

The team has a kitchen near the locker room with a full pantry and fridge. She grabs a Gatorade as she looks over her options. There's a small kitchenette, but she doesn't have the time to cook anything. A salad and a protein shake will hold her over until the interviews are done. She can pick up something more substantial on her way back to the hotel.

"Special delivery."

Sophie spins around in time to catch the sandwich Mathers tosses her from the doorway. He's in loose jeans and a looser T-shirt, his hair damp from a recent shower. He has a brown paper bag tucked under his arm.

"There's another if you want it," he tells her. He abandons the doorway for the island counter and spills three sandwiches onto the granite. "Company too unless you want to eat on your own."

"Shouldn't you be with your family?" She grabs the bag of pretzels from the pantry and two bottles of water from the fridge to add to their pile of food. She doesn't want to eat on her own, but she also doesn't want to use up her teammate's tolerance of her this early in the season.

"I can't do your interviews for you, but I can make sure you don't starve while you do them. Jenna's used to never seeing me during training camp and preseason."

Sophie unwraps her sandwich, relieved there's no sauce or dressing on it. Dry sandwiches aren't her favorite, but there's no sense tempting fate with something that will stain her shirt. They eat in companionable silence, Mathers sensing what she needs between interviews is a chance not to talk.

She finishes her first sandwich then eyes the second, hungry enough to eat it but without enough time. When she finishes her water, Mathers nudges the second towards her. She drinks that one too. "Thank you," she tells him, because he gave up time with his wife and kids to bring her a sandwich and there aren't a lot of people who would do that. "I'm sorry I have to dash, but the next interviews are in-person."

Mathers puts her second sandwich in the fridge. "For when you're done. You should hurry, though. I don't want Mary Beth coming down on me for making you late." He smiles at her, and she offers a hesitant smile before she leaves.

She makes a quick stop in her locker room to brush her teeth before she meets Mary Beth in the press room. It's only her so instead of the long table they sometimes use, there's a smaller one, just enough space for two chairs behind it. The wall at her back is covered with a black screen dotted with the team and League logos.

"It's our core of reporters," Mary Beth says as Sophie sits down. "They're tetchy from two days without access to the team. Be polite, answer their questions, but if they cross a line, I'll step in."

Sophie nods. At a signal from Mary Beth, an assistant lets the reporters into the room. They file in, sitting in the sea of seats in front of her. There will be times throughout the year where it'll be standing room only in here, but she's glad she won't be crowded by reporters and their recording devices tonight.

Marty Owen from *The Concord Courier*, one of the reporters she met at the draft, stands to ask the first question. "Concord took a chance on you. How do you plan to show you were worth the risk?"

Here we go again.

THE NIGHT BEFORE her first preseason game, Sophie can't sleep. She's in bed, because resting is the second-best thing to sleeping, but her brain is buzzing in circles. Tomorrow she plays in a NAHL game. She'll be on her home ice for the first time, donning a red home jersey in front of her fans. There's going to be national coverage for a *preseason* game, and she knows it's because it's her debut. Not her *real* debut. She has to prove she deserves that. But it's still her first time playing a game on NAHL ice.

She's staring at her ceiling, willing herself to fall asleep, when her phone buzzes. At first, she ignores it but then, because it isn't like she's doing anything else, she rolls over and answers the call.

"Dude," Travis says. "*Hockey.*"

"I know!" She grins at her phone for at least a minute, not saying anything, but it's okay because she knows Travis is doing the same thing. They were linemates for three years, playing together at even-strength and on the power play. She misses having him on her wing but, even more, she misses him in the locker room with her or on the bench.

"I get to practice every day with Mikhail Figuli," Travis says. "I played on a line with him today. I thought I was going to shit my pants."

"Charming," she says, dry, but she'll give him a pass because it's *Mikhail Figuli.*

He played for the Edmonton Hydras in his prime, if there's even such a thing given what a dominant career he's had. There were ten years where he and his center, Jonathan Stucki, traded the Maddow Trophy back and forth as the top scorers in the League. She cried when she first watched the old coverage of Stucki announcing his retirement after a knee injury he couldn't come back from. *Figuli* cried then requested a trade, because he couldn't imagine playing for the Hydras without Stucki on his line every night.

"I've seen footage of him before but in-person he's even better," Travis says. "We're playing wing on the same line at tomorrow's game."

"If I watch the recap, how many times will I catch you staring?"

"Too many." Travis laughs at himself, light and easy. "I've already been roasted for it by everyone on the team but, like, it's Figuli. How's your preseason?"

"Well, I don't have any Slovakian superstars on my team but it's been good. Everyone's so big, though. And older than us."

"You don't have to tell me. I'm playing with the League's resident old guy."

"He's still faster than you."

"Yeah," Travis agrees, dreamily. "He fucking is."

SOPHIE DRESSES FOR the game in her own locker room, and there's no one to squeeze her knee to keep her legs from shaking or to give her a friendly nudge and remind her to breathe. Once she's geared up, she goes to the main locker room, her helmet tucked under her arm. If her teammates aren't dressed yet, tough shit. She's a part of this team, and she won't sit alone in her locker room until someone fetches her.

Everyone looks up when she enters, but almost all of them return to their own routines. A couple of guys turn around as they pull their Under Armour on as if they're embarrassed for her to see their bare chests.

Hayes is one of the players who stares, half-dressed, but he doesn't hide from her. The projected lineup has Hayes centering the second line while she plays on Matty's wing on the first. Hayes has their preferred position, but she's on the top line so she's not sure which one of them wins tonight.

She sits between Faulkner and Garfield, careful of stray elbows as they pull their own jerseys on. Her knee bounces up and down again. She's about to face her first test as a Concord Condor, and she's tired of waiting. She wants to be on the ice *now*.

Somewhere in the stands, her parents are watching the game. Colby's watching from school, but he promised he'll fly in for her first regular season game. That seems impossibly far away with the whole preseason standing between her and her first real NAHL game.

Faulkner drops a hand to her knee. "Save some of that energy for the ice, eh?"

She holds herself so still she forgets to breathe.

Faulkner laughs and tugs on the end of her braid. "It's nice to see you get pregame jitters like the rest of us." He's teasing her, but in a team way, the kind that means she belongs, so she doesn't draw her shoulders up to shield herself. "Just remember, if you have to puke, do it in that direction." He points at Garfield.

She punches his arm, the same as she's done to Travis dozens of times over the years.

"Weak," Faulkner tells her. "Hasn't anyone taught you to throw a punch?"

"I'm not allowed." She has to rely on her teammates to stick up for her when she needs it, because while leagues have, grudgingly, allowed her to play, none of them want her to fight. Even the NAHL has "strongly suggested" she keep her gloves on.

"I'll teach you. If you keep doing it your way, then you'll break something."

"You think I'll need to fight?" What she wants to know is *does this mean no one on the team will stick up for me?* She hates how she has to rely on other people to keep her in one piece, but she hates the idea of being left to fend for herself even more.

She's still thinking about it when they troop up the tunnel, but as soon as they're on the ice, she puts it out of her mind. They're in their real rink now, the lights brighter, the stands bigger, and the crowd is louder than at training camp.

She takes a moment to let it sink in, the noise and excitement and sheer volume of people, before she switches into game mode. She goes through her usual warm-up; stick handling near the benches before she joins her team for some laid back three-on-two. The routine almost makes it feel as if this is any other game, in Chilton or Thunder Bay or even Stuttgart, Germany.

But one look at her jersey or the sea of red in the stands reminds her this is far from just any game.

When they skate to the bench, she finds McArthur, and he tosses her his water bottle. "I wish I was on your line tonight."

So does she. They've connected well during practice, and she's studied his game enough to know how she can make it better. "Preseason is for trying different things," she says neutrally.

"I guess. And I don't want Matty centering me. He talks too much on the bench." McArthur raises his voice at the end to make sure Matty, who's nearby, will hear him.

"Only because I have to repeat myself for wingers who don't listen." Matty pulls McArthur into a friendly headlock. "Merlin doesn't focus well."

"Merlin?" Sophie repeats.

McArthur frees himself from the headlock and says, "It's cause I'm magic on the ice." He laughs at the face Sophie makes. "I tried to get The General to stick but no dice."

"He's shit with nicknames," Faulkner says, skating over to join them.

"I got you stuck with Absalom, didn't I?"

"Absalom?" Sophie asks. She hasn't heard anyone call him that, and she feels as if it's something she'd definitely remember.

Faulkner sighs. "It's from a book. No one actually calls me that. They call me Kevlar."

"It's from a *Faulkner* book." McArthur looks young and boyish, pleased with himself. "I'm all about the literary references."

"Name one character in the book," Faulkner challenges.

"Absalom," McArthur says without missing a beat.

"You're an idiot," Aronowitz, another one of their wingers, says. "Absalom isn't a character in the book. He's one of the sons of David. It's supposed to be a metaphor or a reference, some fucking English term I don't know."

They all stare at Aronowitz.

"My mom wanted me in touch with my heritage," Aronowitz explains. "She told me stories on the way to and from hockey practice. Absalom was killed after his hair was caught in a tree."

Faulkner shoves McArthur, almost knocking him off balance. "Worst fucking nickname."

McArthur cackles until Coach Butler calls them in for one last talk. Sophie's nerves, forgotten while the guys joked around, return as Coach reminds them of the game plan. By the time she's on the ice for the anthem, she feels more settled. She looks out at the people jumping and waving, some of them hoisting signs so they'll be caught on camera. All these people are here because they think Concord is a team worth investing in.

It is, Sophie promises them. *Watch and I'll show you.*

She stands on her own blue line, shoulder-to-shoulder with her captain. On the far blue line, in a white jersey, is Shawn Wedin. He looks bigger than she remembers in his skates and full pads. There's a hydra on the front of his jersey, its three heads twisting, jaws wide open.

This is the first time she's played against a former teammate like this. The roster at Chilton was more fluid than she liked, but when her teammates left it wasn't to go to a rival school. They dropped out of hockey or pursued the Juniors route or graduated to the NAHL. Shawn won't be looking to outlet a pass to her tonight, and he won't have her back if the other team plays too physical. She's a Condor, he's a Hydra, and she slots him firmly into the opponent category as the opening strains of *The Star-Spangled Banner* begin.

They play *O Canada* as well, in deference to the Canadian team here, and a slow smile stretches across Sophie's face. The last time she heard her anthem at a hockey game, it was when they were given their gold medals in Stuttgart. Her anthem means home and it means hockey, the two of them impossibly twined together. As the song ends, she mouths the final words with the singer, then it's time to play.

She almost skates to the faceoff dot to start the game before she remembers it's Matty, not her who's playing center tonight. She takes her position next to a kid she's never heard of before. She even checks his nameplate to see if his name rings a bell. He narrows his eyes, clearly having heard of her. He's also over-ambitious, trying to muscle her out of her spot as if she doesn't have at least two inches and twenty pounds on him.

"Your face will get used to feeling the glass by the end of the night," he mutters.

"If you can't knock me out of my faceoff spot, then you won't have much luck checking me."

"Fat ass."

Sophie laughs so hard she almost misses the faceoff. But as soon as the puck's dropped, her body coils, ready. Matty knocks the puck back to her, and she leaves the idiot kid to think up more insults as she drives into the offensive zone. She protects the puck as a d-man challenges her for it and passes back to Matty just as someone's shoulder knocks into hers.

She stays on her skates and uses the momentum from the hit to push away from the guy who hit her. She plants herself in front of the net, and she's immediately welcomed by the goalie poking at her with his paddle. It's harder to hold her position here than it was at Chilton, another reminder that she isn't playing against high schoolers anymore. She's up against men who have years of experience and muscle development on her.

She pushes and shoves with a d-man in front of the net, refusing to cede her ground. Matty aims a shot at her stick, hoping for a deflection, but it rides up the d-man's stick instead and flies out of play.

Their line skates to the bench so Hayes's can take the ice. Matty sits next to her on the bench and gives her a moment to catch her breath before he leans in to tell her what they can do better next time out.

They start their next shift in the defensive zone, but Matty still wins the faceoff. She passes to Faulkner, then hauls up the ice for the exit pass. He slings it up to her, and she's three strides ahead of everyone before they even realize she has the puck. No one can catch her as she goes one-on-one with the goalie.

He pushes out of his crease as if he can startle her with the sudden movement. She fakes a shot and then, once he's bitten, skates around him for an easy goal.

The crowd erupts, and Sophie throws her hands up in the air. It's only a preseason game, but she still scored, and she laughs as her linemates crash into her to celebrate.

ON HER VERY next shift, she turns the D inside out and passes to Garfield. His shot is stopped by the goalie, but Garfield still pats her helmet on the way to the bench. "Beauty of a move there."

"A little more elevation and you have a goal."

Garfield pats her helmet again and opens the bench door for her.

SHAWN'S ON THE ice the next time she has a shift. She knows he likes the stretch pass, because he isn't the best skater, but he'd prefer a D-to-D pass if it's there. He doesn't like the responsibility of outletting the puck ever since his turnover almost lost them the Finals two years ago.

"Pressure him," she tells Garfield and Matty as they skate toward the faceoff dot. "He'll cough up the puck, then he'll probably take a penalty."

Edmonton wins this faceoff, but after some hard board battles, Concord emerges with it. As soon as Sophie sees that Garfield has the puck, she takes off. He passes to Faulkner who slings it up the ice again.

It isn't quite the same play as before, because Shawn's back on defense, but Sophie knows she can take him. She pushes the puck out, tempting, and he lunges for it. She tips it between his legs, then catches her own pass as she blows by him.

She flips the puck to her backhand then lifts her shot, but the goaltender is solid. The puck bounces harmlessly off his shoulder, and Sophie chases it into the corner. She looks to see what options she has. Matty's in the zone and Garfield's dropping down to help and Faulkner's shouting a warning.

A moment later, Shawn slams into her, knocking her face first into the glass. She kicks the puck out to Garfield, then twists and shoves Shawn off her. He shoves back, laughing at some of the surprise that must show on her face. "Did you think you'd get special treatment?"

Faulkner swoops in, knocking Shawn off her and she jumps back into the play.

His words stick with her, though. *Did you think you'd get special treatment?*

SHE BRACES HER arms on the boards in front of the bench as she catches her breath. Shawn barrels into players as if he thinks his key to making the team is how hard he can hit. It was a role he eagerly filled at Chilton. But she's never been on the receiving end of his hits. He was always laying players out for crowding her or slashing her.

Well, almost always. She hit her first real slump in her sophomore year. She went two games without a point. In her third pointless game, some kid from the other team roughed her up on what felt like every shift, and Shawn didn't do a thing about it. He let her be elbowed and tripped and crosschecked. Then, in the third period, she slid the puck to Travis for a goal.

The next time the kid came after her, Shawn threw him down to the ice.

She learned an important lesson that day. If she doesn't contribute to her team, then she isn't worth protecting.

Clive Stanton, a defenseman who makes Shawn look small, flattens Smith into the boards. He turns and smirks at the bench as if to tell Sophie she's next. She meets his gaze evenly, unwilling to be intimidated. But if he comes after her she'll need her teammates to jump in and help her.

SHE OPENS THE second period by tempting the goalie to his near post, then passing the puck to Garfield through both defensemen so he can tap the puck into a near-empty net. He muscles through the Edmonton players to celebrate with her.

Ten minutes later, Shawn lines up a monster hit. She knows it's coming and takes her time anyway. She waits for Matty to break free of the player trailing him and slings the puck up ice. It means she held onto the puck long enough that she's a hittable player, and Shawn slams into her, shoulder first.

Even though she's braced for it, he knocks her breath out of her and puts her on her ass. Her lungs feel too tight as if they squeezed all the air out and don't have the room to draw more in. She braces her stick on the ice to lever herself to her feet, but Shawn crosschecks her across the chest to shove her back down.

It's unexpected enough to catch her off guard, and she stares, mouth hanging open, as she lands on her ass again.

His face twists into a sneer. "Do you know how long I've wanted to do that for?"

She's still staring when Garfield flies in, gloves off. Matty helps her to her skates as Shawn shakes off his gloves and fights. Shawn's hated her all this time? He's wanted to *hurt* her? Sophie's competitive, sometimes to a fault, but there's a line and Shawn crossed it.

"You okay?" Matty asks, concerned, as he skates with her to the bench.

"They'll have to hit me harder than that to keep me down."

"I'd rather you didn't get hit at all."

"Apparently I have a target on my back."

Matty sits her between himself and McArthur on the bench. "You also have a whole team behind you. No one gets away with cheap shots like that on our watch."

If I do my part, then you'll do yours.

SHE ASSISTS ON Garfield's second goal of the night, a thank-you for the five minutes he spent in the penalty box because of his fight with Wedin.

Chapter Six

SOPHIE HAS FOUR missed calls on her phone when she wakes up on Decision Day; one from her mom, one from her dad, one from Colby, and one from Travis. They're all from last night after she turned off her ringer and stared at her ceiling, too wired to sleep and too tired to do anything else.

She doesn't call any of them back, especially not Travis, who she hasn't talked to since her game against Edmonton. If Shawn has been waiting four years to fuck her up, then she doesn't want to know what Travis has been plotting. It's easier to cut off all contact. It's not like they're on the same team anymore; he'll be easy to avoid.

He hasn't gotten the hint, though. He called her after their first preseason games, probably wanting to talk about the goal he scored, but she let the call ring through. She ignored his two texts as well, but he hasn't given up, calling her after all three of his preseason games and even two of hers. And now again, the night before they find out if they start the season with their NAHL teams.

He'll have to find someone else to brag to.

She packs up her hotel room, checks out, then goes to practice even though it's far too early. She had a solid preseason, but it wasn't exceptional, and she can't shake the lingering feeling that it wasn't enough. She plans to hit the weight room and run or lift until she's too wiped out to worry.

Instead, she changes and goes out to the ice. Petrov is already there, skating in slow circles. He smiles when he sees her but it fades quickly. She joins him on the ice, and they skate in silence until they pass the penalty boxes.

"I think this is the last time I skate here for a while."

"You've played well."

"There are a lot of good people here," he says. "At least I'll get a lot of ice time in Manchester."

She doesn't know how to comfort him. She isn't his captain, she's his competition. There are only so many center positions on one team, and she isn't so selfless she hopes he makes the team ahead of her. "We can grab some sticks and play keep away."

He looks at her bare head, then his long-sleeve shirt. Neither of them are in pads or helmets so she shrugs and says, "We can play gently."

Petrov laughs, and they race to the bench to grab sticks and a puck. They goof around until more people trickle on the ice. The older guys don't have the same nerves as Sophie and Petrov do. They've been through this before and most of them know whether they'll make the team or not. Sophie knows she *should* make the team, but she also thought she should've gone higher at the draft.

Coach Vorgen sets them up with shooting drills before he tells Matty to head up to Coach's office.

"Good luck, Cap!" Lindholm yells after him.

Matty tosses off a salute on his way out.

Sophie aims for the targets Coach Vorgen put up. She feels a spark of satisfaction every time she hits one even though no one's watching or taking notes. She's six-for-six when she skates to the end of the line to wait for her next turn.

Merlin watches her skate over, his expression a mixture of impressed and concerned. "You know they've already made their decision, right?"

She checks the flex on her stick. "So I should stop playing my best?"

"You're playing like you're possessed."

She doesn't admit how nervous she is. Instead, she watches as Hayes misses the first two targets. At least she's better than him.

They're only halfway through the line when Matty comes back.

"That was quick," Sophie says.

"Coach doesn't need to have a long talk with him right now. All they do is have long talks. Once, Butler joked to the media that he talks to Matty more than his wife." Merlin winces at the memory. "He doesn't joke with the media anymore."

"So?" Lindholm asks. "Can I stop holding my breath?"

Matty rolls his eyes. "Yes, I made the team. Your turn."

Lindholm slaps Matty's ass on the way by then laughs all the way down the tunnel.

"Captains and their goalies," Sophie says, unable to hide her longing. Colby was her first goalie, and they were obviously close, but she's been close with all her goalies throughout the years. Goalies, like captains, often have the weight of the team on their shoulders. And goalies, like captains, can single-handedly change the course of a game.

"Lindy's a softie," Merlin says. "I'm sure he'll slap your ass too if you ask nicely."

Sophie arches her eyebrows, and Merlin's face drains of all color as he realizes what he said. He's still spluttering when she cuts in front of him to have the next go at the drill.

THEY'RE CALLED INTO Coach's office in order of seniority. She's the first of the young players to be called in. Stepping into Coach's office is a little like stepping into the hotel room after the draft. Coach Butler, Mr. Wilcox, and Mr. Pauling are all there on Coach's side of the desk, and they still hold her career in their hands.

She sits in the chair on the side of the desk closest to the door and folds her hands in her lap so no one can see how they shake.

"You've had a good preseason," Coach Butler tells her. "You're versatile, you can play multiple positions, and you don't look like you're plotting my death every time I put you somewhere you don't want to be."

That's another point for her over Hayes. She played two games on Matty's wing and even though it isn't where she wanted to be, she showed that she can do it. Hayes didn't take his assignment on the left wing with grace, complaining when Coach was out of earshot, but word got back to him anyway.

"I just want to play hockey," Sophie says. She'll play wing for the rest of her career if it means playing in the NAHL.

"You will," Mr. Pauling promises. "Welcome to the Concord Condors."

She's stunned at first, and then her face breaks out into a wide smile. "Thank you, sir."

"You'll start the season centering the second line and playing with Mathers on the first power play unit," Coach Butler says. "You two had chemistry during the preseason and we want to build on that."

"The hockey is the easy stuff, though," Mr. Pauling says.

"You'll stay with me and my family like we discussed at the draft," Mr. Wilcox tells her. "We have a basement suite so you'll have some privacy. Jessi's already trying to bring you in for show-and-tell."

"I can do that."

"We'll talk about it. For now, we want a place where you can feel comfortable. How have you been settling in? I'm sure this hasn't been an easy experience for you."

"It's good."

All three men give her identical expressions, amused and slightly exasperated, but it's Mr. Pauling who talks. "You're the first woman in the NAHL. We don't expect everything to be perfect."

"If I have a problem I can't handle on my own, I'll ask for help." All her life, coaches have told her to alert them to any problems she has. None of them meant it. They say they want to know because they feel as if they have to, but if she brings something up, then she's the problem. She refuses to be a problem. She won't give Concord an excuse to drop her.

"One last thing," Coach Butler says.

Psych! We're sending you to Manchester.

"Your number." He slides a piece of paper across his desk to her.

It has the numbers 1-99 printed in three columns, excepting the numbers retired by the NAHL. Some of the numbers already have names next to them.

24. Dan Mathers

36. Jeff McArthur

39. Benoit Delacroix

93.

She takes the pen Coach offers her and prints her name without hesitation, each letter bold against the page. All three men look at her selection.

"It would be easier…" Mr. Pauling falters, unsure if he should finish.

"I've never done anything the easy way," Sophie says. "Ninety-three is my number. I've earned it."

She dares any of them to contradict her. They have to know she and Hayes want the same number which means they have to know whoever they called in first would take it. They picked her, because she's better. It doesn't make up for the draft, but it's a start.

"Of course you have," Mr. Wilcox says. "I'll show you the way to my house after practice. Will you send in Hayes for us?"

She waddles out of the office, awkward in her skates. When she reaches the ice, she notes the mixture of surprise and relief and irritation. She does her best not to memorize the faces of her teammates who wish she hadn't made the roster.

She skates up to Hayes. "They want you." *They want me more.* She doesn't say it, but he scowls at her as if he heard her think it.

As soon as he's gone, she's swept off her skates. Merlin laughs as he twirls her around. "You were gone for a long time. I wasn't sure you were coming back."

"Speak for yourself." Smith somehow lifts *both* of them off the ice in a hug before dropping them back down.

"I was talking about living arrangements. I'm staying with the Wilcoxes this season."

"Ronnie's a good guy," Merlin tells her. "His kids are cute. It'll be good for you to have people your age to play with." He laughs which means he's making fun of her, so she shoves him even though she doesn't get the joke.

Once everyone has their meeting, Coach Butler and Mr. Pauling address the players who made the team. Afterwards, they're sent to the locker room to change and with strict instructions not to celebrate too much, because they have a long season ahead of them.

She breaks off from Smith and Faulkner so she can go to her locker room. She'll have to do something about this now that she's made the team. It's stupid to be separated from her teammates. She's almost to the door when Hayes catches up to her. She looks over her shoulder in time for him to shove her up against the wall.

"What the hell?" she demands. She knocks his hands away and shoves him back.

He steps right back into her space. He has the same look in his eye he had when they were across each other from the faceoff dot, as if he wanted to grind her face into the glass. She's pretty sure the looks she gave him back weren't any nicer, but they're not facing off against each other anymore. At least, they shouldn't be.

"You took my number."

"*My* number."

"I was their first-round pick. You were *last*."

It's something that will always sting, but she's made the team, she has her rightful number, and it gives her the confidence to push into his space, backing him up against the far wall. "I guess the front office cares more about skill than draft order."

He growls, but she doesn't back down. He came in here acting like he deserved to have everything handed to him while she's had to work twice as hard as him her entire life. Maybe it would've been easier if she'd let him have number 93. Maybe they wouldn't be standing here, on the verge of a fistfight, but she *earned* her number. She was better than him during the preseason and everyone saw it. It's not her fault his ego can't handle the truth.

They're still staring each other down when a burst of laughter draws their attention. Down the hall, the main locker room door opens. Hayes steps back as Nelson and

Garfield come out of the locker room, laughing and shoving at each other.

Nelson looks up and huffs when he sees Hayes. "Hurry up, rookie, or I'm leaving without you."

Dropping his voice so only Sophie can hear, he says, "This isn't over," before joining the other two wingers. Nelson pulls Hayes into a friendly headlock, and Garfield messes up his hair, laughing because Hayes can't do anything about it.

Sophie ducks into her locker room.

THE WILCOXES LIVE in a nice neighborhood in Hopkinton, about twenty minutes from the practice rink. Their house sits in a cul-de-sac, and every house in the circle has a hockey net set up in the driveway.

Mr. Wilcox takes one of her suitcases out of the trunk of her car. "We'll return your rental after practice tomorrow. I can drive you most days, and a couple of the guys live out here. Carpooling is good for the environment."

Mr. Wilcox laughs, and she forces herself to laugh along even though she'd prefer to keep her car. She likes the freedom to be able to go anywhere she wants whenever she wants. Relying on her teammates seems like a bad idea.

She grabs her other two suitcases and trails behind Mr. Wilcox. He gives her the code to the garage and makes her punch it in before they head inside. They stop in the basement first to drop off her things. The stairs lead into a large, open entertainment room. A pool table and ping-pong table share the center of the room. Along the back wall is the biggest TV she's seen outside a movie theater.

Tucked into the corner is a small kitchenette with two stove tops, a microwave, and a refrigerator. The bedroom has a king-size bed taking up most of the space and there's an attached bathroom that will be all her own. She sets her suitcases at the foot of the bed. She wants to unpack or maybe faceplant on her bed and try to process the excitement of the day, but Mr. Wilcox continues the tour.

There's a laundry room to the left of the kitchen. "Amber might come down here to do laundry, but she won't bother you. The kids..." He offers Sophie a smile. "I've talked to them about boundaries, but they're young and excited to have you stay with us."

Sophie nods and follows him up the stairs. The entire first floor is done in smooth hardwood, perfect for sock skating. She catches a glimpse into the family room and the formal dining room before they're in the kitchen.

Mrs. Wilcox is at the kitchen counter. Her brown hair, threaded with a few grays, is pulled back in a ponytail to keep it out of her face. She's wearing a red and black apron with a condor on one of the pockets. She's making biscuits, but she looks up and offers Sophie a warm smile. "I'm Amber. I'd shake your hand but..." She wiggles dough-covered fingers.

"I'm Sophie. Thank you for inviting me into your home."

There's a giggle somewhere behind her. When she turns, she spots a flash of blonde hair before two bodies dart behind the doorway they're hiding behind.

Mrs. Wilcox sighs. "Kaylee, Jessi, come say hi to Sophie."

Two young girls poke their heads back out. The taller one shoves the shorter one forward, but she grabs her sister's hand and they approach Sophie together, a united front.

"I'm Kaylee," the taller one says. "I'm in third grade, and Miss Donovan says we're too old for show-and-tell but if you go to Jessi's class, then Mom says I can skip mine and go too."

"I'm Jessi!" The shorter one beams, showing off two missing teeth. "I'm in first grade, and I've lost teeth just like Theo, but Daddy says I look prettier than he does."

It takes her a moment to connect Theo with Theodore Smith. When she does, she smiles and nods, and hopes she isn't coming off as awkward as she feels.

"Well, that's the whole family," Mr. Wilcox says.

Kaylee gasps.

"What about Biscuit?" Jessi asks.

Kaylee plants her hands on her hips and fixes her dad with a look which terrifies Sophie, and she spends almost all her time with hockey players. "Biscuit is part of the family."

Apparently overcoming her shyness, Jessi clutches Sophie's hand and tugs on it. "We'll show you."

"Twenty minutes to dinner," Mrs. Wilcox says and it's all the permission the girls need to drag Sophie upstairs.

The two of them share a room, and the walls are covered in a bizarre mix of cat posters and hockey posters. Their comforters are Condors themed, but underneath them their sheets are white and covered with pink and purple butterflies.

"This is Biscuit," Jessi says. When Sophie looks away from the eclectic style, Jessi's holding a hamster in her cupped hands. It's tiny, gray with a black stripe down its back. It does its best to wiggle its way to freedom.

"Oh, um, it's a pleasure to meet him."

"Biscuit's a girl," Kaylee says. "I wanted a puppy, but Dad said no. He says it's not the right time yet, but he says that every year."

"We ask every Christmas," Jessi says. "Both of us. Kaylee asks Dad and I ask Santa, but Santa hasn't said yes either."

Behind Jessi's back, Kaylee holds a finger to her lips. Biscuit makes her escape, wriggling out of Jessi's hands, and Sophie gasps as the hamster drops to the floor. Fortunately, it isn't far to fall, and the hamster doesn't seem to suffer for it. She bolts for the open door, but Kaylee leaps into action and slams it shut before Biscuit can make a break for it.

"Now we have to catch her again," Kaylee says.

"Mom doesn't like it when Biscuit poops on the floor," Jessi says.

"I told her we could house train a puppy. Hamsters can't be house trained."

They manage to catch the hamster, then they sit with their feet pressed together and let Biscuit run around, their legs acting as a wall to keep her from escaping again. When Biscuit runs up the inside of Sophie's sweatpants, she squeaks, startled.

"Doesn't it tickle?" Jessi asks, delighted to share this experience with Sophie.

Sophie would rather not have a rodent crawl up her leg.

She's relieved when Mrs. Wilcox calls them for dinner and Biscuit's returned to her cage. She washes her hands thoroughly before sitting down at the table. They pass dinner around in a circle and Jessi takes two biscuits from the basket. When she realizes her parents aren't watching, she takes a third.

"You're welcome to join us for every meal," Mrs. Wilcox says. She notices Jessi trying to sneak a fourth biscuit and plucks the basket from her hands. "But there is a kitchen down there if you ever need some space."

"Thank you."

Does she look as overwhelmed as she feels? It's a little pathetic how she can handle double practices on top of media availability day in and day out, but it's a *family* that frazzles her. She doesn't examine too closely what that says about her.

After dinner, she calls her parents. She unpacks while her mom fills her in on everyone back home. Her chest is tight when she hangs up. She's a little misty eyed as she brushes her teeth and changes into her pajamas. It's stupid to be sad. She is living her dream right now.

There have been some bumps along the way, and she's sure there will be more as the season progresses, but she's a Concord Condor. She made it to the NAHL. And with that knowledge, she can handle anything.

Chapter Seven

NOW THAT SHE'S made the team, some things need to change. Having a separate locker room to shower in makes sense. She doesn't want to shower in an open room with her teammates, and she doesn't want to wait for them all to be done like she had at Chilton. It doesn't mean she wants to be isolated from them either.

If she's a part of the Condors, which she's proven she is, then she should be in the main locker room. It means she has to talk to Ben Granlund, and she catches him the day after Decision Day. He's in one of the supply closets, clipboard in hand as he counts the rolls of tape they have.

She knocks on the open door so she doesn't startle him. "Sophie," he greets. "What can I do for you?"

"Could you put my gear in the main locker room from now on?" She's probably supposed to run this by someone first, Coach or maybe even Mr. Pauling, definitely Mary Beth, but if she asks then they might tell her no. Granlund looks hesitant so she forges ahead. "Just my gear. I'll still use the other locker room to shower and put my Under Armour on and everything, but for the rest of it, I want to be in the locker room."

"Of course you do." He nods and makes a note on his clipboard. "I can certainly do that for you. Congratulations, by the way. My kids are already bugging me for your jersey."

"I'll sign it for them if you want." She'll even meet them as long as there are no hamsters involved.

MONDAY IS THE first day she uses the big locker room. They still have a few days before their first game, enough for her to adjust to a new routine and for the guys to do the same. She isn't superstitious the way some hockey players are, because she's never had the luxury of depending on a pair of socks or a certain pregame meal to make her a better player. If she wanted a good game, she had to rely on herself; the time she put into practice and the effort she put into the game.

Routines are a different matter entirely, and she won't test a new one out the day of a game. Even a day before seems like it's pushing it. So, after she does her warm-up in the gym before practice, she heads into the main locker room.

A bunch of the guys are already there, dressing for practice. Kuzmich, one of their defensemen, is the first to notice her. Despite being a grown man, he *yelps* and slaps a hand over his bare chest.

"It isn't anything I haven't seen before," Sophie says.

"Uh." Nelson's gaze seeks out Matty as if he's looking for help. Their captain is in his spandex shorts and nothing else, but he doesn't try to cover up. He lifts his eyebrows as if to ask *really* and reaches for his jock.

With their captain's approval, everyone settles until Sophie pulls her shirt over her head. Kuzmich makes another strangled sound and this time Sophie rolls her eyes.

"I'm wearing a sports bra," she says. Because *honestly*. She's covered enough to be decent and she's in a locker room, half-dressed people are normal. Hell, *naked* people are normal.

"Just keep your bathing suit parts hidden and we're good," Merlin says.

"Bathing suit parts?" Faulkner repeats with the glee of a man who's just been handed prime chirping material.

"Are you five?" Smith adds.

As the locker room turns to its usual shit-stirring, Sophie pulls her shorts down, revealing a pair of spandex shorts beneath them. She changes into her hockey gear, careful to keep her gaze on the ground.

"You're not showering with us, are you?" Merlin whispers.

"No. I'm not here hoping to catch a glimpse of your dick." She feels a spark of satisfaction at the way he flinches back. "I'm here because I'm on this team and this is where the team gets ready."

The locker room is dead silent after she answers, as if they'd all heard her. Good. She's had teammates hit on her before, a waste of everyone's time, but that was in high school. She expects the NAHL to be different. To be *better*. Merlin used the one stupid question pass.

"Our first game is Thursday," Matty says, too loud but it means everyone's paying attention to him now instead of her. Their first three games are on the road. She supposes it's good to get a couple of games under her belt before putting on a show for their home fans, but she wishes her first NAHL shift could be on home ice. "Montreal then Quebec. We're going back-to-back to start the season."

"The hockey gods hate us," Lindholm sighs.

"Note it!" Smith tosses a whiteboard marker to Faulkner. "Day Four of the regular season, and Lindy's already bitching."

Faulkner catches the marker with ease and scrawls *Day 4–Lindy* on their board. "For the record, are you whining because of the back-to-back or because we have Quebec right off the bat?"

"Careful of your answer," Delacroix, their veteran defenseman, says. He thickens his accent for show.

Lindholm says something in Swedish and from the big grin on his face it isn't anything nice. Delacroix answers in rapid French that Sophie can't follow. Her *mémé* tried to teach her the language growing up, but Sophie's always been more interested in hockey than anything else. Her grasp of hockey terms is strong, and she can muddle her way through a conversation, but she can't keep up with a fluent speaker like Delacroix.

The two men continue to chirp each other, laughing at their own jokes, until Matty claps his hands sharply together. "Game plan." He holds his hand out for the marker.

Faulkner hands it over, and Matty turns to their board. As soon as he isn't looking, Delacroix blows Lindholm a kiss. Lindholm flips him off.

"Settle down," Matty says but there's no real heat in his voice. He sounds amused as if he's used to this.

"I think Matty has eyes in the back of his head," Smith stage whispers.

"I also have two fully functioning ears."

This sends the locker room into an uproar. By the time Coach Butler comes in, half the guys still aren't dressed, and Matty hasn't written a single thing on their board. Coach takes a long look around the room and says, "I see focus is a problem today. We'll take care of that."

HAYES TOOK #2 on Decision Day. Maybe it's supposed to be a reminder that he went second overall at the draft, but it serves as a reminder to her that he's second best. The coaching staff is impressed with her, and she'll only improve with each day she practices.

Today, she taps a nonsense rhythm against her thighs as she enters the locker room. Her cheeks are warm, flushed from her off-ice workout. They have one last practice before Montreal. They'll have a light morning skate tomorrow, but this is her final fine-tuning before her first NAHL game.

She's limber from her stretching, and her body feels *good*, the way it does at the start of a season before she's run down by the games played and sheer number of hits she's taken.

The locker room is fuller than it normally is at this time, and her steps slow, wary. A couple of the guys glance at her then obviously return to their conversations. Her shoulders creep up toward her ears, ready for whatever joke is about to come. Pranks are important and her reactions even more so. They help bond a team and being a rookie again means she has to put up with bad jokes and worse pranks.

She gathers the courage to cross the room to her stall. Her skates hang up like they have the past few days, but today they're knotted with pink, sparkly laces.

"Thank you," she manages to say without a waver in her voice. "For a second I almost forgot I was a woman."

There's some scattered laughter. She twists her fingers in the hem of her T-shirt to hide the way they tremble. If her team messed with her skate laces what else did they mess with? Are her blades loose? Is there a rock in the toe meant to irritate her all practice? Are they lined with itching powder?

She can't skate in these.

She lifts her skates out of her stall so she can bring them to Granlund, but she pauses when she sees the Condors shirt hanging in front of her practice jersey. She pulls it out and turns it over. FOURNIER is printed across the back as usual, but instead of the 93, there's a 224 instead.

"Huh." She works her jaw so she doesn't clench it. Tears prickle behind her eyes, but she forces them down. She hasn't cried in a locker room since she was twelve.

She changes as fast as she's ever changed, getting into everything but her skates. Those she carries out with her shirt. She speed-walks to her locker room where she shoves her skates into the top of her stall. It isn't a good hiding place, but it isn't as if anyone will come in here looking for them. She stuffs the shirt up with them and goes to Granlund's office.

He's in a red polo today and smiles at her when she comes in. "I don't have jerseys for you to sign yet. They can't decide whether they want the black ones or red ones."

"Just let me know. Um, can I have a new pair of skates today?"

"Of course." He pushes away from his desk. "Something wrong with your usual ones?"

Maybe. She doesn't know and won't risk it. "They just don't feel right." She laughs, the self-deprecating laugh of a superstitious hockey player. Granlund doesn't know her well enough to know she isn't superstitious.

"Can't have that. It's the season opener tomorrow. You need to be at your best." He brings her into the equipment room and they pick out a pair of skates she's already had molded to her feet. The laces on them are bright white and brand new.

"Thank you," she says.

She takes her skates to the rink and puts them on there so she doesn't have to be in the locker room.

THE SKATE PRANK isn't a surprise to her. It's actually pretty standard, but this team doesn't know that one time her bantam teammates filled her skates with baby food so it oozed out when she put them on without noticing. It was an unimaginative prank, born out of an even more unimaginative nickname. She was the youngest player on the team and had a reputation for whining to the refs because she wanted to be protected from illegal crosschecks to the head. Baby was one of the kinder things they called her.

Itching powder was another common prank, so was a piece of clear tape on the blades so she'd fall on her face when she tried to skate. It was a risk moving to the main locker room where people had access to her gear, especially when she hates that more than anything. Hockey is supposed to be the one thing she can trust.

But when she can't trust her stick to hold up under a shot or her skates to carry her across the ice, hockey becomes tainted. She almost asks Granlund for completely new gear but that's paranoid. So instead, she hits the ice early and takes a few test strides to make sure her new skates are okay. Then her neck itches and she wonders whether it's just an itch or the prelude to something more sinister.

Don't let them get in your head. You have an important game tomorrow, she tells herself sternly. She skates a few slow laps and resists the urge to check all her pads to make sure they haven't been tampered with.

She works on her stickhandling, figure-eights, and some juggling. She glances up when she hears her teammates. Hayes is one of the first on the ice, and he meets her gaze, a smile tugging at his lips.

Do you think you'll chase me back to the other locker room? Do you hope you'll run me out of the League? I've faced worse than you. She flips the puck up and bats it out of the air and into the net. She gathers the puck and does it again.

She's poised to do it a third time when Faulkner skates up to her. "Is that the signature Fournier move? Will you score like that tomorrow?"

"Probably not." She laughs and slides the puck to him. "But I wouldn't mind putting one in the back of the net in my first game."

"If any of the rookies are going to do it, it'll be you."

She appreciates his faith in her. She appreciates even more that he doesn't try to talk about earlier. They pass the puck back and forth like it's any other day, and when it's his turn to show off, she laughs as he tries to pull off a spin-o-rama.

"Maybe leave the cool-looking goals to the forwards," she says.

His shot goes wide, cracking off the glass, and she laughs even harder as she hunts down their puck. She spins through the same shot, the puck clinging to her stick until it isn't. Her shot hits the back of the net, and she arches her eyebrows at him, challenging.

"I dare you to score like that tomorrow," he says.

"It's a low-reward shot. Besides, Coach Butler doesn't seem like the kind of coach who likes the extra flairs."

"Naw, he's a bread-and-butter kind of guy. Speaking of—" Kevlar looks over at where Coach is by the bench. "I think he's about to blow his whistle."

DESPITE THE SHAKY start, practice is good. It contributes to her long-standing theory that hockey makes everything better. Coach reminds them they're flying out tonight, and she smiles all the way back to her locker room. Tonight will be her first plane ride with her team and her first hotel stay with her team and tomorrow is her first *game*.

She's still smiling when she emerges from her locker room, freshly showered, and her bag slung over her shoulder. Her smile falters when she sees Matty waiting for her. Being singled out by her captain is never a good thing.

"I told Ronnie I'd give you a ride home."

She follows him out to the parking lot, because she doesn't have any other option. This has all the hallmarks of a captain lecture. It's been a while since she was on the receiving end of those. She's more used to giving them these days.

When they reach his car, she sits up front and rests her bag on her lap. Maybe if she's really quiet he'll forget she's here. He turns the radio on, and she's forced to listen to country music for the whole drive. It makes her wish he'd just come out and say what he has to say so that she can bolt as soon as they reach the Wilcoxes'.

Instead, she listens to some guy croon about his dog and his favorite pair of boots.

Matty parks the car in the driveway and turns the radio off, plunging the car into strained silence.

She wiggles the zipper on her bag.

"I let the guys re-lace your skates," he tells her. "I didn't know about the T-shirt. That was too far."

Honestly, the skates bother her more than the shirt. Can she say that to him? He's been chill so far, but maybe he has a patience quota and she's pushing its limits. But if she can talk to anyone it's her captain. And if she wants things to change, then she has to say something.

She keeps her gaze firmly fixed on her bag as she says, "The shirt doesn't bother me. I *did* go last in the draft. If I can't handle my team ribbing me about it, then I'll never survive when the rest of the League does it. They can plaster #224 stickers in my stall or paint the walls pink, whatever. But I don't want them touching my gear."

"Okay," Matty says, inflectionless, no hint at what he's thinking.

"I can take a joke. I know how to be pranked, I'm not asking for special treatment. I just—" *don't trust my team.*

"Okay," he says again. This time, he covers her hands with his, calming her frantic fidgeting. "No one touches your gear."

She nods but still doesn't meet his gaze. Will he turn around and tell Marty Owen and *The Concord Courier* that Sophie Fournier is a head case? Will he tell Coach Butler she shouldn't play tomorrow? She shouldn't have said anything. She should've kept her mouth shut. She—

"Don't forget to set an alarm for your nap today." Matty sounds more like the captain she's used to as he pulls his hand back.

"I won't be late for the plane."

"Bring a book or something. Road trips can get boring."

Now, Sophie looks at him. Is he joking? How can she be bored when they're leaving for their first game? Tomorrow she'll put on her game day jersey for the first time so she can make her NAHL debut.

It's going to be *amazing.*

Chapter Eight

TAKING THE ICE for warm-ups in a regular season game is nothing like doing it for a preseason one. The stands are fuller, the crowd is louder. Her jersey is heavier and her skates are lighter. She looks around the Montreal stadium, unable to believe she's standing here.

Whenever she went to her grandparents' house as a kid, she would watch Mammoth games with them. If it wasn't hockey season they'd watch reruns of the good old days. She still has a youth-sized Bobby Brindle jersey tucked away at home, a Christmas present from her *mémé*. Watching Brindle lift the Maple Cup five years in a row on grainy VHS tapes is what first inspired her to want to lift the Cup herself. She saw the longing and pride on her grandparents' faces as they watched with her, and she decided then and there that she would win the Cup and share it with them.

She spent her entire childhood looking up to the Mammoths and now they're her first measuring stick of how far she's come.

When the game begins, she's on the bench. It's weird not to be out there for the opening faceoff. She's earned herself a place on the team but not a starting spot.

Yet.

Matty and Korhonen set up across from each other. The official drops the puck, and they both lunge for it. They tie each other up long enough for Garfield to knock the puck back to Delacroix who passes to Nelson, who carries the puck into Montreal's zone.

Korhonen knocks the puck free, and Garfield hunts it down. He battles two Montreal players as he keeps the puck locked up. Nelson flies in, four guys battling for the puck now. Finally, Montreal works the puck free, but Delacroix bats down their breakout pass.

Matty scoops up the loose puck and flings it toward the net. It deflects off Garfield's skate, but LaJoie slaps his glove down, trapping it. The official blows the play dead, and Coach Butler taps Sophie's shoulder. "You're up."

She goes over the boards with Merlin and Aronowitz. Matty taps her skates with his stick as they pass each other. "You've got this."

Does she?

She skates to the faceoff dot on shaky legs. All around her, the fans boo, drowning out everything else, even though she hasn't even logged her first minute in the League. She takes a deep breath. As she breathes out, her nerves and excitement and anticipation settle into her body. She's taken thousands of faceoffs in her life. She can do this.

She takes her place opposite *Gabriel Ducasse* and her nerves slam back into her, full force. He smirks at her. "Nervous?"

She doesn't waste breath responding. When the puck is dropped, she's the first to it. She slides it over to where Merlin's waiting. "Nothing to be nervous about."

Two shifts later, he lands a hit on her that is probably deserved.

"Welcome to the show," he tells her, then steals the puck and sends it up ice for a three-on-two.

She hauls back to play defense and they scramble to keep the puck out of their own net. It's a piecemeal change to get off the ice, but it doesn't end with a goal against so she'll take it as a win.

She sits on the bench and braces her elbows on her knees as she catches her breath. Merlin is the next to sit by her, then Aronowitz.

"You good?" Aronowitz asks her.

He thinks the hit rattled her? "I'm not made of glass."

"She's good," Merlin translates. He nudges Sophie with his elbow. "Pass before he hits you next time."

"Let me know he's coming and I will."

He nods and tells her the best way to weather big hits. As she listens to him, a smile spreads across her face. This is why she loves hockey. There's no awkwardness, no dancing around how she's the first woman in the League. They're hockey players talking hockey.

They're given another shift before the fourth line has their first. She feels Hayes's glare the whole way out to the faceoff. She wins it and the crowd boos. They cheer when she and Ducasse collide in the neutral zone even though she doesn't go down.

None of this is new to her. She's faced tough crowds and players who want to prove their worth by knocking her around the ice. The guys are bigger now, and it's harder to stay on her skates, but she takes it as fuel to be better.

And it means her victories feel even bigger. She slides the puck through Ducasse's legs and picks it up on the other side of him. *Take that, Captain Canada*, she thinks as she brings the puck into the zone. They get their cycle going, moving the puck to shift the defense and try to create a shooting lane.

Sophie's the first with a view of the net. She hits iron on her shot and the clang reverberates through her skin. Merlin gathers the careening puck and sends it to Kevlar at the point. He tosses it to Smith, who takes his own shot.

The puck ricochets off LaJoie's pads. Sophie beats Ducasse to it and uses her body to shield the puck. He shoves her twice with his stick and once with his arm, but she doesn't cave. Instead, she passes to Aronowitz, and they get another two shots before Ducasse finally has the puck on his stick long enough to ice it.

Sophie leads her line off for a change.

"We wore 'em out for you," Merlin tells Matty.

Matty taps his helmet and lines up across from Ducasse for the faceoff. He wins it clean to Delacroix who wastes no time before shooting, and the puck finds the back of the net. She and the guys on the bench leap to their feet, arms thrown up in celebration. On the ice, Matty almost tackles Delacroix to the ground.

The first goal of their season.

The first of many.

It feels like a promise and for a moment, she sees their season stretched out before her—full of cellies and hugs and big wins. She snaps back to the present as her teammates skate by for their fist bumps.

"Thanks for softening them up for us," Matty says as he squeezes onto the bench next to Merlin.

"Hey!" X protests. "Are you giving them credit for *my* goal?"

"How the hell did we let a d-man score the first goal of the season?" Nelson complains.

"Power of the D, baby," Smith says, and their half of the bench cracks up.

IT'S STILL 1-0 headed into intermission, and the game isn't won yet, not by a long shot, but the locker room is relaxed. If they keep playing the way they did in the first period, then they can win the game. She knows Concord has never broken .500 on a season. Winning the first game is a step in the right direction.

You made the right choice drafting me, she wants to say. *I'll help turn this franchise around.* She can't say it. At worst, no one will believe her. At best, they'll call her arrogant. She has to show them.

So of course she loses a faceoff to Ducasse on her first shift of the second period.

"Relax," Merlin tells her. "You can't win them all."

She'll never improve with that attitude. She scowls at her skates instead of her teammate as they take their places on the bench. Hayes's line is out, banging and crashing, making life difficult for Montreal. If he scores his first goal before she does, will they give the second line to him? She can't let that happen. If she slips, it's a quick slide out of the League.

If you're not the best, then you don't get to play.

On her next shift, she leaps over the boards, switching for Matty. She skates straight for Ducasse, shouldering him into the glass then hip-checking him off the puck. When he tries to reach around her for the puck, she elbows him, gently enough that the refs won't call her on it.

She springs free with the puck, and he cusses her out in French. *Those* words, she knows, but she pretends she doesn't when Merlin demands to know what he was saying. There's a fine line between her team being protective and overprotective. One is good, necessary even. The other makes her a liability on the ice.

She's on the bench when Montreal scores to tie the game.

After that, her line absorbs minutes from the fourth line. Sophie has an almost-goal, but almost doesn't count.

The score stays 1-1 through the second period and through the third as well. They're given a five-minute intermission before a ten-minute overtime. If the score is still tied after that, then they'll go to a shootout.

"Stop smiling like that," Merlin says as he hands her his water bottle.

"Extra hockey," she says.

"You won't think this way a month into the season."

She can't imagine there ever being a time where she doesn't want to play hockey, but she keeps the thought to herself. Her line's given the overtime start, but they spend the whole shift pinned in their defensive zone. Her line swaps out for the third line, but she doesn't have much time to be annoyed with her first shift.

Coach Butler sits her near him on the bench. "Switch with Nelson. You're on Mathers's wing."

She barely catches her breath before an on-the-fly change. Matty's the one who gets the puck deep, and he traps it in the offensive zone while he waits for Sophie and Garfield to join him on the ice. She flies in, banging her stick and shouting for a pass. When the puck comes to her, she shuffles it to Garfield who passes to X.

Montreal's defense scrambles to react, but they're too slow to keep up. When Sophie has the puck again, Korhonen steps up to challenge her, exactly like she knew he would. She's able to blow by him and by the time he changes directions, she's flicked the puck at LaJoie's pads. He kicks the puck out, but it lands on Matty's stick. He lifts it up and over LaJoie's outstretched leg.

Matty punches his fist in the air as the goal light flashes. Sophie's the first to reach him, and he pulls her in for a hug.

"First NAHL point," he tells her.

First NAHL game.

First win.

She smiles and hugs him back, laughing as the rest of the line crashes into them.

AFTER THE GAME, she sits in her stall in her Under Armour, sweat making her shirt stick to her back. She has a hat jammed on her head to cover the worst of her helmet hair, but nothing can help with her flushed cheeks or the sparkle in her eyes. Sitting still seems like an impossible task as Mary Beth lets the media into the room. Almost all the reporters swarm her stall.

Merlin, who sits on her left, flees to the shower. Garfield, on her other side, leaves too. She recognizes most of the reporters from various scrums throughout training camp and preseason. Marty Owen is here in a rumpled sweater. Ed Rickers, from *The Granite Sports Network*, is wearing a tie with hockey pucks all over it in honor of their first game.

It's Rickers who starts them off. "How does your first win feel?"

"Good." She smiles, sharing a bit of her happiness with them. "The preseason is full of changing lines as we test chemistry, and it's nice to see all that hard work pay off in our first game."

"Do you think these lines will stick?"

"That's up to Coach Butler."

Danielle Rossetti, from *The Burlington Times*, steps forward. "Your line could use some work."

"For sure. There's always work to be done, but we saw glimpses tonight of what we can be. Now we chase that."

"You and Ducasse looked like you had some things to say with each other," one of the Montreal reporters says.

"We're hockey players. It's hard to shut us up."

There's quiet laughter before Marty Owen says, "Did you hear about Ivanov? He scored his first goal tonight on his first shift. You only had an assist tonight, and it took you to overtime to get it."

Of course this is the direction he's going in. The rest of the reporters crowd closer as if she's about to drop a headline-worthy soundbite. It's another reminder that everything she's doing is new. Her reporters back at Chilton learned in her freshman year she's as bland and boring as mayonnaise.

"Do you know who had a goal *and* an assist tonight?" She tips her head toward her captain. "Matty had a solid game tonight."

She successfully steers her scrum back to her own team. After they clear out, she waits in her stall for her team to shower and change so she can use the showers. Concord made adjustments to their rink, but Montreal clearly didn't see a need to do the same. It means she takes a hurried shower to wash off the worst of the sweat and pulls her suit on over damp skin. Maybe one day, if she plays well enough that more women are drafted into the NAHL, locker rooms will come with two shower rooms.

One game at a time, she counsels herself. She can't set her sights too far ahead or she'll lose focus on what's in front of her. At the same time, it's impossible not to think of the possibility. She could have a teammate to share a hotel room with, maybe even a teammate to rent an apartment with. She wouldn't be alone as often as she is.

She's the last one on the bus, but some of the guys are still finding their seats so she isn't holding them up. She takes the window seat, five rows back and sits down. So far, she doesn't have a seatmate on the bus or the plane. It means more space for her to stretch out.

Smith peers over the back of her seat. "Your hair's dry."

"I'll wash it at the hotel tonight." Or tomorrow morning, depending on how tired she is when they get in. Either way, she'll wait to take a long shower until she doesn't have to worry about delaying anyone.

They stop for dinner on the way out of the city. Sophie ends up between Smith and Kevlar. She's worried at first at getting in between the d-pair but then they just talk over her. It means she can pull out her phone guilt free. It's her first chance to look at it since before the game, and she has nearly fifty text messages.

Over half of them are Colby, live-texting her the game she played in, complete with selfies. There's picture after picture of him, the Jumbotron in the background every time it showed her taking a faceoff or even just sitting on the bench.

She texts him back. *Dork.* Then, *Sorry I couldn't come up and say hi. Things are hectic with the back-to-back.*

She has to text her mom next, then her dad. She has a voicemail from her *mémé* but it will have to wait until she isn't at a table full of rambunctious hockey players. She's tempted to slip her phone into her pocket and be done but then she sees her chat with Ivanov. He's in her phone as "DI" in case anyone steals it or looks over her shoulder. She should probably say something. It's what a friend would do, right? But they're rivals, their teams and for the Clayton, and she doesn't *want* to congratulate him on his goal.

Guilt wins out. *Heard you scored your first goal. Congrats.* Her finger hovers over the send button. Is this an appropriate not-quite-rivals text? She hits send and holds her breath as if he's going to answer right away. When he doesn't, she worries her bottom lip between her teeth. Maybe she should've sent an emoji so he knew she was happy for him? Maybe she shouldn't have sent anything at all.

"Dude," Kevlar says after the fourth time Sophie checks her phone for an answer. "You're making *me* anxious."

"Sorry." She tucks her phone out of sight.

"Who are you texting anyway?" He gives her a considering look. "Boyfriend?" The face she makes is so horrified he laughs. He keeps laughing even after she steps on his foot and elbows him. He has to wipe tears out of his eyes once he's finally calmed down. "Guess that's a no on the boyfriend."

"No boyfriend."

Perhaps she's too emphatic in her answer, because Kevlar studies her, assessing. But whatever conclusion he draws, he doesn't share it with her.

She's halfway through her dinner when her phone buzzes between her thighs, startling her. She pulls it out as discreetly as she can. It's easy now that food is here and everyone is focused on eating.

Ivanov has sent her a picture of himself holding his first goal puck. There's a giant grin stretched across his face. His hair is sweat-tousled, and there's a mark across his forehead from his helmet.

game 4 u 2??? he asks.

SOPHIE: *It was good. We won in OT. I had an assist on the game-winning goal, but the reporters only wanted to talk about you.*

Worried the message is too harsh, she sends a smiley face.

DI: *I'm best))))))*

Satisfied that she has a handle on this friend thing, she puts her phone away for real this time and digs into her dinner. She needs to replenish and do it quickly since they have another game tomorrow night.

IT'S LATE WHEN they arrive in Quebec City, but she's too tired to sleep. She ignores the missed call and two texts she has from Travis and calls her parents instead.

"Good game, honey," her mom says. "We're all proud of you." There's some commotion on her end of the phone. She laughs before adding, "Colby wants you to know he wanted to fight all the people booing you, but your father didn't let him."

"It's the thought that counts." Sophie stretches out across her bed. She's in her pajamas already, and her teeth are brushed. Her body is ready for her to sleep, but her mind is spinning in too many different directions.

"I was worried when they kept hitting you."

It's a familiar refrain. Her mom has always worried about her playing hockey, and it will only grow worse with Sophie playing against men. Her side aches from Ducasse's constant hits, and she has a bruise blooming across her thigh, but those are part of hockey. She'll have worse before the season is over.

"I held my own."

"I know. Your father says you did a good job keeping your skates under you."

Pierre Fournier had a strong Juniors career before he put hockey aside to have a family and a nine-to-five job. He's been Sophie's greatest support and biggest critic as she's pursued her own hockey career. The two roles are intertwined to the point where they can't be separated. She wouldn't be as good as she is without his critiques or the patience with which he ran her through drill after drill to improve the small parts of her game.

To hear she did well…it makes her smile.

"You can do better," she hears her father say, his voice muffled as if her mom is trying to shield the phone from him.

"There's always room for improvement," she says, echoing what she told the media earlier.

Her mom sighs, then the phone makes a strange noise before Colby exclaims, "Victory!" his voice clear in her ear. "Sorry, Mom was hoarding the phone. Tell me *everything*. Was it amazing?"

"So amazing. I played in a *NAHL* game. And we *won*."

"You beat Captain Canada. He was fuc—freaking pissed about it too."

"You know how it is. Guys don't like being beaten by rookies and they really don't like being beaten by women."

"They'll have to get used to it," Colby says. "You should've seen his face when you didn't go down on that open ice hit. Didn't he watch you play in Stuttgart? Ugh, Dad wants the phone. Kick ass tomorrow, okay?"

She can hear her mom scolding Colby for his language as the phone is handed off.

"Chin up, tomorrow," her dad tells her. "And keep your temper in check. Quebec's rough."

"I won't let them rattle me."

"You need to sleep and eat plenty of protein in the morning. You caught Montreal off guard, but you'll need to be better to beat Quebec."

"I will." *Did I play well?* she wants to ask. *I'm the first one in our family to make it to the NAHL. Doesn't that mean something?*

He passes the phone off to her mom so they can say goodnight.

"I'm so proud of you, sweetie," her mom says. "Sleep well and we'll see you tomorrow night."

QUEBEC CITY IS a...special place.

There's a saying in the League that if you want to see two teams brawl you go to a Boston-Philadelphia game but if you want to see the *fans* brawl you go to a Montreal-Quebec game. Like any good Mammoths fan, Sophie grew up despising Quebec.

In the '80s, Montreal won the Maple Cup in five straight seasons, setting a record no one thought would be beaten. Their quest for a sixth was stymied by Quebec who then went on a run of their own, tying Montreal for the Five-Cup record.

They even had a chance to make it six and take sole ownership of the achievement. In Game Seven of the Finals, in triple OT, the puck trickled through William Loiseau's pads. It was an anti-climactic end to a wild series and what would've been a history-making playoff run. Loiseau had to be smuggled out of the arena afterwards. He never showed up for clean-out day. He left the arena after Game Seven and no one's ever seen him in Quebec City since.

Well, they haven't seen him in person.

Outside the stadium is a statue of Five-Hole Billy to remind everyone of what they almost had. Or maybe it's to scare goalies away. Ever since Loiseau disappeared, they've had trouble keeping a goalie. Sophie's *mémé* says he cast a curse on the city before he left.

On their way into the rink, Lindy stops in front of the statue and stares it down before he leads the team inside.

THEY PLAY TWO really good periods against Quebec.

Then they play a really shitty one.

Sophie had an assist on Merlin's goal to make the game 3-0 then the primary assist on Matty's power play goal that put them up 4-0. Lindy gave up goals on back-to-back shifts to start the third, and Coach Butler yanked him. That's when the team really fell apart.

Five unanswered goals in one period. She takes an extra second to pull her jersey over her head in the locker room so she can make a face without anyone seeing it. Then she settles into her stall for a long, uncomfortable scrum.

LATE IN THE third against Toronto, the game is tied. She skates around the back of the net and threads a pass through two defenders to put the puck right on Aronowitz's stick. He roofs it and points at Sophie as soon as the goal light flashes.

His goal stands as the game-winner. It feels good to win the game, two of their first three. It's almost as good when Aronowitz bumps her shoulder with his as they head down to the locker room.

See, she thinks as he gives her a friendly facewash, rubbing his glove in her face. *I can do this. If I give them goals, they like me.* Last game, she assisted on Matty's goal, because he's her captain and an important person to have on her side.

Her scrum tonight is lighter than last night's, a byproduct of the win. Rickers is wearing a tie patterned with hockey nets today. "You have assists in your first three games. How does it feel?"

Sometimes, she thinks talking to the media is like talking to a therapist. They always want to know how she *feels.* "It's obviously a good feeling when you're contributing to your team."

"You aren't worried that you haven't scored any goals yet?" Marty Owen asks, continuing his work to make himself her least favorite reporter.

"If I notch an assist, then it means someone on my team scored a goal, and I'm a team player. As long as we score more than the other team then I don't care how we get there."

"Hayes got his first goal tonight," Owen says, testing her for weakness.

How does that feel? She forces a smile onto her face, because Hayes is her teammate, and his goal opened the scoring and set the tone for the game. "He started us out right."

"It was a short-handed goal on an arguably bad call," Owen persists. "He made quite a statement with his goal. When can we expect the same from you?"

It isn't like I'm not trying. "Hayes has always been a threat on the penalty kill. It's one of the strongest parts of his game. Still, that's a heck of a way to score his first."

"Your home-opener is against Boston," Danielle Rossetti says, switching gears. "It's your first match-up against your rival, Dmitri Ivanov. How do you plan to prepare for the game?"

"Same as any other game. Practice, make the adjustments Coach Butler asks me to make, then play hard."

"Do you have any plans for Canadian Thanksgiving tomorrow?" Rickers asks. It's a softball question, and a couple of the reporters groan, but it isn't as if they were going to trick headline material out of her.

"The team's getting together at Matty's place. I'm looking forward to it."

She answers a few more questions about their Thanksgiving plans, then the media disperses and she only has to wait a few more minutes before she can shower and change. As she did after the past two games, she has to wait until her teammates are done showering to take her turn.

She's in and out quickly which means she won't have a proper shower until they're in Concord, late tonight, or tomorrow morning. She dresses and wrings her hair out one last time before she hurries to the bus. She isn't looking where she's going, and she almost runs Nelson over exiting the locker room. The winger plays on the top line with Matty and Garfield, and she almost doesn't recognize him without Garfield at his side. They're like Smith and Kevlar, joined at the hip.

He looks equally startled to see her even though he was clearly waiting for her.

"Um, hi?" she says. "Did you forget something in the locker room?" It's the only reason she can think of that he's out here. At least he was polite enough to wait until he was sure he wouldn't catch her while she's undressed.

"I thought I'd walk out with you."

She laughs a little before she can help it. "It's Toronto." She isn't exactly worried about something happening between the visitors' locker room and the bus.

He shrugs, and they walk the first few steps in silence, long enough to confirm their part of the rink is deserted. That's when Nelson says, "You have a problem with Haysie, and the media will use it to drive a wedge into our team. They aren't on our side."

Like she needs a lecture on media coverage. She doesn't lash out at Nelson, because he's a veteran member of the team, and she thinks he means well. Also, she doesn't want a reputation for being difficult. "I meant what I told them tonight. He had an impressive first goal."

Saying it, even to Nelson, leaves a sour taste in her mouth. But she knows how to say the right things to the media. She's a team player before she's anything else, and if she has to praise Hayes's game, then she'll do it. She'll hate every second of it, but she has years of practice shielding what she actually thinks.

Though, maybe she's not as good at it as she thinks if Nelson is calling her out.

"Your whole 'we're teammates not rivals now' thing might work better if you didn't call him Hayes."

Like *hell* is she calling him Haysie. Given the history they have, the fact she says his name instead of spitting it is a compliment. She considers pointing out that he does his best to avoid saying her name altogether, but figures pointing her finger and saying "he did it first" isn't the way to show she's a mature player.

"Look, I get that it isn't easy for you," Nelson says, and she can't wait to see where this is going. "But it isn't easy for him either. He was the second overall pick at the draft and from the moment his name was called, all anyone has done is talk about you."

Her stride falters as she realizes Nelson is telling her to feel sorry for Hayes. She'd say she can't believe it, but she's grown up amongst hockey players. Some of them are actually this dumb. "You're trying to tell me that it's been hard for *him*?" All he had to do was show up. Until two months before the draft, she didn't even know if she'd be allowed.

"Not that it's been easy for you," Nelson's quick to say, "but cut him some slack."

Cut him some slack. What the actual fuck? She resumes their walk to the bus because the sooner they're with the rest of the team, the sooner he'll drop this. "I treat him like a teammate." He won't ever be her friend. Nelson can go cry about it if he wants.

"Team chemistry is as important as skill," he says, and it sounds like a warning.

Are you saying my place on the team is in jeopardy unless I link arms with "Haysie" and sing "Kum ba yah"?

They reach the bus before she has to come up with a response. Nelson motions for her to go first, and it isn't worth putting up a fuss. She boards the bus and takes her customary seat. Smith leans over the back of it. "You're not the last one on the bus."

She gives him a thumbs-up, then leans her head against the window. The glass is cool against her face. She bristled when Nelson brought it up, but he has a point. If she's a problem in the locker room, they'll trade her or bury her in the minors. If that happens it could be years before women are given another crack in the NAHL.

Being friendly with Hayes makes her want to vomit but it's better than losing her dream.

Chapter Nine

MERLIN PICKS HER up from the Wilcoxes, and she isn't surprised to see Smith and Kevlar already in the car. Merlin tries to joke about them being lazy, but she knows Mary Beth talked to the team about the optics of being alone with her. The short version was: don't. They don't want to give any ammunition to the inevitable rumors that she's sleeping with one, or more, of her teammates.

Honestly, last night was probably pushing the envelope. Not that there was anything she could do about Nelson waiting for her outside the locker room. *He* should've known better, but it isn't something the guys think about. For her, it's always on her mind. Is she laughing too much at a teammate's jokes? Is she standing too close? She's used to people watching her, their gazes hungry for any tiny seed they can grow into a scandal. Her teammates will get used to it too.

Smith doesn't bother covering a yawn with his hand, which makes Kevlar yawn then reach out to punch him in the shoulder. "What are you tired for? You slept until Merlin showed up."

"I'm like a bear," Smith explains. "I require a lot of food and a lot of sleep."

"You better not fucking hibernate, we have a whole season to play."

"A non-hibernating bear," Smith says which is a ridiculous thing to say and both Merlin and Kevlar are quick to make sure he knows it. They're still talking shit when Merlin parks behind a long row of cars.

Sophie picks up her bowl of fruit salad, her contribution to today's party, and waits for the other three to be ready. Smith has a cracker platter which makes sense when Faulkner retrieves a cheese platter from the trunk. Merlin shows all three of them up with some kind of cookie-brownie hybrid.

"There's no way you made those," Kevlar accuses as they walk down the street to Matty's house.

"There are peanut butter cups in the middle," Merlin says smugly.

Smith snatches one off the plate and takes off running, surprisingly fast for a man carefully balancing a plate of crackers. Merlin chases after him even though the dessert is long gone. Kevlar looks at Sophie, questioning.

"I already had my workout this morning."

"It's an off-day. Not even Butler made us go to the rink."

"Our first home game is in two days. I needed to work on some things."

If it was Matty or even Merlin she said that to they'd give her a lecture on taking breaks and being *patient*. But Kevlar just says, "Let me know if you need a second body. I can't play goalie, but we can work on outlet passes."

"How about keeping my skates under me? My lower body strength is good, but I need to adjust to the heavier hits. Ducasse got me good in our first game."

"Then you recovered." Kevlar waves off her protests. "Theo and I will help. He'll bitch about staying late, but he could use the extra exercise."

She doesn't think that's true, but she appreciates that he says it instead of "we need a chaperone."

Matty lives in a neighborhood like the Wilcoxes. It reminds her a little bit of home except the houses are bigger and the lawns are manicured. Even if she couldn't tell Matty's house by the scent of the grill and the sounds of people in the backyard, she would've been able to pick his house out from the others. For one, there's a Condors flag on one side of the door, opposite an American flag. There are also three hockey nets of various sizes and the garage door is scuffed from errant pucks.

"Allison has a wicked wrister, but she's still working on the accuracy part of it," Kevlar tells her. "Clayton wants nothing to do with hockey. He wants to be the next Tom Brady."

"Who's that?" Sophie asks. She holds a straight face for all of two seconds, until Kevlar's horror makes her burst into giggles. She's still laughing when they round the corner of the house. The patio is covered with long tables, loaded with food, because everyone was tasked with a side or dessert.

Matty, X, and Thurman are in charge of burgers, hot dogs, and sausages. The grill is going already, manned by Matty, who's laughing at something Lindy said. The patio gives way to a large, grassy backyard. There are lawn games set up along with a badminton net and a soccer goal, both of which are being used by her teammates and their kids.

This is one of the biggest differences now she's in the NAHL. Her teammates are adults with wives and kids and *houses*. At Chilton, some of her teammates had girlfriends, but nothing so settled or permanent as this. She wants it. Not a partner or kids but a house. She wants to be so sure of her place on the team that she can put down roots.

Kevlar nudges her toward the tables. She sets her fruit salad down in between a garden salad and something that looks like it's coated in mayo.

"Kuzy brought that," Kevlar says, following her gaze. "He brings it every time we have a thing, but it looks like something the trainers would kill me for eating."

Merlin drops in on them with an exasperated, "Where have you been?" as if he hadn't ditched them the moment they arrived. "I want to introduce you to Matty's wife. She's a classic case of having a better-half."

"You're too sweet." The speaker is a woman in a fashionable pair of jeans and a practical ponytail. She offers Sophie a warm smile. "I'm Jenna. You must be Sophie. I've heard a lot about you."

"Thank you for inviting us to your home."

Merlin groans. "Do you have to be nice to *everyone*?"

"It's called being polite, and I'm not nice to everyone. I got two minutes for high-sticking Marcus last game."

"That was an accident." When she doesn't say anything, he turns to her, eyes narrowed. "That was an accident, right?"

"For sure. Is there anything we can do to help out?" she asks Jenna.

"Enjoy yourselves and don't humor Dan when he starts calling himself King of the Grill." She looks fond even as she teases her husband.

"King of the Grill?" Sophie repeats.

"Being captain has gone to his head. Everyone indulges him too much."

Matty wanders over to them, a plate of uncooked sausages in one hand and a plate of burger patties in the other. He's wearing plaid flannel and a backwards baseball cap. "Are you trying to turn my rookie against me?"

"Would I ever?" Jenna asks.

He kisses her, a quick touch of their lips. "I'm going to grill. Be nicer to me."

"If I help, then can I be Prince of the Grill?" Merlin asks with a smirk.

Sophie stays rooted to the spot as they chirp each other, stuck on *my rookie*. It's tradition for older players to take younger players under their wing, but she wasn't sure it was a tradition she'd be a part of. And now her *captain* wants to mentor her?

It's almost too much, her chest swelling with pride and hope and a desperate need for him to be telling the truth. On the other side of the patio, Hayes is in deep conversation with Nelson and Garfield, each of them holding a beer even though Hayes is still a few years too young. Unlike Sophie, Hayes is allowed to live with a teammate, Nelson offering a place in his house.

She couldn't have that, but apparently, she can have this, her captain smiling and calling her *my rookie*. She can't help her own smile.

"Hello?" Merlin waves a hand in front of her face. "You want to come help grill?"

She shakes her head. As much as she'd love to hide by the grill with Matty and Merlin, she should make an effort to mingle with her teammates. Nelson's warning the other night sticks with her. She isn't willing to strike up a conversation with Hayes, but she fills a bowl with fruit and meanders over to where Kuzmich is watching a game of cornhole devolve into dodgeball with beanbags.

"They're cute," Kuzmich says. There's something wistful in his voice as they watch the kids gang up on Smith, abandoning their beanbags so they can pull him to the ground.

"I guess." Objectively, the kids are cute. But then she thinks about how Kaylee insists on playing with Biscuit after dinner every night and how Jessi cackles when the rodent runs up Sophie's pants. When the kids successfully haul Smith down, they clamber over him, uncaring of their elbows and knees. "I'm not like them."

"They just want to have fun. Surely you know how to do that."

"If you put a hockey stick in my hands." She didn't come over here to talk about herself. "Kevlar says you brought a salad. I've never seen it before."

"It's Olivier salad. My mama taught me how." His accent thickens as he talks about home, and he looks sad, gaze lingering on the kids. "She lives in Russia with my wife and my children."

Oh. She wants to ask why they aren't here or why he isn't there, but they don't know each other well enough for such personal questions. "Do you want to throw beanbags at someone else's kids?" she asks instead.

He laughs, some of the homesickness lifting from his shoulders. They wade in to rescue Smith from playing human jungle gym. Kuzmich appoints each of the hockey players team captain and they split the kids between the three of them. Flinging beanbags at each other keeps them entertained until Matty announces the first round of food. Immediately, the kids abandon them as they sprint for the best spots in line.

Matty refuses to give them anything from the grill until they show him they have fruit, vegetables, or both on their plates. After that, he lets them pick what they want, handing out mostly hot dogs which the kids take to the condiment table to smother with ketchup.

"This is different," Sophie says. It feels more like Canada Day than Thanksgiving. There's no turkey being served and no cranberry sauce in sight. She hasn't been home to celebrate in years, thanks to billeting and boarding school, but even at an American school they had enough Canadians on the team that Coach would take them out on Thanksgiving.

Kuzmich squeezes her shoulder. "Team is a different kind of family so we have different traditions. These will become just as important."

She can only imagine what he's had to give up, moving here from Russia. She knows he doesn't celebrate Canadian Thanksgiving, but how many holidays has he spent without his kids or his wife with him?

"It looks like we're in for a long wait," she says. "Come get some salad with me."

Her desire to cheer him up doesn't extend to trying his dish. She likes her salad more green than beige. She fills a plate with spinach then piles on vegetables, crumbled egg, and two spoonfuls of sunflower seeds. Kuzmich wanders off while she's debating dressings. One minute, he's by her side, the next, he's sitting down with Nelson and Hayes.

Hayes happens to catch her gaze, and he looks surprised. She offers a smile that feels wrong, but she told Nelson she would try harder. Surprise gives way to confusion, then a frown. Sophie drizzles a vinaigrette on her salad. Is it possible to be teammates with someone and never speak?

"Jenna made lemonade," Smith says, coming up beside her. "Do you want some?"

Her mind flashes through how many people are here— teammates but also wives and girlfriends and *kids*. It's probably safe, but her stomach churns in warning. "Which one of us is the rookie?" She keeps her tone light and even manages half a smile. "I should be getting *you* a drink. Lemonade, you said?"

Smith's face goes through a complicated series of expressions before he settles on what she interprets as *I'm lazy, but someone warned me against taking advantage of the rookies*. She makes the decision easy for him. "Claim a table for us, and I'll handle drinks."

He takes her plate of salad and she weaves in and out of teammates until she reaches the part of the patio closest to the house. There's a table with plastic cups and pitchers of lemonade. It looks like Jenna made enough for a party twice their size. There are also coolers with bottles of water, Gatorade, beer, and one with cans of soda.

Merlin's there pouring himself a cup of lemonade. He drinks the whole thing in one go before he refills his glass. She writes *Smith* on a plastic cup and fills it before she grabs a purple Gatorade for herself.

"You don't want to try the lemonade?" Merlin asks.

"I'm not very adventurous."

"Steer clear of the sausage then. Matty likes to buy weird shit and use us as test subjects." Too late, he glances around to make sure there aren't any kids in earshot.

"Thanks for the heads-up. Do you want to sit with me and Smith?" They head together to where Smith has claimed not only a table but an entire plate of cheeseburgers.

"I picked up a stray," Sophie says as she hands him his lemonade.

"You're alone?" Aronowitz asks, because Smith apparently picked up some strays of his own. "Where's Marissa?"

"Working."

Marissa, as Sophie has learned, is Merlin's girlfriend. According to Kevlar, she's way too good for him, something Merlin has never denied. All Sophie knows about her is she's a nurse and has enough patience to date Merlin.

Merlin takes a drink of his lemonade to console himself. "Are you sure you don't want to try it?" he asks, holding the cup out to Sophie.

"I've seen this PSA. Next you're going to offer me drugs." She takes the lemonade anyway. It's good, cold and sour enough to remind her of lazy summer afternoons playing road hockey with her brother.

"Just say no," Merlin says, solemn. "Unless they're from the trainers. In that case, say yes every time."

"Don't drink with them," Smith warns. "Alcohol and painkillers don't mix."

"I learned that one the hard way," Merlin says.

Kevlar smacks the back of his head. "Your girlfriend is a nurse."

"Like she has enough time to be successful *and* keep his dumb ass out of trouble," Smith says.

"Hey!" Merlin protests, but they're all too busy laughing to listen.

Sophie takes a big bite out of her burger and happily fades to the background as they tease each other with years of ammunition to use. One day, she'll be a fixture of this team the way these guys are.

Smith nudges her. "What's the dumbest thing you did in high school?"

"Like I'm stupid enough to tell you. But one of my teammates had never done laundry before Chilton and he used dishwasher detergent instead of laundry detergent and flooded the laundry room with soap suds."

"Aronowitz did that his rookie season," Merlin says. He looks happy to shift the group's focus to someone else.

"How many times do I have to tell you, it wasn't me!"

The guys laugh and all loudly talk over each other as they fill Sophie in on the best stories from the previous years.

THEY HAVE A day between their Thanksgiving celebration and their first home game. It's too much time and not nearly enough. In some ways, the three games that kicked off the season were a warm-up for the real start. Sophie hopes to play her whole career for Concord. She wants management, but also the fans to want her here as much as she wants to stay. It's silly, and dangerous, putting her happiness in someone else's hands.

Practice is tense, the game on everyone's minds. For the rookies and the new players to the team, it's their first time playing in the Northeastern Mountain Sports Arena, NEMSA for short. Even for the players who have been Condors before this season, there was no hockey last year. Everyone is itching to play again and to apologize to the fans by putting on a good show. Kevlar stays an extra half hour with her but then he's also the one who herds her off the ice, ignoring her pleas for just five more minutes.

"Five more minutes won't make a difference," he says as they head down the tunnel. "You're either ready or you're not."

"I'm ready." If she says it enough times, will it make it true?

"Merlin and Witzer are coming over for smoothies if you want to join us. I'm pretty sure Theo can get Merlin to drink a kale shake."

"That sounds disgusting. I'll be there."

As soon as she makes the promise, Derek Napoli rounds the corner. He's the producer of CondorsTV which makes him in charge of episodes of *In the Nest* and little video clips to share with the fans. She understands that the work he does is important, but he's always trying to draw secrets out of her. She's afraid by the end of the year she won't have anything that's only hers.

"Raincheck?" Kevlar guesses.

She sighs and breaks away from him to meet Napoli. He's doing a special on the rookies' first home game which means she has to sit and answer a bunch of questions. At the end of it, he brings Hayes in for a double feature and it's so painfully awkward he gives up on that angle after only a couple minutes.

It does mean she and Hayes are the last two at the rink, and they walk to the locker room together, because there's nowhere else to go. Silence stretches between them, painful.

"First home game tomorrow," she says.

"The cameras are gone, you can quit pretending to be perfect."

I tried, she thinks. Then she gathers her stuff and retreats to her private locker room to shower.

SOPHIE PULLS ON her red home jersey for the first time this season. They wear white on the road, then switch between red and black for home games. The black ones are sleek, but the red ones make a statement. They're bold, impossible to ignore, and she feels a mixture of giddy and nervous as she stares at it in her hands.

She looks around the room. Matty's jersey has a crisp white C on it. Delacroix and Thurman each wear the As, marking them as alternate captains. Theo and Kevlar have their heads bent together as they reach whatever wavelength they need to be on as a d-pair. On the opposite side of the room, Lindy's already in his goalie pads, and he rests his elbows on his thighs as he stares at the floor, finding his goalie-zone.

All around her, her teammates are going through their pregame routines. She goes through her own, checking all her gear to make sure it's strapped into place then closing her eyes. She visualizes a faceoff win, then a breakaway. She scores on the backhand, over and over. The cheers of the crowd fill her ears.

She's knocked out of her thoughts when Merlin bumps her as he fiddles with his elbow pads.

"Sorry," he says. "I didn't mean to. Go back to your meditating."

"I'm not meditating." Then, because he looks guilty, she adds, "You didn't throw off my game. I'm not that fragile."

It's a sign of his nerves that he doesn't crack a joke. It's her turn to nudge him. "The shine of the season's already worn off?"

"It's Boston."

He sounds defeated before they've even stepped onto the ice. It's a lopsided rivalry, but it's a new season and the beginning of a new era for the Condors. He doesn't believe it and, from the general mood of the locker room, no one else does either.

That's okay. She believes, and she'll drag them along with her.

The fans cheer from the moment they take the ice for warm-ups, and it helps her set aside things like team rivalries and personal rivalries. She skates a few half-laps and then grabs a puck to go through her stickhandling. She picks a spot by the bench where the Ben & Jerry's logo is, tracing the puck over the letters.

She's curling around the J when she hears the first trickle of boos. At first, she thinks it's because the Barons are on the ice now but when she looks up, the stands are a sea of purple. The fans weren't cheering *Concord* earlier, they were cheering for Boston. And now she's being booed in her own stadium by fans in snapbacks who slosh beer everywhere as they pound the glass.

No, she thinks as she stares down a man with a full beard who flips her the double bird as his buddy films it. *This isn't where you come for cheap tickets. Next time we play Boston at home, the stands will be filled with* our *fans.*

She finishes her warm-up, rage and determination rising in equal measure. When the starting lineups are announced, Matty's name is welcomed by lukewarm cheers. *Ivanov* is greeted by a roar of noise so loud that the air vibrates with it.

Fuck that.

She takes the ice for her first shift, ready to make this crowd hers. Concord is a young franchise, and they've never given their fans a reason to believe in them. That changes now. Sophie's going to win in this building. Together with Matty and Lindy and X, she's turning this team around. She'll build a fan base as she builds up the franchise.

And no one—not even Dmitri Ivanov—is getting in her way.

She races Carlton for the puck and wins. She reaches the puck with enough time to settle it then pass it up to Merlin. Carlton slams her into the glass a second later. He snarls at her, and the fans pound the glass, hoping for a fight.

Idiots. She spins away from him and circles the net. She smacks her stick on the ice, demanding the puck. Merlin passes to her, and she takes a point-blank shot from the hash marks. Hippeli makes the stop, but the puck bounces off the crown on his jersey and onto the ice. Sophie whacks at it again. She hits Hippeli's pads, but the play hasn't been blown dead so she does it again, trying to score on willpower alone.

Hippeli finally covers the puck, and the official blows the whistle. Sophie's grabbed from behind and hauled away from the net. They're immediately separated by two guys in stripes.

"Play stops when the whistle blows," Delmonte reminds her and Dubya, the Boston d-man she tangled with.

Sophie skates with Merlin back to the bench, furious that she hadn't been able to put the puck away and even more furious that the building cheered for Hippeli's save. "Barons don't even wear crowns," she mutters, and Merlin laughs even though she wasn't trying to be funny.

On her next shift, she makes herself a nuisance in front of the net again. This time she's crosschecked twice for her efforts, but she secures another offensive zone faceoff. They're building to something good. She and Hayes pass each other as his line takes the ice and she taps his glove. "You've got this."

He looks surprised that she's talking to him. "I know."

She wrings her hands on the bench as Hayes wins the faceoff. Merlin hands her a water bottle. "Breathe." She squirts a bit of water into her mouth, then some on her face and under the collar of her jersey. Hayes is knocked around by Boston's fourth line tough guys, and she narrows her eyes.

Newton throws his shoulder into Hayes, knocking him flat on his back. He scrambles back to his skates, but it's too late to prevent Newton's breakout pass to Roberts. Roberts carries the puck into Concord's zone, and Sophie stops breathing again. A quick shot and—Lindy bobbles the puck but manages to keep it out of the net.

"Get it out," she mutters as Kuzmich scoops up the puck. She puts her mouth guard back in so she has something to bite down on as her team panics and sends the puck two hundred feet for an icing.

Ivanov and the rest of the first line take the ice, fresh, against Concord's tired fourth line. It's the kind of match-up coaches patiently wait all game for and they've handed it to Boston in the first fucking period.

"Win it," she whispers as Hayes lines up for the faceoff.

He loses it and Boston sets up in Concord's zone. They toss the puck around as if they're on the power play. Sophie's team is out of position. By the time they're where they're supposed to be, the puck's moved again and they're in the wrong place. They're too slow. They—

The puck whips past Lindy's shoulder.

The crowd cheers as seemingly the entire stadium leaps to their feet.

Sophie grinds her teeth into her mouth guard and she nudges Merlin. "They'll be cheering for the right team by the end of the night."

"Okay," he says, a weary note in his voice as if he's used to games like this.

She elbows him, too hard to be friendly. "I mean it." She pulls on Aronowitz's sleeve. "This is what we're doing next time we're out there." Using three water bottles and a lot of pointing, she diagrams a play.

She's the first to change as Matty skates to the bench. "I'll find you," she tells her linemates before she hits the ice.

She skates down to relieve Garfield who trapped the puck against the boards, giving Concord enough time for a partial change. She shoulders Dubya off him, then pins the puck with her skate so Garfield can get off the ice.

"Here!" Aronowitz calls.

She works the puck free and passes up to him. He immediately passes to Merlin who is at the blue line and gaining speed as he receives the puck. She races to catch up to him.

"Watch your left!" she calls as Carlton gains on Merlin.

He checks over his shoulder before he slides the puck to her. She catches it on the tape of her stick and comes at the goal from the left because Merlin's coming at it from the right. Hippeli's big in net, and there's no space for her to shoot, but he's shifted toward *her* which means—she passes through Dubya's legs, and the puck lands on Merlin's stick. Hippeli pushes off his post, but he isn't quick enough. Merlin squeezes the puck between the far side post and his skate.

Goal.

She slams into Merlin, shouting as she slaps his helmet. "Fucking right!"

Aronowitz crashes into them both, knocking them into the boards. "Just like you drew it up!"

The Jumbotron pans around the building, capturing elated fans in Condors jerseys. Sophie nods to herself, because *this* is the team they can be. Big goals in big moments.

SHE ENDS THE game with an assist on each of her team's three goals.

Boston scores four, Ivanov notching the game-winner.

With twenty seconds left in the game, and Lindy on the bench so they had an extra attacker, Merlin rang a shot off the post. She wonders if he'll hear the echo of the missed goal as he tries to sleep tonight. Her dreams will be haunted by the crowd cheering for Ivanov's goal.

At the beginning of the season, Coach Butler sat her down to talk about realistic expectations. Winning the playoffs this year isn't realistic. Even making the playoffs will be a stretch. He told her there was nothing wrong with reaching for high goals but to keep in mind how long her arm is. He ended the session by telling her to think about what she wanted to accomplish this season.

She wants to fill their stadium with their own fans. She wants her team to get a standing ovation when the starting lineups are announced, and she wants their goals to be the ones celebrated.

She wants to make this city hers.

Chapter Ten

MY ROOKIE.

Matty's words from their Thanksgiving party stick with her long after the party itself. He's taken to staying after practice with her to work on her faceoffs, because her win percentage isn't as high as she wants it to be. Players in the NAHL *cheat*, which is allowed so long as they aren't caught, but it means she needs to learn a lot more tricks.

They're also two of the people who are kept the longest by the media, both after practice and games. It's normal for the two of them to head out of the rink together along with X or Lindy or Thurman, depending on who the unlucky guy who's tapped to do media with them is.

Tonight, it's X with them. His stubble is speckled with gray, and he rubs his hand over it. "I should've shaved in the locker room. Aline won't kiss me like this."

"I don't think shaving will help," Matty says. He laughs and dodges as X takes a swing at him. "That all you got, old man?"

"Once you're approaching the wrong side of two decades in the NAHL we'll see how quick *you* are."

They bicker as they walk her to Mr. Wilcox's car. It's locked which means he's still finishing up a meeting. Ever since Thanksgiving, she's thought about getting a car of her own. Between her salary and her endorsement deals she has more money than she knows what to do with. Most of it goes to her savings account, because there's very little she actually needs. The team provides her with gear, Mrs. Wilcox cooks for her more often than not, and she doesn't have the time to do anything outside of hockey.

It means she has plenty of money to buy a car. She knows Mr. Wilcox is happy with the elaborate carpool situation, but it's frustrating always having to wait for someone, and it's doubly frustrating, because she can't go anywhere with one teammate. There always has to be two she inconveniences. Having a car of her own would solve a lot of her problems, but she doesn't even know where to begin the process.

My rookie.

Does that extend outside of hockey? She's careful not to be a burden, because she doesn't want to wear out the few friendships she has, but she doesn't know who else to ask. Ivanov is just as clueless as she is and too far away. Mr. Wilcox doesn't want her having a car. Matty's her best option.

"Can I ask you a question?" she blurts out as Matty and X turn away.

X, solemn, says, "If a boy tells you he's too big for a condom, punch him and run."

"Not that kind of question." Sophie's face is bright red, and she wishes she could hide it. "Besides, my mom taught me that one years ago."

"Your mom taught you to throw a punch?"

"I can show you next game."

"No fighting," Matty tells her. "What was your question?"

"I want to buy a car, but I don't want to go by myself. I tried doing some research, but all I figured out is I want four doors and enough space for hockey bags in the trunk." She braces herself for one of them to laugh at her.

"That's a better start than you think," Matty says. "You have no idea how many guys I have to talk out of little sports cars. Low riding cars and New Hampshire winters don't mix."

She wants something practical but more than that, she wants something that's *hers*. Matty promises to help her set up an appointment on their next off day before he and X head out. Sophie digs her iPad out of her bag and pulls up footage from their last game so she can at least do something useful as she waits for Mr. Wilcox.

THEY LOSE AT home against DC in overtime, but she adds another assist to her point total for the season. She drew the Founders out of their careful defensive position, daring them to try to steal the puck from her. When they bit, she made a cross-ice pass to Matty, and he knocked it home.

I'm your best rookie, she thought as he opened his arms to her for a hug. *I'll set you up on every power play we have so long as you don't replace me.*

It wasn't enough to win them the game. It means they haven't won at home yet and, even more troubling, they're on a five-game losing streak. She'd known Concord wasn't a good team, but she'd hoped she'd make a major impact right away.

"It's been eight games without a goal for you," Marty Owen says.

"It has." She waits for the follow-up where Rickers or maybe even Rossetti mentions how she's racking up assists. She's on an eight-game point streak to start her NAHL career, two games from tying Kyle Sorkin's rookie record. When no one says anything, she adds, "I've never been a pure goal scorer. I'm a playmaker."

As a threat on the ice and as a woman, she draws extra attention from the other team, which gives her teammates more space to work with. Over the years, she's learned to protect the puck from two or three players at a time, and she can make near-impossible passes through traffic. She's adapted her game to how she's covered, and she's one of the best in the world at it.

Only, no one values what she does.

Okay, that's unfair. The *media* doesn't value what she does. Coach Butler is impressed with her possession numbers, and Matty's pulled her aside more than once to tell her he's proud of how she's a team player. Merlin always has a big smile for her when she assists on his goals, and he jokes about how he'd be looking at third line minutes if she didn't pass to him all the time.

Her team values what she does and that's what matters.

"You're not a goal scorer at all right now," Owen says. "Do you think it's a sign you aren't ready for the NAHL?"

She's currently leading her team and all rookies in points right now. That means more than the zero next to her goal count.

"Hayes has more goals than you, and he plays half as many minutes a night," Owen continues.

She has to draw on every ounce of her patience to make it through her press.

AT LEAST ENDURING Marty Owen's critique of her play prepares her to hear the same from her dad. She's in the Wilcoxes' basement, showered and in her pajamas, by the time he calls, and she's braced for his lecture on shooting the puck or a promise of a few drills for her to try.

"They won't give you a second chance," he says.

She sinks down on her bed, disappointment weighing her down. *Not good enough* isn't a label she's normally pinned with. It sucks that on the biggest stage of her life, she's falling short.

"I know." She scrubs a hand down her face. "The chances are there, but I'm not converting on them. I'll be better."

It isn't like she's sinking the team. She puts up assists, and she plays good defense, and there's no one on the team who can stick lift better than she can. She doesn't throw big hits like Smith, and she isn't scoring goals like Matty, but the goals will come. She has to be patient and trust the system.

Eight games in and her patience is wearing thin.

New articles after every game highlight her lack of scoring. There's always at least one comparing her to Ivanov who's scoring enough for them both and another saying she's proof women can't handle playing in a league full of men. It's a constant reminder that she doesn't play only for herself. Her success, and her failures, reflect on her entire gender, whether it's a fair projection or not.

It's a lot of pressure.

"I know I've hammered team-first into your head since you were old enough to skate, but sometimes you need to focus on yourself. Score a couple goals and they'll get off your back."

As if it's that easy. "How can I be better?"

"I've found some videos. I'll send them to you."

Sometimes, her dad is more overwhelming than supportive, but no one can say he isn't invested in her success. This isn't the first slump she's had, and she'll pull out of it. She just needs patience and faith in the system.

She has a feeling that will become her mantra over the next few weeks.

"DO YOU THINK I need to do more?" she asks Matty when he picks her up to go car shopping.

"It's an off-day. No talking about hockey."

She opens her mouth then falters, unsure what to talk about if hockey's off the table. What do they have in common outside the team? He's almost twice her age with a wife and kids and a house. Will she ever be settled like him? Will she wake up one day with a husband and kids and a house?

She laughs quietly to herself. She's the first woman in the League. As soon as she shows interest in dating, they'll drop her for not being focused enough or try to write a clause into her contract saying Concord has the right to break it if she's pregnant. And she doesn't even *want* any of that. She grew up in locker rooms, surrounded by guys, and she's never wanted to kiss one let alone marry one. She's seen how their mouth guards fall out then they pop them back in. She doesn't want their dirty mouths touching hers.

Besides, after years of guys slamming her into the boards and trying to break her wrists and listening to what they'd do to her if the officials weren't there to stop them, she has no desire to get *closer*. She's gotten as close as she wants to be, thanks.

"So," Matty says after a few minutes. "How's staying with the Wilcoxes?"

"It's good. They're nice." Does he care about Biscuit or Jessi's campaign to drag Sophie to show-and-tell? Probably not. "How're your kids?"

"They're good."

They lapse into silence again. It lasts until Matty pulls onto 89, then he takes pity on her. "Okay, we can talk about hockey."

Thank goodness. "We're passing too much on the power play."

"That's rich coming from you," he says but he listens as she dissects their power play. They're debating the advantages of one d-man versus two when they pull into the Manchester Subaru parking lot. "They're good New England cars. I was thinking a Forester, because you wanted space, and the guys would never let me live it down if I got you something station wagon-y. X left me three voicemails reminding me not everyone is in the minivan stage of life."

"No minivans," she agrees.

The salesman they work with keeps addressing all his questions to Matty, which is annoying, but Matty looks to her to answer each of them. Eventually he shows them outside to a line of Foresters. She finds one in black.

"Does it have heated seats?" she asks. She peers through the back windshield. There's definitely enough space for her gear.

"And a built-in GPS," the salesman says.

"I'll take it," she says. "Where do I need to sign?"

Matty laughs as the salesman scrambles to keep up with her. They troop back inside, and Matty leans in to whisper, "Remember, no 93 after your name here."

"Hilarious," she deadpans.

At the end of the afternoon, she's the proud owner of a brand-new car. Matty takes a picture of her standing next to it so she can text it to her parents and her brother.

THE FIRST PLACE she takes her car is the grocery store.

Between boarding school and hockey teams, she's always had her meals provided for her. She still could; between the team and Mrs. Wilcox, she doesn't need to cook for herself, but she wants to try. She has a job with a steady paycheck and she has a car. Learning to cook seems like the next logical step.

As soon as she's in the store, she flounders. She's used to snack runs with her teammates, where the bus pulls up at a gas station on long road trips so they can use the bathroom and load up on junk food. This is completely different.

She stares at the wall of lettuce, unable to believe how many different types there are.

She tucks her cart out of the way and Googles basic recipes. She makes a list and then winds her way through each aisle, loading up her cart. By the time she reaches the checkout, her cart is heavy enough that pushing it through the store has to count as a workout.

The man who rings her up has a brace on his left wrist. His nametag says *Brad*, and he does a double take when he sees her. "You're the girl who can't score."

Her smile freezes on her face. "That's me." She eyes the six-pack of Snickers bars and wonders if she should've left them on the shelf. The last thing she needs is Brad giving *The Sin Bin* her grocery list.

He takes her bananas and sets them on the scale. "You should stop looking for deflections in front of the net. You're too small."

Her smile slips into a media smile, practiced with no real feeling behind it. She isn't too small. She knows how to hold her ground in front of the net.

Brad drags her strawberries across the scanner. "You should pass more on the power play. You aren't letting it develop enough."

"Hmm," she says, non-committal.

"The season will turn around. And if not, we're used to this by now." He laughs but she doesn't laugh with him. "I play in a men's league." He shows off his brace. "Maybe what you need is a new stick. Or a fight. Those always give me a good wake-up call."

This is turning into the longest checkout of her life.

When she escapes back to the Wilcoxes, she puts her groceries away and flops down on her bed. She scrolls through her phone contacts, hovering over "Colby" before continuing down to "DI". She hits call before she can overthink it.

"Friend!" Ivanov greets with more enthusiasm than Sophie deserves. "Call to celebrate win?"

"Congrats," she says even as she scrambles to pull up the NAHL website on her computer. The Barons won today, and the headline picture on the site is Ivanov with the goal light on behind him. Jealousy unfurls deep in her chest.

"Big win," he says happily.

"A goal *and* an assist for you," she says, forcing her tone to stay light. Wins haven't come easily for Boston either. "I can go if you're busy."

There's background noise; muffled voices and the occasional shout. "I always have time for you."

"I was recognized at the grocery store today," she says.

"Most famous," he teases.

"It wasn't like that. The guy who rang me up told me I should get in a fight to fix my scoring problem. Or try a new stick."

"Your stick good for assist. And for streak."

Her eight-game streak puts her two away from tying the record of an opening point streak by a rookie. Kyle Sorkin set it in the 1982-1983 season while playing for the Quebec Bobcats. She has the opportunity to tie, maybe even break, a twenty-nine-year old record and all anyone wants to talk about is how she isn't scoring.

"Can get three more," Ivanov tells her, sounding confident that she'll not only tie the record but break it. Then, "Knock on wood?"

"Nah, I make my own luck."

"I need to make too. Competition for rookie trophy is tough."

Her heart feels as if it's being clenched in someone's fist at the mention of the Clayton. Clayton Maddow was the top player in the NAHL's inaugural season, the best rookie in a season full of rookies. He had such a dominant season they named two trophies after him, the Clayton for the top rookie and the Maddow for the point leader at the end of the regular season.

She's had the Clayton in her sights since the draft. If she's the best rookie in the League, then she proves she's as good as she knows she is. But she doesn't want to talk about this with Ivanov. He's her competition for it, and she doesn't want to sour the conversation.

"Have you had any fun fan encounters yet?"

"Lady give me baby," he answers. "Thought she wanted me to sign. Almost write on head."

"You did not."

"It's true!" He laughs. "She snatch back and give me mean look."

The background noise on the bus grows louder and then an unfamiliar voice demands, "Who the fuck is this?"

She hangs up. A couple minutes later, Ivanov texts her, *sorry team nosy*.

SOPHIE: *Enjoy your win.*
DI: *You get one soon. Get goal too.*

He sends her a picture of himself flashing a thumbs-up. She shakes her head but sends him a couple of emojis back before she puts her phone aside in favor of her laptop. Her dad's combed through her shifts from the past few games with advice on where she can improve.

Chapter Eleven

SHE DOESN'T SCORE a goal in Philadelphia, but she puts up another assist, extending her streak to nine games. If she scores or tallies an assist against Vancouver she'll tie Kyle Sorkin's record.

And, in a nice change of pace, Marty Owen is giving Hayes a tough time instead of her. Tonight is shaping up to be a good night, at least until Owen says, "You've only had a handful of points to start the season while Fournier has at least one in every game."

Hayes clenches his jaw and curls his hands into fists. It isn't subtle and Owen, like an instigator on the ice, can tell when he's gotten under someone's skin.

"She's producing while you aren't," Owen presses. "Is it a matter of playing time? If you were on the second line would you have more points?"

Rickers clears his throat to draw Sophie's attention back to her own scrum. "I heard you took Matty with you to buy a car." He sounds disappointed as if he hoped she would bring a camera crew with her. She has enough cameras prying into her life without inviting more. Napoli, the producer for CondorsTV, is *everywhere*. He recently did a special on her stay with the Wilcoxes, bringing a camera crew by to go through her room and her fridge before they camped out in the dining room to watch the family eat. At least Jessi was too shy to invite the cameras upstairs to play with Biscuit.

But there are cameras in the rink and in the locker room and the hallway, and there's always someone who wants her for a brief segment or an interview. She has to talk about her day, her experience in the League so far, give up piece after piece of herself so they can pick her apart and criticize her.

They're exhausting because she always has to be on. Her answers have to be thoughtful and funny, but she can't give away too much. She has to be conscious of every word she says and how it may be misconstrued, then she's labeled a hockeybot for coming across as stiff and practiced.

So no, she didn't invite anyone to watch her buy her first car.

"The next game is a big one for you," Rossetti says, bringing them back to hockey. "Will you score a goal or are you saving your first for when you break the record?"

"I'm not focused on the record," she says, and half the reporters roll their eyes. "I'm focused on playing my best and contributing to my team."

"Do you think you can contribute more?"

"I can always contribute more."

BETWEEN A LATE dinner in Philly and an even later flight to Manchester, she forgets about Hayes's interview. She makes plans for breakfast tomorrow with Merlin and Aronowitz, then waves off Theo's offer to walk her to her car. It's the first time she's driven to the airport on her own, but the airport's basically deserted at this hour. No one's going to jump her in the parking lot.

Just in case, she tucks her keys between her fingers, the way Colby taught her before she went to Chilton. The streetlamps cast long shadows as she weaves through the rows of cars to find where she left hers.

She's out of earshot of her teammates by the time she spots her car, nestled between a hulking SUV and a sleeker Mercedes. She curls her fingers on the handle of her door, and then a hand slams against her window to hold the door shut.

Her heart leaps into her throat. She elbows her attacker in the gut and spins, shoving him against her car. She pulls her keys back, ready to punch when she realizes who it is.

"*Hayes?*" she demands, too angry for her voice to tremble the way her body does. "The fuck?"

Who the hell sneaks up on someone in a dark parking lot? She forces herself to take a step back, arms dropping to her sides, as her heart does its best to beat right out of her chest. Her legs shake from a rush of adrenaline with no outlet. She's tempted to punch him anyway.

He scowls at her as he smooths out his suit. "You aren't better than me."

She stares at him, unbelieving. They're not doing this right now. Tonight was a tough game; tough to play and tough to lose. Her side aches from O'Reilly taking runs at her every shift, and her patience is frayed from the shit he spewed between whistles. She wants to climb into her bed and sleep, then she wants to wake up tomorrow and tackle all the things they need to fix so they can beat Vancouver.

She definitely doesn't want to be alone in an airport parking lot with Michael fucking Hayes.

"*I* was the first-round pick."

"Yes," she snaps. "You were Concord's first pick and I was their last. Can I go home now?"

She's done her best to avoid him, difficult because they're on the same team, but since he's avoided her too it's worked. Tonight, she doesn't have the time to cater to his ego. They're on a six-game losing streak. They've lost seven of their first nine games, an abysmal start even for Concord. She hasn't scored a goal yet and if she doesn't fix her game, doesn't fix this *season,* she might not play next year.

Hayes could be sent down to Manchester midway through the season and start next season with Concord. He could be a fourth liner all season and then get bumped up next one. If she isn't good, if she isn't *the best,* she doesn't get to play.

"I'm better than you," he says as if he needs her to admit it.

She takes a step closer, crowding him against the side of her car. He has two inches on her, but she's the heavier of the two, and she likes her odds if this turns into a real fight. "You haven't shown it so far."

He grabs her by the lapels of her suit jacket and slams her back against her car. Her keys slip from her hand and fall to the pavement. He presses closer as if he can intimidate her. "You're an experiment and with every game, you prove it's a failed one."

He stalks off before she finds her voice.

She doesn't know how long she stands there, shaking, until she bends down to pick up her keys.

MARY BETH CALLS Sophie into practice early, never a good thing. When she arrives in Mary Beth's office, Coach Butler and Matty are there too, standing on either side of her. Her desk is covered in newspaper and internet articles. Each one has a picture from Hayes's interview last night—eyes hard, hands curled into fists. It reminds her of their encounter in the parking lot, and she drops her gaze to the articles, hoping to hide the flicker of fear.

She slept restlessly as she played out all the ways last night could've gone worse than it did. She skims one article which cites trouble in the locker room. Another is full of anonymous sources who claim having a girl in the room is a distraction. Another says what she brings to the team isn't worth the hassle she brings with her.

At least there's no hint of what happened in the parking lot. She would've had a very different phone call with Mary Beth this morning if any of that had leaked. She's lucky none of the airport cameras picked anything up. She can't count on being so lucky again. She needs to control herself better.

She glances from the articles to where the three adults are lined up on the other side of the desk.

"Is this going to be a problem?" Coach Butler asks.

Are you going to be a problem? She can't help but notice she's the one in Mary Beth's office first thing in the morning. And Matty's with Coach and Mary Beth, leaving her on her own. So much for being his rookie. But this isn't the first time she's dealt with inter-team issues, and it certainly isn't the first time she's had to handle things on her own. She squares her shoulders. "It was a tough loss. The question caught Hayes off guard."

Coach Butler nods. "That's what I thought."

That's what I wanted to hear.

Next to Coach, Matty frowns. Mary Beth, so far, hasn't reacted to anything. Hoping to assuage the worries in the room, Sophie says, "We talked it out last night."

Now, Mary Beth reacts, eyes widening. "You talked it out?" She shakes her head. "We need to do something to counter these articles, a fluff piece either with *GSSN* or CondorsTV."

"Whatever you have to do," Coach Butler says. "All I want is to coach hockey." He leaves the office, but his disappointment lingers, a solid weight on Sophie's shoulders. He's a no fuss coach who expects the best out of all his players. He won't like the distraction of the articles, and it won't take many more of them for him to decide *Sophie* is the distraction.

"You and Hayes will do a video together," Mary Beth says. "You'll wear makeup and you'll let someone curl your hair. I'll write out some nice things for you two to say about each other and then you'll play a friendly game of ping-pong in the Wilcoxes' basement and we'll put this behind us."

Sophie nods.

Mary Beth's quiet for a moment. Her gaze flicks between Sophie and Matty. "What did you mean when you said you talked it out last night?"

"We talked." She should've kept her mouth shut. Now, Mary Beth will pry into things Sophie would rather keep secret. She doesn't know if she and Hayes can put last night or the past four years behind them, but they definitely won't if more people get involved.

"When?" Matty asks. "You didn't sit near each other on the plane."

"We parked near each other." She smiles, hoping to reassure them. "It's nothing to worry about. Just two hockey players having a chat."

"Is that what Michael will say when I meet with him?" Mary Beth asks. Sophie's gaze snaps up to hers, surprised. Mary Beth stares back evenly and unimpressed. "Did you think you were the only one we were going to talk to?"

Yes. "I don't know what Hayes will tell you. It's been a tough string of losses. People get frustrated and they say things they shouldn't." She looks down at the articles again.

"We'll fix it," Mary Beth promises, then her expression turns serious. "No more late-night talks."

Sophie nods. She wouldn't have had this one if she could've avoided it. "May I dress for practice now?"

"Go. It's an open practice. All the cameras will be focused on the two of you."

Of course they will be. She's already tired, and she hasn't even warmed-up yet. She heads out of Mary Beth's office, but leans against the wall to fish her phone out of her pocket. It buzzes angrily at her with a call from Merlin. Her stomach sinks as she answers it. Between last night and the early morning, she completely forgot about breakfast.

"I'm so sorry," she says. "Mary Beth called me in."

She walks down the hall as he asks, "Everything okay?"

"Nothing you need to worry about. It's fine." She runs a hand through her hair and wishes, not for the first time, that her hockey path wasn't so damn complicated.

"It doesn't sound fine. We just sat down. We can order you something and bring it in with us. Did you eat breakfast?"

"I had a shake."

"I don't care what the strength and conditioning coaches say, protein shakes don't count as meals. Yeah, we're definitely bringing you something. Blueberry crepes? Stuffed French toast?"

"I'll make something in the team kitchen."

"Not even a little chuckle there? We'll be there as soon as they can pack our food in boxes."

"You really don't have to do that," she says but Merlin's already hung up. She shoves her phone back into her pocket and enters the locker room.

Matty follows her in a minute later, and he looks around the room before he pokes his head into the shower room. "A late-night talk? Is everything okay?"

"It's *fine*." She turns her back so she can change into her practice clothes. "Contrary to what everyone in this organization thinks, I have played with teammates who didn't like me before." *I'm not a problem. I don't need to be fixed.*

"That's not—" Matty breathes out, frustrated.

Sophie tosses her shirt into her locker and pulls out her practice shirt. "We've been on a losing skid, and I want to score a stupid goal. That's what I'm focused on right now."

"I'll stay an extra half hour to work on shots with you."

"Thanks."

Matty waits until her shirt is on to clasp her shoulder. "You're my rookie. That means I look out for you."

Am I?

THEY'RE DOWN 0-2 after the first period against Vancouver. The crowd in the stands, already thin, has thinned further by the time they take the ice for the second. It's a small consolation that Concord is too far from Vancouver for the stands to be flooded with Vancouver fans. Would it be better to have the seats filled with green uniforms than be mostly empty?

So far, her quest to turn Concord into a hockey city has been a failure. With each loss, fewer and fewer fans turn out to watch them. There's rumblings that the sponsors might not renew their contracts when they come up again. If the funding is pulled from the team, does it fall apart? There's talk of New York wanting a second team, and they have the fanbase and the funding to support it.

She doesn't want to move. If her franchise is bought out and relocated, it's a failure and one she'll take on her shoulders. They have an opportunity to cement the Condors' place in Concord.

She switches for Thurman, hopping on the ice while he meanders off it. She has to avoid the puck, because he still isn't on the bench, and there's no way she's risking a penalty for having too many men on the ice.

"Good! Good!" Matty shouts from the bench.

She pulls the puck away from Hatch. While he's still recovering, she blows by him, carrying the puck into the offensive zone. She drives the net, two defenders swarming her then makes a back pass to the point. Smith is there to settle the puck and fire it at the net.

Enzi, the goalie, flails, and the puck deflects off his blocker and into the glass. The puck makes a sharp cracking sound before it drops harmlessly to the ice. Sophie tries to push through the defenders to reach it first, but they sandwich her between them, holding her still.

Aronowitz slings the puck up the boards to Merlin. Sophie frees herself in time for his shot to be blocked, sparking a rush in the other direction.

FOUR MINUTES INTO the second period, Kevlar tosses the puck up to her. She's a step ahead of every player on the ice and with two powerful strides, she's on a breakaway. It's her and Enzi, and she has a whole arsenal of moves. Two more strides, and she'll fake a shot then go high glove side, because he's looked weak there all game.

One stride then—

Something catches her ankle and *pulls*.

She loses her balance. The puck trickles harmlessly off her stick as she falls on the ice. She scrambles back to her skates, because there's still time to salvage the play. Enzi covers the puck and the official blows his whistle, arm raised in the air.

"Are you fucking kidding me?" Hatch demands, skating up to the official. "I barely fucking touched her!"

Maxime Proust looks unfazed by Hatch's rant so the forward turns to Sophie, a sneer on his face. "You went down fucking easy. Are you a little bitch or a hockey player?"

Merlin reaches Sophie in time to plant a hand on the logo on her jersey to keep her from stepping up and snapping back at the opposing player. It's Theo who steps in front of Hatch, completely blocking him from Sophie's view. "Go take your time out. Maybe when it's over you'll have calmed down enough to play with the big kids again."

Hatch snarls a few more insults, but he isn't stupid enough to throw down with Theo.

Since she drew the penalty late in her shift, she sits as the second power play unit takes the ice. Thurman wins the faceoff, and then her team goes to work. They pass, a dizzying pattern that Vancouver can't keep up with. Point-to-point, down low, back up until X winds up and shoots. By chance, Enzi's in the right place, and the puck hits his shoulder then the crossbar then drops to the ice.

Thurman's right on his doorstep, and he tips the puck in.

Sophie jumps to her feet along with the rest of the players on the bench. A power play goal and the game is 1-2. Tying the game is within their reach, and then they can push to win it. They can snap their losing streak, and maybe the stands will be fuller for their game against Cleveland.

"I don't think his break was long enough," Theo says as Hatch does the skate of shame from the box back to his bench. He scowls at Sophie on his way. "You let me handle him."

"Nothing stupid," Sophie says.

"I'll leave that to him."

VANCOUVER TAKES ANOTHER penalty late in the period. Coach Butler looks down his bench with a frown. Matty and his line were on the ice before the penalty, and even though Matty stands tall next to his bench, it's obvious his breathing is labored. And, on the shift before, Thurman blocked a shot, and he's wincing at the end of the bench as the trainers hover.

"First unit out," Coach Butler finally says. "Hayes is your fifth. Fournier, you take the faceoff."

It's the first shift they've ever played together, and Sophie looks over, willing to set aside her frustration with him if it means tying the game. He meets her gaze and nods. Okay, then.

She skates to the faceoff dot. A glance at the crowd shows them leaning forward in their seats. Concord's already scored once on the power play, and it was enough to make them believe. Sophie smiles and adjusts her grip on her stick.

The puck is dropped and she moves first, knocking it over to Hayes. He passes to Kevlar and they set up. It's different having Hayes on the ice instead of Matty, but he plants himself in front of Enzi, and she can work with this. They move the puck around, quick, crisp passes. Hayes holds his ground. He'll be a screen, or he'll deflect the puck. They just need a shot.

Sophie passes to Kevlar then switches with him, drifting lower as he skates to the point. She fades out of the play until Vancouver forgets about her. Kevlar fakes a pass to Garfield and then slings it down to her. She shoots a one-timer, the puck flying on goal. Enzi doesn't even come close to stopping it.

The puck hits the back of the net, and Sophie's frozen for a moment, unbelieving, before she throws her arms up.

Her first fucking NAHL goal!

Behind her, the fans pound on the glass and chant her name. Garfield crashes into her, then Kevlar. Merlin and Hayes join them a moment later. Merlin's smile isn't as bright as she was expecting, and Hayes looks...guilty?

Kevlar rubs her helmet and she looks up at the Jumbotron.

Her stomach sinks as she watches the replay. The reason Enzi doesn't stop her shot is because Hayes's stick is on Enzi's, holding it down. And since Hayes is in the crease... Her excitement fizzles out as Vancouver challenges for goaltender interference.

The crowd boos, the loudest they've been all night. They pause when Maxime Proust announces that the goal has been called back, and then they start up again with even more force.

Matty pats her helmet after the announcement. "You'll get it."

"You rested after that nonsense?" Coach Butler asks. The players on the ice nod. "I want the first unit out there. Score and make sure it counts this time."

She takes the ice again, Matty with them instead of Hayes. Vancouver doesn't forget about her this time. When she and Kevlar switch like they did before, she's shadowed by a Vancouver player. It doesn't stop Kevlar from passing to her. As soon as the player defending her steps up, she slides a pass through his legs and past another defender. Matty catches the puck on his tape then shoots.

This time, Sophie looks at the officials before celebrating.

THEY LOSE 2-3.

She allows herself to be frustrated on the long walk down to the locker room and then she shoves it aside, because she needs to put her best face on for the reporters. She strips down to her Under Armour and sits in her stall. She's surprised when Matty comes over.

"The press will be brutal tonight," he says. "Everything will be about your non-goal."

"I figured." Matty lingers which means he has more to say but isn't sure how to word it. There's only one thing he could be trying to say diplomatically so she beats him to the punch. "It wasn't Hayes's fault. He was being a nuisance in front of the net like he's supposed to. I'll have other opportunities to score."

Matty taps the brim of her hat and heads over to have a similar conversation with Hayes. She braces her elbows on her thighs and takes a deep breath.

When her reporters swarm, she tells them what she told Matty. She even believes it. Would she like to have scored there? Obviously. But she isn't holding a grudge against Hayes. There are plenty of legitimate reasons she has to hate him. One goalie interference call doesn't even scratch the surface.

By the time she's done with her media, the only person still with reporters around him is Hayes. She shoves her feet into her sliders and goes down the hall so she can shower. Let someone else be the last person here tonight. She wants to go home, fall into bed, and dream about scoring against Cleveland.

When she emerges from her locker room, Theo and Kevlar are waiting for her.

"Hi?" she asks.

"I had to talk to the trainers," Theo says. "We're just heading out."

"What a coincidence." She wonders if Matty told them she isn't allowed to be by herself in parking lots anymore. It isn't worth being resentful over, so she just sighs and lets them flank her. "Are you going to follow me home too? It'll put a damper on my plans to sneak through the McDonalds drive-thru."

"You're hungry?" Theo asks. He laughs. "Stupid question. We'll stop somewhere real. Where do you want to go?"

She's not sure she'll stay awake long enough for somewhere real, but she shrugs and lets Kevlar pick. Honestly, so long as she eats, she doesn't care what it is.

WHATEVER TENUOUS TRUCE she and Hayes built in the game yesterday evaporates while *GSSN* films them in the Wilcoxes' basement. For one, Sophie's in stiff designer jeans and a floral blouse, which means she's in a real bra and the straps dig into her skin. Second, she's in *makeup* and they curled her hair, the way they do whenever they want her to look soft and approachable.

It's bullshit.

At least Rickers doesn't ask Hayes about "ruining Sophie's big moment last night" the way Marty Owen did after the game.

IN ALL THE coverage of Sophie's goal-that-wasn't, the fact she tied Kyle Sorkin's record was lost. Even Sophie forgot about it, too frustrated by losing her goal, then losing the game, then having to play nice with Hayes.

She's preparing for the game against Cleveland when she sees she has a voicemail on her phone. She listens to it, laughing at her *mémé*'s message.

"Yeah?" Merlin asks. He looks as if he could use a laugh. They all do, worn down by their now seven-game losing streak.

"Just my *mémé* reminding me there's nothing a Bobcat can do that I can't do better."

Merlin raises his eyebrows. "Oh, right, you were a Mammoths fan growing up."

"*Oui*," she says and shakes out her shoulders.

While her accomplishment last game was glossed over, everyone knows what tonight could mean. *TNSN* flew Brindle and Sorkin to cover the game. It's their first game on a national broadcast which makes it even more important that they win this one. She takes a deep breath and puts her headphones in.

It's Aronowitz's week to pick the music for the locker room, and he listens to weird dubstep.

SHE RINGS THE puck off the crossbar twice in the first period. The second time, the puck dings off the side post then the crossbar then drops into Augereau's glove. She almost snaps her stick.

In the second period, she takes two penalties. The hook was an honest accident. The slash...was not. She sits in the box and fumes. Hayes scores a shorty, bringing the fans to their feet. *That should be me*, she thinks, bitter. She splashes some water on her face, but it doesn't cool her off any.

Going into the third, they're up 4-2; a goal apiece for Hayes and Theo, and two goals for Matty. She hasn't assisted on any of them. She tries to tell herself it doesn't matter. Her team's on track to snap their losing streak and team comes first.

But she wants the record.

Her line has an extended shift in Cleveland's zone, and she takes what feels like a dozen shots on Augereau, Cleveland's backup goalie, but none of them go in. The goalie finally dives on top of the puck and doesn't move until the official blows his whistle.

Sophie's line switches out with Hayes's and as they pass each other he mutters, "Tick tock."

She looks at the game clock. 11:27. She narrows her eyes at him but doesn't have a chance to snap anything back, because Merlin nudges her toward the bench.

CLEVELAND SCORES WITH 3:47 left in the game to put them within one.

With 1:38 left on the clock, the Presidents call a timeout.

Sophie crowds closer to Coach's clipboard and ignores Hayes's quiet *tick, tock*. She tied a twenty-nine-year old record. What has *he* done this season?

After the timeout, Augereau is on the bench so that Cleveland has an extra attacker. Sophie sits on the bench as Matty's line is sent out. She chews on her mouth guard as Matty loses the draw. Her team tries to clear the puck twice and fails. Cleveland sets up their cycle and she bites down harder on her mouth guard. They only need to hold out a little longer then they'll have their third win of the season.

Matty's line switches out for the third.

"Fournier, you're replacing Nelson," Coach Butler says. "Mathers, as soon as you have your breath back, you're on the ice."

Sophie shifts on the bench so she's next to Matty and Garfield. Nelson doesn't look happy to be pushed off his line, but he moves over so there's space for her.

"Passing lanes," Matty says, breathing hard. "Stick on ice."

Sophie nods. A couple seconds later, Farage's shot deflects off Kuzy's stick and out of play. Matty stands up. Sophie and Garfield follow him over the boards.

There's 0:37 left in the game.

Sophie takes a deep breath as she skates onto the ice. Is this a test? If it is, she'll pass it. She'll prove to Coach Butler that she'll put the team before herself. If she can keep Cleveland from scoring, she doesn't care if she breaks Sorkin's record. Will that be enough to show her commitment to this team?

Matty wins the faceoff to Garfield. The winger is swarmed by Cleveland players and coughs up the puck. Sophie challenges Farage, Cleveland's captain, and manages to take the puck from him. Her clearing pass is knocked down by Olsson. The defenseman passes to his partner who passes to McGuire. Sophie steps out to challenge him, only to chase down Farage after McGuire passes.

She darts between players, always a step too slow. Garfield blocks a shot. He grunts with the impact but doesn't go down. X swings his stick at the puck and it somehow misses two Cleveland players as it skitters down the ice. Sophie doesn't bother chasing after it. She does her best to catch her breath as a whistle blows for the icing.

Garfield skates off the shot block.

She glances at the clock.

0:14 left.

Tick, tock.

Her breathing is ragged and too loud in her ears as she jostles with McGuire for position. Matty cheats on the faceoff, blatant enough to be given a warning. It buys Sophie another deep breath. He cheats again, and he's tossed from the dot. He taps her skates. "You can win this."

"Aww," Farage drawls.

Sophie rolls her eyes, then beats him to the puck. As soon as she knocks the puck back, she skates up to her defensive coverage. Matty passes up to Garfield, but Olsson is there to take the puck. Sophie's there a second later. She knocks the puck off his stick, toward the blue line. Olsson's the last line of defense for the Cleveland team so she snaps up the puck and *goes*. She flies down the ice with a clock counting down in her head.

If she makes it to the red line, then she can't ice the puck.

Or she could *score*. There's no goalie for anyone to interfere with this time. She can cement their win, break a record, *and* get this damn goal.

"Behind you!" Matty shouts. She glances to see Olsson gaining on her. He isn't fast enough, but Matty's skating up the other wing, using the last of his energy to give her an option if she needs it. She glances at the open net then over at her captain. A flick of her wrists, and she can put all the stupid storylines to rest.

She passes.

Matty bobbles the puck, surprised it's on his stick, before he nets an easy goal.

The goal light flashes.

The fans leap to their feet, shouting and screaming as they toss their hats. Sophie grins and scoops the puck out of the net, offering it to her captain. "Hatty for Matty."

He doesn't take it. "It could've been yours."

I put the team first. I gave up my first goal so you could have a hat trick. Does this mean I'm your rookie again? Are you on my side? Against Coach Butler and Hayes and everyone out there who wants me gone?

She presses the puck into his glove. "I'll get mine." Before he can protest further, the rest of their line reaches them, full of expletives and helmet pats for the first hat trick of their season. The bench is jubilant as they skate through for their fist bumps. Sophie's still grinning as she takes her customary seat next to Merlin.

"Eleven-game point streak and a record. Not bad, rookie."

SHE HANGS OUT at ice level after the game is over so she can skate out as she's announced as the second star of the game. She lifts her stick to the fans who stayed to cheer. *Come back and we'll show you more games like this.* She skates back, and the stadium grows louder as Matty's announced as the first star.

They head to the locker room together, but Matty lags behind as they reach the door.

"Don't tell me you're tired," she teases as she opens the doors. He just grins, and she walks face first into an aluminum pie pan full of whipped cream. In the background, her teammates whoop and cheer as she splutters and tries to breathe.

"Is that even on your diet plan?" Merlin asks as someone puts a towel in her hand.

"You're right." She wipes the worst of the whipped cream off her face. "I shouldn't have this all on my own." It's Merlin's only warning before she lunges and rubs the towel all over his face. He yelps and tries to jump back, but Theo and Kevlar grab him and hold him still.

Within minutes, the whole team is laughing, loose with the win and the hat trick. Matty gives her the puck back with a strip of tape on it.

Sophie Fournier – 11-Game Point Streak 10/26/11.

She clutches it to her chest. This is the best night of her career so far.

Chapter Twelve

THEY GO TO New York and beat the Empires, which marks their first back-to-back wins of the season. She extends her point streak to twelve games but still doesn't have a goal. Atlanta is another win and another assist for her. October ends with the Condors on a three-game winning streak, and she's finished her first month in the NAHL with at least a point in every single game she's played. She leads the League's rookies in the points race and all players in assists.

Now, all she needs is a goal or two.

They have an afternoon skate on the 31st, Coach Butler's attempt to keep them from starting their Halloween party too early. But, in acceptance that a party will happen, tomorrow's practice is also slated for the afternoon. It should give her teammates enough time to sleep off their hangovers so no one vomits on the ice.

She's nervous about tonight's festivities. She's been to backyard cookouts and team dinners, and they've gone out to celebrate a couple of their wins, but tonight is a *party*. She'll be the only one there not drinking, because if she's caught underage drinking, then she won't be slapped with community service or healthy scratched for a game or two. It'll be the end of her career.

And she can't skip. It might be a party but it's still team building, and if she doesn't show up then she drives another wedge between her and her team. She has a headache building when she reaches the locker room, and she really isn't in the mood for whatever prank has drawn her teammates to her stall.

Last week someone hung up a side-by-side comparable of her and Ivanov, but the joke ultimately was on them, because she left it hanging there as motivation to be better. Two days ago, someone hung embarrassing baby photos in Merlin's stall, and there are certainly enough biographies and articles with pictures of her if someone wanted to pull the same prank again.

She fixes a smile on her face—*be nice, be grateful*—and elbows her way through her teammates.

"Sophie, don't," someone says. She thinks it might be Merlin.

She knocks his hand away. There's a mini-dress hanging in her stall where her practice clothes should be. It's red with a plunging neckline and double stripes on the sleeves like her hockey jersey. Instead of a condor on the front, though, there's a hockey puck. Pulse pounding between her ears, she takes the dress out and turns it over.

She's ready for another 224 joke. She isn't ready for the big capital letters that spell out SLUT.

"Oh." Her voice sounds far away. "Puck slut. Hilarious."

"Sophie—"

This is supposed to be her team. When the media comes down on her, when other teams come after her, she's supposed to trust the guys in this room. SLUT, the dress accuses. *Not one of us.*

"What's going on?" Matty demands.

Everyone turns to his voice.

Well, everyone but Sophie. She's still staring at the dress. Things were getting better. They won three to end October and more than doubled their wins for the season. She's assisted on goals in every game. Matty's leading the League in power play points because of her right now.

She balls up the dress and shoves it into her gear bag.

She changes for practice and hits the ice before any of her teammates. She grabs her stick and tips a bucket of pucks over the bench. The rubber discs scatter across the ice. She picks one at random and fires it on net.

It goes in.

She shoots another.

Then another.

She doesn't know how many she's flung at the net before Coach Butler says, "I didn't realize this was one of the shots you needed to work on."

Startled, she drops her stick and it clatters on the ice. "I'll clean them up." She grabs the empty bucket and skates toward the net to fill it.

Coach Butler joins her on the ice, but he doesn't help her with the pucks. "If you're going to practice, then do it right."

"I will," she promises. She fills the bucket and returns it to the bench before she picks one puck to juggle with. It gives her something to do as her teammates file on the ice. She tosses it up in the air, catches it on the blade of her stick, then flicks it up in the air again.

She can feel McArthur staring at her; he hovers on the edge of her vision as though he wants her to look over. She acts as if her puck has her full attention. Is he like Wedin, pretending to like her so long as she's useful to him? She'd rather he be like Hayes. It isn't as if she'll stop passing to him if he tells her the truth. She's a hockey player and she wants to win games. She won't sabotage the team because her feelings are hurt.

McArthur can't take a hint, though, because when they line up for their first drill, he bumps her shoulder the way he's done a dozen times by now. "Sophie—"

"Is this about the drill?" she interrupts. She takes fleeting satisfaction in the way he flinches back. "Because that's all I'm focused on right now."

His mouth hangs open, nothing to say.

"Okay then." She turns back to Coach Butler.

SHE'S NEVER BEEN more grateful to have her own locker room than she is today. As soon as practice is over, she books it for her sanctuary. She strips with record speed and hops in the shower so she can pretend the tears running down her face are actually from the spray.

She slams her fist against the wall. It isn't *fair*. The NAHL was supposed to be different. She thought she was leaving behind all the petty posturing and the egos. When she was younger, her teammates hated her for having a better shot at the NAHL than them. But everyone on the Condors is in the show. Why are they still trying to drag her down?

Playing NAHL hockey has been her dream her entire life and, for the first time, she wonders if maybe she picked the wrong dream.

When the League was still dragging its feet on whether or not to let her play, she had her agent put feelers out to the Swedish Hockey League. She could've been in Gothenburg right now, playing with Elsa Nyberg, a Swedish winger who caught her eye at a couple of U-Tourneys. And even if she was on a different team, she could call Elsa and talk to her about what it's like being a woman in a league of mostly men.

Here, she can call Ivanov to talk about what it's like playing with the pressure of a franchise on her shoulders. They can talk about being rookies in the NAHL and how it's amazing and scary and overwhelming, but she can't talk to him about this. She can't talk to anyone about being a woman in the NAHL, because she's the only one.

She emerges from her locker room with dry eyes and wet hair. She catches a glimpse of Mathers, McArthur, and Faulkner hovering outside their locker room. They start toward her once they spot her, and she isn't in the mood for whatever intervention they've cooked up. She wants to run to the Wilcoxes and collapse on her bed and not move until tomorrow's practice.

Running away from her captain seems cowardly, and a better option presents itself when she sees Mary Beth coming from the other direction.

"You need me?" Sophie guesses.

"Only if you have the time. I know the team has something planned tonight, but Derek promises it'll be quick."

Napoli is never quick, but Sophie says, "Of course I'll do it," and turns away from her teammates to meet Mary Beth. Her PR manager frowns once she's closer. Sophie scrubbed her face, but there's no mistaking the puffiness around her eyes. She heads off the question by saying, "It was a tough practice. Coach Butler wanted us to know that we can't slack even if it's a holiday. Can you help me with my makeup before I'm on camera?"

Mary Beth raises her eyebrows, but she doesn't say anything about how this is the first time Sophie's volunteered to put on makeup. It makes her Sophie's favorite person in the Condors organization right now. They make it to Mary Beth's office without any of her teammates following, and Mary Beth not only helps her with her makeup but tells her she can do the interview in her Condors hoodie.

They meet Napoli in one of the media rooms, and she sits on a plastic chair while he adjusts his camera and the lighting. Once he's set, he sits across from her. "Tonight's Halloween, and we have quite the collection of your costumes from over the years." He shuffles through a stack of cards and holds up one of her in her Bobby Brindle jersey. Napoli makes a face. "Brindle? Really?"

She's answered a version of this question throughout her entire career. She smiles as she says, "My dad's family is from Montreal so I grew up watching the Mammoths play. Brindle was a little before my time, but my *mémé* made sure I looked up to the right players."

"He was quite the star for Montreal. Are you gunning for his record now you have Sorkin's?"

Bobby Brindle's seventeen-game point streak is the longest in NAHL history. He set it in 1982, the same season Sorkin set his rookie streak. She's definitely thought about how his record is in her reach too. Claiming them both in her rookie season would be quite the statement, but she won't tell anyone that's her goal.

"I'm taking one game a time."

Napoli, picking up on her reluctance, shuffles through his pictures again. "This is my favorite of you. Most kids go as a pumpkin for their first Halloween, but you were a hockey puck." She's a little more than four months old, in a gray onesie with a hockey puck drawn on the front. Napoli leans in, conspiratorial. "I heard you had to be rescued from your brother."

"Colby's a few years older than me, and someone dressed his sister up like a puck. I'm not sure why anyone thought he *wouldn't* try to push me around with his stick."

"You two are close." Napoli finds another picture, but this one isn't from Halloween. It's one of her and Colby playing in their backyard. She's in a puffy snowsuit and stuck on her back in an orange plastic sled. Colby has the string wrapped around his waist as he skates her around the ice on their pond.

"We are." Sophie pauses. So much of her life is public knowledge that she hates giving more of it up. She tries to remember what's already known and what isn't. "He wanted someone to play hockey with, but I was too young, so he found another way to get me on the ice with him. In a couple more years, I took my first skate on that pond."

"Sweet," Napoli says. "Speaking of sweet, I heard Snickers are your favorite candy." Napoli seamlessly transitions into a quick-fire favorites clip. He probably would've tried to make her stay for a third special, but Mary Beth looks up from her phone, and he hastily wraps things up.

WHEN SOPHIE GETS to the Wilcoxes, she drops her stuff in her room then realizes she isn't in the mood to be alone right now. She doesn't exactly want to be with other people either, but maybe Mrs. Wilcox will let her help with dinner. Upstairs Mrs. Wilcox is, in fact, cooking, with the girls nowhere to be found.

"Can I help with anything?" Sophie asks.

"It's nothing fancy, just some pasta before the girls head out tonight."

As if they were summoned, Jessi and Kaylee barrel down the stairs. They skid to a stop in the kitchen on the off chance their mom couldn't hear them run. They aren't in their costumes yet, but Jessi has black face paint in her eyebrows and streaked across her forehead.

Mrs. Wilcox sighs as she closes the oven. "I told you to wait for costumes until after dinner."

"Are you eating with us?" Kaylee asks Sophie. "We're having spaghetti."

"I'm eating mine cold so it'll taste like brains!" Jessi exclaims.

"There's plenty if you want to join us." Mrs. Wilcox looks tired as she stirs the spaghetti then checks the meatballs.

"I'll eat with you," Sophie says. "Afterwards, I can even help you get ready."

Both girls cheer. She knows from previous dinner conversations that Kaylee is going as a Viking shield maiden, because she's been obsessed since they did a Viking unit to start the school year. Jessi's going as a black cat. Someone told her that hockey players are afraid of them so Sophie has spent the last week pretending to run away every time Jessi popped out from behind a door or bookcase with her cat ears on.

"Will you come trick-or-treating with us too?" Kaylee asks.

"She has her own party to go to tonight," Mrs. Wilcox says.

Jessi's bottom lip wobbles. It isn't as if Sophie *wants* to go to her team party, and babysitting their GM's kids is a good excuse to stay home. "I can take you."

Jessi punches the air. "Yes!"

Mrs. Wilcox watches her like she wants to pry but then the oven beeps and she has to pull the garlic bread out of the oven. By the time she sets the tray on a cooling rack, the spaghetti is threatening to boil over. After that, there's the sauce and when it's all said and done, Sophie escapes any uncomfortable conversations about what she's supposed to be doing tonight.

AFTER DINNER, SOPHIE draws Jessi's whiskers on her cheeks and helps Kaylee strap all her armor into place. A lot of her armor is hockey pads covered in tinfoil, but she designed her own shield, a large piece of cardboard that was painted gray before she painted a condor on it. Once the girls are ready, they turn their attention to Sophie.

"Where's your costume?" Jessi asks.

"We can't leave until you're dressed," Kaylee tells her.

"I don't have a costume. Besides, you're the ones trick-or-treating, not me."

Kaylee sighs, sounding exactly like her mother. "We'll have to improvise."

"What's that mean?" Jessi asks. She trails after her sister as Kaylee leads them down to the basement.

Sophie ends up going as a hockey player. Well, she goes as *herself*, in jeans and a Fournier jersey. It probably defeats the purpose of Halloween, but she doesn't say anything, because Jessi was making noise about having a second pair of cat ears.

Mr. Wilcox is home when they troop back upstairs. He looks at Sophie, then his girls, and frowns. "You're still here."

"We're on our way out now," she says, purposefully misunderstanding. Her phone buzzes in her pocket and she digs it out to see that she has a text message.

MCARTHUR: *Where are you?*

Sophie switches her phone to camera-mode and holds it out to Mrs. Wilcox. "Will you take a picture before we go?" Maybe this can go in next year's Halloween special on her.

They have to go outside for the pictures, because Jessi wants to scare Sophie so then Kaylee insists on protecting her. The final picture comes out weird, but she still sends it to Mrs. Wilcox. After a moment of deliberation, she sends it to McArthur too. *Girls night*, she writes underneath it.

It's dusk as they go to their first house, and there are other kids out. They're mostly younger, accompanied by a parent. Sophie stands with the adults as Kaylee and Jessi troop up the first walkway. They come back to her with giant smiles. Jessi shows off her pillowcase—she already has three pieces of candy—then takes off running.

"You'll tire yourself out!" Kaylee shouts and runs after her.

Sophie follows them at a more sedate pace. Halfway through the night, she's tasked with carrying their pillowcases, because they're too heavy for the girls.

"They'd be lighter if you let us eat the candy," Jessi says, which is a surprisingly good argument for a six-year-old. Fortunately, Sophie was prepared by Mrs. Wilcox before leaving the house.

"You were allowed two pieces and you already ate them."

Jessi huffs and slumps her shoulders as if Sophie's ruined her entire life.

By the end of the night, Sophie has both pillowcases and Jessi. They called Mrs. Wilcox for permission to go to a second neighborhood, but it might've been too ambitious. Jessi's sleepily clinging to Sophie, her face tucked against Sophie's neck. She'll have to check for black face paint there later tonight.

Kaylee's dragging her feet. She's in charge of Sophie's phone, the flashlight app on to light their way. She keeps looking at Sophie as if there's some way for Sophie to grow a third arm and carry her too.

"Sorry, kid. We're almost there."

Kaylee yawns and shuffles closer to Sophie. "Thank you for taking us."

"It was fun," Sophie tells her. She's surprised to realize she means it.

"Tomorrow, we'll sort and trade our candy. You can have all our Snickers. They're your favorite, right?"

At the house, Sophie hands the girls over to their parents and retreats to the basement before anyone can ask about the team party. She changes into her pajamas, scrubs the smears of black face paint off her neck, and brushes her teeth. When she gets into bed, her phone is full of pictures from Ivanov.

They're of him and his teammates, dressed up for their own Halloween celebration. Ignoring her pang of jealousy, she texts back, *looks like a good time*, then puts her phone on silent.

Chapter Thirteen

UNLIKE THE REST of her teammates, Sophie doesn't show up to practice and wince against the bright locker room lights. No one is in the mood to talk as they dress for practice, which suits her just fine. When they hit the ice, Coach Butler blows his whistle gleefully and grins as most of the team flinches.

By the end of practice, *Sophie's* head hurts from the shrill sound of his whistle, and she didn't even stay up late last night let alone have anything to drink. At least no one throws up. One time at Chilton the team was caught drinking and Coach set up trashcans on each end of the ice then bag skated them, forcing them to skate until half the team vomited.

They leave from practice for the airport and fly out to Detroit. She takes her customary seat on the plane and balls up her sweatshirt and pretends to doze until everyone around her is asleep. Then she pulls out her iPad. Her dad's sent her the latest compilation of her shifts, and she studies them as if she can find the secret to why she isn't scoring any goals.

THEY START NOVEMBER by being shut out by Detroit.

Goodbye, win streak.

Goodbye, point streak.

Five articles come out after the Detroit game heralding the end of her career with headlines like *End of Beginner's Luck?* and *Streak Snapped: Unlucky 14.* There are copies of each article plastered in her stall in Milwaukee. There's also an article from almost thirty years ago, celebrating Bobby Brindle's record-setting streak, the one she's no longer a couple games shy of.

She crumples all the papers and tosses them in the trash. She dresses for practice and goes through the motions without having to talk any more than necessary. Afterward, she keeps her head down as she skates off the ice, ready to shower then hole up in her hotel room.

Her teammates are all clustered in the tunnel, clogging up her exit. She pushes through until she sees what's caused the logjam. It's Travis, leaning against the wall in an Engineers sweatshirt. She completely forgot that he plays for Milwaukee.

"What're you doing here?" she asks. "Isn't your morning skate over?"

Travis ignores the hostility in her tone. "Lunch?"

She hasn't listened to a single voicemail he's left her or answered a single text since they played Edmonton in the preseason. Why is he still bothering her?

"Lunch?" Mathers asks.

Her entire team stops shuffling toward the locker room to watch the unfolding entertainment. Travis looks uncomfortable for the first time, pulling out of his slouch then rethinking it and slumping his shoulders again. "Uh, yeah." He looks to Sophie for help, but she just stares evenly back at him.

"Where're you going?" Mathers asks, sounding less like her captain and more like her dad.

"Forbsie's. I mean, Richard Forbes. I'm living with him this season."

Mathers glances at Delacroix and, after a nod from his d-man, he relaxes. "You can go."

Sophie's gaze snaps to Mathers as Zhang mutters, "Oh, shit." Her captain winces, knowing he's said the wrong thing, and even Delacroix shakes his head and takes a step back, letting Mathers bear the brunt of his mistake on his own.

Sophie has a dozen responses on the tip of her tongue; *thank you for your permission* and *go fuck yourself* fighting to escape first. But then she takes a deep breath and smooths her expression into something less murderous. Mathers is the one who crammed his foot in his mouth, but if she responds the way she wants to she'll be the one labeled a bitch and a problem. There's already enough strain on the team because of her and Hayes; she won't add to it by feuding with her captain.

"Lunch sounds good," she tells Travis. Her skin prickles, uncomfortable with the way her entire team watches her as if she's an exhibit at the zoo. "We might have to wait a bit. I can't shower until the guys clear out."

"We'll wait here," Mathers says, a peace offering.

A few of her teammates look pissed that they have to wait so she hurries down the tunnel and takes a lightning-fast shower. When she rejoins them, there's a guy she doesn't know chatting with Delacroix. He's tall like Mathers but slimmer, not as much muscle packed onto his frame.

Travis is the first to spot her. He waves her over as if there's anywhere else she might be going. "Sofe, this is Forbes. He's giving us a ride back to his apartment."

Forbes looks up from his conversation with Delacroix to wave at her. She waves back then grabs Travis's wrist and says, "We'll just catch up until you're ready to go." She drags him down the tunnel then away from the locker room so her teammates can't eavesdrop.

"Dude!" Travis exclaims once they're alone. He yanks his wrist out of her grasp and glances at his reddened skin. "What the hell?"

"What is this?" she demands. She might have to tiptoe around her teammates, but she won't do the same with her opponents. "Lunch? We haven't talked to each other since the preseason."

"And whose fault is that? I've been *trying*."

"Maybe I don't want you to try."

Travis flinches as if she hit him, but he's a hockey player so he rallies quickly. "What's your fucking problem? We were teammates. You were my *captain*."

"I was Wedin's teammate too." She snaps her mouth shut and looks away, but it's too late to take back what she said.

Travis flips from pissed to concerned in seconds. "What happened?"

"Nothing."

"Sophie—" Travis groans, used to her stubbornness. "Have you seriously been ignoring me because Shawn Wedin is a dickhead?"

"Dickhead? Are you five?"

"Fuck you. I thought we were *friends*. I've been shitting my pants before every game because we're finally in the NAHL, and you haven't picked up the damn phone because of Shawn Wedin?"

"Whatever." Her attempt to storm off is ruined when Forbes rounds the corner and they almost collide. He reaches his hands out to steady her, but she bobs and weaves to avoid the contact.

"My car's in the other direction," Forbes says.

She's about to tell him that she isn't going to lunch but then she'll have to explain to her teammates why. She takes a deep breath, locks all her feelings under tight control, and offers Forbes a media smile. "Lead the way, then."

"It's still fucking creepy to watch you do that," Travis says.

"I'm a woman of many talents," Sophie says.

No one says anything else on the way to the car.

THEY STOP TO pick up sandwiches and bring them back to Forbes's apartment. His place is spacious and surprisingly clean. It implies they cleaned for her. Guilt needles at her for being tetchy earlier. She nosily looks at all the pictures in the living room.

She pauses at a familiar one. It's the men's Team Canada picture from the Stuttgart Games. It's right after the gold medal match, everyone still in their uniforms. They're wearing their medals. Ducasse is front and center. Pearce, the goalie, is easy to spot, because he's still in all his gear. She didn't realize Forbes had been part of the team.

She watches him pull down plates from the cabinet and tries to remember seeing him there.

"I was an alternate," he says as if he guessed her question.

She looks back at the picture. In the back row, wearing a Team Canada tracksuit rather than a jersey, is Forbes. She joins them in the kitchen and Forbes hands her a plate. He hands one to Travis next who stares at it, bewildered. She stifles her laugh as Forbes unwraps his sandwich and puts it on a plate of his own instead of eating off the wrapper.

"Mullet says you two are friends." Forbes doesn't sound as if he believes it. Given that Sophie's ignored Travis all season, she can't blame him. But maybe Travis is one of the good guys. And it isn't like she's flush with friends right now.

"We are," Sophie says, and Travis looks surprised, then pleased.

"We're just going to catch up," Travis tells his teammate. "It'll probably be boring for you."

It isn't exactly a subtle request to leave, and Sophie's sure if she was a guy Forbes would already be in the living room or hanging out with his other teammates. As it is, he hesitates, glancing between them. Sophie takes pity on him. "He should stay. I'm not supposed to be alone with anyone. Who knows what rumors might be started."

"Ew." Travis wrinkles his nose.

Sophie laughs. "Same. Of course, maybe Forbes like to watch."

Travis chokes on his first bite of sandwich. Forbes looks pained as he pulls a pair of headphones out his pocket. Once he's given them as much privacy as he's going to, Sophie takes a giant bite of her wrap.

They don't talk until they've each put away their first sandwich. It's Travis who nudges her and asks, "So? What's it like playing with Hayes?"

She glances at Forbes who seems absorbed in his phone but... "It's been an adjustment, but we're teammates now and that means more than a high school rivalry."

Travis looks ready to call bullshit when he remembers his teammate sitting only a couple of feet away from them. Maybe Sophie's paranoid, but her team has enough problems without her telling anyone she wishes Hayes wasn't on the team.

"What about you?" she asks. "What's playing with Figuli like?"

Travis's entire face lights up, and Sophie knows it was the right question to ask.

AFTER LUNCH, SOPHIE finds herself homesick for a team she won't ever be a part of again. It's stupid to miss her prep school team when she's in the *NAHL*. She spends the night moping in her room, then continues her moping the next morning as she eats room service so she doesn't have to face any of her teammates yet.

She's contemplating a pre-practice pity shower when she decides enough is enough.

Who cares if her teammates are dicks?

Who cares if the media doesn't believe in her?

Growing up, the NAHL was her dream, the one thing she wanted more than anything. She wanted to wake up every morning and play the sport she loves. She's living her dream and instead of enjoying every second of it she's feeling sorry for herself?

Not anymore.

When she boards the bus for morning skate, she sits down next to Merlin. He looks surprised to see her, which she deserves, but she brushes it aside. "Liney lunch after practice."

"What?"

"You, me, and Witzer."

"I know who our line is."

"Theo and Kevlar can come too if they want."

Kevlar leans across the aisle to join their conversation. "Did you say lunch?"

"I know a good wrap place," Theo says.

"No." Kevlar claps a hand over Theo's mouth as he tries to defend himself. "He told me the same lie in Pittsburgh. The sandwiches had coleslaw and French fries in them."

"*In* them?" Sophie asks.

"I like wraps," Aronowitz says. "You know, if my opinion counts for anything."

"Great, we have plans," Merlin says. "Now, can you sit in your usual seat?" He looks almost sheepish as if he doesn't want to kick her out but—

"You and your fucking superstitions," she says. She hops across the aisle to sit in her usual row. "You better score a hat trick tonight."

Merlin groans and knocks quickly on the window. Sophie grins and settles in for the short ride to the rink.

AFTER A SOLID morning skate and a good lunch, she only needs one more thing to be ready for tonight's game, a nap. She's headed for her hotel room when Merlin jogs to catch up to her. "Running away again?"

"I don't run away."

He rolls his eyes. "We're watching TV in your room."

She's about to ask who *we* is when Kevlar and Theo catch up to them. She should've known. She looks between the three of them and raises her eyebrows. "Really?"

"I mean, we can ask Matty for permission," Kevlar says. His d-partner smacks him and he grins. "Too soon?"

Sophie laughs and opens her door for them. They poke through her room, going into the bathroom and looking around the beds. Merlin even opens one of the dresser drawers and makes a face at Sophie's T-shirts, neatly folded inside.

"It's the same as your rooms." She takes her shoes off by the door and climbs onto her bed. The comforter is rumpled, because she put the "Do Not Disturb" sign out this morning. She doesn't need someone to make her bed so she can mess it up again when she naps.

"How come you have two beds if there's only one of you?" Theo asks, dropping down onto the second bed.

Kevlar joins him, and between the two of them, there isn't enough space left for Merlin.

"It's easier to book this way. Maybe next year I'll have a roommate."

"Like another girl? Ow." Theo rubs his shoulder after Kevlar hits him. "Sorry. So, you're hoping for another woman on the team?"

"It could happen." Sophie rolls her eyes at Merlin as he hovers awkwardly next to her bed. "Get the remote then sit your ass down."

"Bossy," he says.

"I'm feeling more like myself."

FOR THE FIRST time all season, Sophie's glad to be on the bench for the first shift of the game. It means she can just stare as Figuli makes her team look like amateurs. He isn't the fastest player on the ice, not anymore, but he's unpredictable. He twists around Matty until her captain falls on his ass.

Two shifts later, Hayes is out against him. They battle along the boards and Figuli sneaks an extra slash in. The next time they come together, Figuli throws a shoulder into him. He says something too, but Sophie's too far away to hear it. Hayes keeps his cool until Figuli slashes him again. The two of them are behind the play, out of the officials' sight and care.

It isn't a particularly hard slash, but Hayes still brings his stick up and crosschecks Figuli hard enough that he stumbles. *This* the officials see. Delmonte raises his arm and as soon as Concord has possession, he blows his whistle.

Figuli cheerfully waves at Hayes as he skates to the box.

"Fournier," Coach Butler snaps and Sophie's halfway over the boards before she realizes they're on the penalty kill. Coach points to the spot on the bench closest to him. She sits. "It's your turn to defend against Figuli unless you aren't finished gawking."

She blushes, embarrassed at being caught. "I'll shut him down."

They kill off the penalty thanks to a strong effort from Rodriguez and two shot blocks by Zhang, then Sophie heads over the boards with her line. Figuli's a winger so she doesn't go head-to-head with him on the faceoff, but it's only a matter of seconds before they're jousting for a loose puck. They lean into each other, each trying to trap the puck until they can pass to an open teammate.

Figuli flicks the puck to a teammate and twists away. Without his weight to counter against, Sophie almost falls on her face. She recovers but she's a step behind where she needs to be. She pushes, one powerful stride after another until she catches up to Figuli. She pokes the puck off his stick and it trickles harmlessly to Lindy who covers it.

Figuli looks surprised to see it was Sophie who caught him. "I thought I bought myself a little more time than that. You've got some wheels on you, kid."

"Uh, thank you?" She skates to her bench, confused. She's been chirped, insulted, and flat-out threatened on the ice before, but she's never been complimented.

She assumes it's a fluke, but the next time she's on the ice, he does it again. She boxes him out of the crease and after Lindy makes another save, he pats her shoulder and asks, "Have you been hitting the weight room?"

"Fuck off," Merlin says, skating between them as if Sophie needs protecting.

"I can give you some tips," Sophie offers.

Figuli laughs and skates with her toward their benches. "I'm not as young as you. I do all my weightlifting in the pool."

Merlin, deciding Figuli is a lost cause, pushes Sophie toward their bench.

"Focus," Coach Butler tells her.

She sits at the end of the bench and takes a deep breath. She's survived two shifts against one of the greatest NAHL players of all time. Time to get ready to do it again.

TIME IS WINDING down in the first period when one of Milwaukee's defenseman gets too ambitious and pinches. No one comes up to cover him. As soon as Theo knocks Travis off the puck, Aronowitz takes it, and Sophie starts skating.

"Pass!" Matty shouts from the bench.

Aronowitz looks up, spots Sophie, and airmails a pass up ice. She knocks it out of the air and settles it as she skates into the offensive zone. It's her and Palmer, the goalie for the Engineers. She gains speed with each stride, flipping the puck between her forehand and backhand. Palmer skates out to challenge her and scoots backwards as he realizes she isn't slowing down.

She's running out of space, but she's practiced this thousands of times with Colby on their backyard rink and in their driveway during the summer. It's a game of chicken; one of them has to flinch first. She's inches from colliding with Palmer when she abruptly turns, dragging the puck with her. Palmer's frozen in place, and she skates arounds him and knocks the puck in before her momentum carries her into the glass.

Without the time to brace herself, she slams into the glass. Her arms windmill as she fights to keep her balance. The goal light flashes above her as she loses the fight with gravity and falls on her ass.

It isn't the goal celebration she's dreamed of, but it's okay because she just scored *her first goal*.

She scrambles to her skates in time for Merlin to slam her back into the glass, screaming and shouting as the fans behind her boo.

"No fucking goalie interference this time," Sophie says. "That was a fucking beauty!"

She beams as Merlin herds her toward the bench so the rest of the team can share in her celebration.

THEY WIN 1-0, making tonight Lindy's first shutout of the season. But it's Sophie who's presented with the game-winning puck. Someone used a silver Sharpie to write *November 4, 2011. Concord @ Milwaukee. 1st Goal Sophie Fournier* around the rim of the puck.

She allows Napoli to take a picture of her with it, then she drags Theo and Aronowitz in for the next round of pictures. She turns the puck over in her hands as the media pour into the room. She held her own against Mikhail Figuli and scored her first goal. Not bad for a night's work.

Once the media clears out, Merlin stands up on the bench. "We're celebrating tonight!"

The room cheers as Sophie tugs on his suit jacket to make him step down. "We're flying out tonight."

"We have to eat." Merlin slings an arm around her shoulders, pulling her close. She's a little embarrassed at how easily she lets him hug her, but she can't remember the last time someone other than Mrs. Wilcox or the girls hugged her. "We'll buy you a beer. Matty'll turn his back and everything."

"How about a candle in my dessert?" she offers.

"Your big celebration is dessert?"

"It's not even a cheat day," she says.

He stares at her for a long moment, before she cracks up laughing. He shoves her shoulder. She shoves him back, and they slap at each other until they're both laughing too hard to keep it up.

Chapter Fourteen

SOPHIE'S FIRST GOAL doesn't open the floodgates she hoped for. She scores her second in the next game, against Memphis, then goes two games without a point of any kind. They limp through the beginning of November, losing three straight midway through the month, including a 1-6 loss to Kansas City.

The Cavaliers aren't even a good team, and Coach Butler is so pissed by second intermission he doesn't talk to them. Everyone looks to Matty, but he bows his head, absorbing their failure until his shoulders slump, defeated.

It's a silent flight home, no one daring to speak in case they draw Coach's attention. He promised the media there would be consequences for the way they played, and no one wants to bear the brunt of it.

For once, Sophie doesn't watch the game tape on the plane. Coach Butler will dissect the game tomorrow and then fix their mistakes. Her job now is to make sure she's rested enough to keep up with his demands. She balls up a sweatshirt and leans her head against the window. She doesn't sleep, but she relaxes and that's close enough.

THE NEXT MORNING, the locker room is eerily quiet. Everyone is here, and early, but no one speaks as they dress for practice. Lindy, once his pads are strapped into place, sits deep in his stall and closes his eyes. Dark circles make him look far older than his twenty-eight years.

With no one goofing off, they're ready sooner than usual, but when Matty stays in his stall, the rest of them follow suit. Sophie taps her fingers on her knees. She could be stretching or passing with Merlin or doing *something*. Instead, they sit and watch the clock tick, the room growing more suffocating with each passing second.

At 10:00 a.m. exactly, Coach Butler enters the locker room. The players draw up even tighter, braced for him to yell. Coach Richelieu follows behind him with an iPad in his hands.

"Your effort was abysmal last night," Coach Butler says. "Ronnie won't let me scratch the whole lot of you even though it's what you deserve, but I can promise that not everyone in this room will be on the ice tomorrow. I don't care how long you've been on this team or in this League. I don't care if you have a letter, play top minutes or barely any at all. Today, you have to prove to me that you deserve to be in the game." He points at Richelieu. "We're recording you today. You'll be compared, side-by-side, with your competition. One person from every position is being scratched, more if you look like you did last night. Coach Vorgen is in Manchester to see who we're calling up. Any questions?"

She's not sure anyone even breathes.

"Let's go."

Coach Butler leads them to ice level where several of their trainers and strength and conditioning coaches are in tracksuits and armed with iPads. The message is clear; every single thing they do today is being watched and recorded.

Coach Richelieu takes them through some basic skating drills. They weave in and out of cones and practice quick stops and even quicker reversals. Sophie's edgework is one of the strongest parts of her game, and when they move into two-person skating drills, more than one of her teammates falls on their ass trying to keep up with her.

Matty's the latest victim, and she offers him a hand up. For a moment, she's afraid he won't take it. He was just embarrassed on camera by one of his rookies, and apparently this is a practice where any slipup can cost them ice time.

He clasps her hand and lets her haul him to his feet. Coach Butler makes a note on his iPad. Is Matty weak for accepting help? Is she too soft for offering it? She wants to ask someone what the hell she's supposed to be doing, but the rink is still silent. She won't be the first to speak.

No one offers encouragement or chirps their teammates. There aren't any side conversations either. There's the sound of skates slicing through ice and sticks banging and Coach Butler's bark as he orders, "Next!"

After skating drills, they move into passing drills. One player stands by the left faceoff dot while another skates through cones and chairs. There's a bar they have to jump over and three different points where they must receive a pass from the player at the dot and then return it. At the fourth point, they're required to shoot into the open net.

It's a basic drill, but the pressure is ratcheted up with all the coaching staff watching and the knowledge that this drill could be the reason they don't play tomorrow.

Kevlar's shot on goal misses, the puck clacking against the glass. The sound echoes through the rink.

Coach Butler taps something on his iPad. "Next."

Kevlar moves to be the passer. Theo steps in to be the skater. Theo's first pass is shaky, and Kevlar takes an extra second to settle it. Coach Butler's whistle pierces the silence.

"Be better," he says.

Both defensemen press their lips together, blaming themselves.

After a few rotations, Wilchinski is the skater with Aronowitz passing. Aronowitz's first pass isn't right on Wilchinski's tape. He has to reach to catch it. Coach Butler blares his whistle. Wilchinski jumps then fumbles his pass. The rest of their sequence is a mess and ends with Wilchinski shooting wide of the net.

He skates straight for Aronowitz and plants himself in front of the other winger. He mutters something too quietly for Sophie to hear. Aronowitz snaps back. They're two seconds from crosschecking each other or dropping their gloves. Sophie looks to Matty to do something, but he just watches.

Right as Wilchinski raises his stick, Coach Butler blows his whistle. "Next!"

BY THE END of practice, tempers are short. There were another three almost-fights. Coach Butler seems cheerful when he tells them they'll find out tomorrow morning who's playing. She doesn't understand why he wants the team divided. They have enough problems without inviting more.

As the two rookies, Sophie and Hayes stay to clean up the pucks. Sometimes Kevlar or Merlin stay to help or, more likely, mediate, but today everyone is too focused on themselves and how fast they can get out of the building.

At first, they pick up pucks in silence, Sophie on one end and Hayes on the other. Eventually, they meet at center ice.

"This is bullshit," Hayes says.

Maybe he's looking for someone to commiserate with. But maybe Coach Butler wants data on this too, who complains as soon as he's out of earshot. She wouldn't put it past him, and she remembers seeing him talk to Hayes as he handed him one of the puck buckets.

"We weren't good enough," Sophie finally says. "Either we improve or we don't play." That's always been the reality for her, which is probably why the pressure of today's practice didn't rattle her the way it did other people.

Hayes stops and stares at her. "How did people play with you for four fucking years without punching you?"

Her stick is on the bench with her gloves and her helmet, because she needs both hands to haul her bucket around. If Hayes takes a swing at her she has nothing to defend herself with.

"Winning championships probably helped," she answers.

"You're not winning now."

"No, we're not. We will, though. With you, me, Matty, and Thurman down the middle, we have strong center depth. We build from there." She isn't in the mood to argue so she skates her bucket to their bench. "There's a reason Concord had the second overall pick at the draft. There's work to do."

Hayes skates over with her. "Which one of us do you think they're scratching?"

"Not Matty." No matter how pissed off Coach is, he won't scratch their captain. Right?

"Probably not Thurman either."

Which means one of them. Sophie glances at Hayes. He frowns and, by unspoken agreement, they drop the subject.

SOPHIE HITS THE weight room with Zhang and Rodriguez and then she heads to the Wilcoxes. Her plan for the afternoon is to eat, nap, eat again and try to distract herself from wondering whether or not she's in tomorrow's game.

Mr. Wilcox is out raking the yard when she pulls into the driveway. She says goodbye to her plans and allows herself one deep sigh before she slaps a smile on her face.

"Sophie!" her GM greets as she gets out of her car. "You're home late."

"We had a lot to work on." Does he know who Coach Butler's scratching? Is he part of the decision? Does she have to be on her guard at home too? "Do you need some help?"

"That would be great." He points at the two rakes leaning against the big tree in the front yard. "The girls were helping but they got tired."

She rakes leaves for an hour, then heats up some chicken and pasta. Too tired to deal with extra dishes, she eats out of the Tupperware. She wakes up groggy from her nap and feeling vaguely nauseous. At first, she's worried there was something wrong with the chicken. Then she remembers one of their four centers is being scratched for tomorrow's game and it'll probably be her or Hayes.

She chokes down an early dinner as she runs through her performance at practice. Her effort was high and her execution was good but was it better than Hayes's? Does Coach put more weight on her failures because she plays on the second line?

It's too late to do anything now. Either she was good enough or she wasn't.

She calls Ivanov, hoping for someone to commiserate with.

"Sophie!" He always sounds so happy to hear from her, and she doesn't understand why.

"Practice was brutal today," she says.

"Ice bath?"

"Not that kind of brutal. Coach is playing head games. Does yours do that?"

"He likes—how do you say—blender?"

"He mixes the lines up all the time?"

"Yes! Hard to find rhythm."

She wants to tell him about the threat of being scratched and how Coach Butler seemed as if he was trying to provoke a fight, but she's not sure if she can. Will Ivanov use it against her? Or leak it to a reporter? He probably wouldn't, but some things are best kept in-team. She wishes she had a close friend on the team, someone she could talk about these things with.

"How'd you like your first trip to Quebec?" she asks.

"Statue is weird."

"Did Hippeli spit on it?"

"What?"

Sophie laughs. "To ward off the curse."

"Statues can't curse."

"This one can."

"What?" he asks again.

She explains the curse of Five-Hole Billy to him. It isn't the same as venting her frustrations with her coach, but she still feels better afterward.

THE NAUSEA IS back the next morning, and the only reason she keeps her breakfast down is because she'll need the energy for morning skate. Her eggs sit heavy, like stones in her stomach, as she drives to the rink. Will she play tonight? If she doesn't, what then? What will she have to do to claw her way back into the lineup?

The players' lot is pretty full which means she isn't the only one who had trouble sleeping. She half expects the whiteboard in the locker room to have the list of players who aren't in today, but it still has a play from last week drawn on it.

The locker room is as quiet as it was yesterday, but there are a few new faces. Petrov is one. He sits in his stall and looks around, uncertain. He offers Sophie a tentative smile and she smiles back, because it isn't his fault Coach Butler is changing things. The two guys next to him must be the other call-ups. A center, a winger, and a defenseman?

The one on Petrov's left is older than Petrov but not by much. He looks equally nervous as if he knows he's here to take a NAHLer's place and isn't sure he should. The other guy looks ready to take someone's place and keep it.

He's the one who stares as she pulls her shirt over her head.

"Eyes down in the locker room," Merlin snaps.

She turns her back as she finishes changing. The place between her shoulder blades tingles, a warning that at least one person is still watching her. She takes her practice jersey from her stall, red today, and pulls it over her head.

"Me too," Merlin says, holding up his own practice jersey.

Something in her chest eases when she sees the matching jerseys. They wear different colors to make drills and scrimmages easier, and she wears the same color as her linemates more often than not. If she and Merlin both have the same jersey then that's a good sign. Right?

"Want to hit the ice?" she asks.

Kuzy and X enter the locker room together, laughing at some story Kuzy's telling. Already, today feels better than yesterday. Until Kuzy pulls a yellow jersey out of his stall.

They never use yellow.

Red, black, white, and gray but never yellow.

Kuzy pulls the sweater out of his stall and looks at it before looking at X. His d-partner takes a black jersey out of his locker. Sophie glances across the room at where one of the call-ups is wearing a black jersey. And, from the way he tries to sink deeper into his stall, he plays defense.

"Is this a joke?" Kuzy demands. X raises his hands, placating, but Kuzy knocks them away and says something in rapid Russian. Now it's Petrov's turn to edge backward as Kuzy's rant grows louder and, Sophie's guessing, more profane.

"Oh, shit," Merlin mutters.

At first, Sophie thinks he's talking about the d-men drama. But then she sees Lindy pull a yellow jersey from his locker. *Oh, shit* is right. Their starting goaltender stares evenly at the brightly colored fabric, then tosses it in the bottom of his stall and stalks out of the room.

Matty hurries after him.

Sophie's relieved to see a black jersey in his stall. If she's playing and Matty's playing, then it's down to Thurman or Hayes who's scratched. She looks at Hayes's stall and sees a pop of yellow poking out from behind his pads.

She nudges Merlin. "Ice?" she asks again.

"I should've said yes the first time."

Kevlar and Theo join them. Hayes is a healthy scratch tonight. She wanted to prove herself better than him but not like this. Coach Butler has his job for a reason, and she knows he's won a Cup, that he has valuable experience, but she doesn't understand how this is supposed to make them better. She and Hayes had struck an uneasy truce. There was a chance they might manage to be cordial even if they'll never be friendly.

After this...she has to be on her guard. There's another mean-spirited prank headed her way. Maybe he'll confront her in the parking lot again. Would Theo be suspicious or pleased if she finally takes him up on his offer to walk her to her car after late games or flights?

"Sophie?" Merlin waves a hand in front of her face like an asshole. "Did you fall asleep on us there?"

"Sorry, I was thinking. Guess we better bring a big game tonight, eh?"

"Eh." He laughs but it's weak, his heart not in it.

Sophie elbows him anyway.

WITH HAYES OUT of the lineup and the threat of it happening to any of them, Sophie has to play hard tonight. More than that, she needs to show Coach Butler another dimension to her game. If she doesn't, then she could be scratched next time.

She keeps the threat in the back of her mind as she jumps on the ice for her first shift. She skates right for the forward back behind the boards. She throws her shoulder into him to separate him from the puck. Merlin scoops up the puck, and Sophie follows but not before she's crosschecked by Richards.

"I'm coming for you," he threatens as she skates away.

"You have to catch me first."

TWO SHIFTS LATER, it's her turn to defend the puck as he barrels in to try to take it. She braces her arm against the glass so he can't shove her out of the way and uses her stick and skates to protect the puck from him.

Merlin hovers nearby, waiting to see who'll win the battle. She fights for a sliver of space then kicks the puck up to him. Richards shoves her again even though there isn't a puck to fight over anymore.

She skates around the back of the net and taps her stick on the ice. Merlin passes back to her and she skates right on goal. She widens her stance to make it more difficult for Markstrom, one of Houston's d-men, to poke the puck away. As she defends from him, someone comes up behind her. She tucks her stick between her legs and passes the puck up to Smith at the point.

Richards slams into her, knocking her into Markstrom. She wobbles but, sandwiched between the two players, stays on her skates. The three of them are a tangle of sticks and arms. Richards holds her stick so she holds Markstrom's and they create enough of a commotion that the goalie can't see around them.

Theo's slapshot rockets past all of them and into the net.

Sophie whoops and frees herself so she can jump onto her d-man.

"Between the legs?" he asks as he catches her. "You almost tricked *me* with that one."

COACH BUTLER HAS seen her assist on goals before. She needs to show him something *new*.

Three shifts later, Richards lines up a big hit. She sees him coming the whole way in, and she can avoid the hit or she can make a play. She holds onto the puck, waiting for the pass she wants. As soon as Aronowitz is open, she slings the puck up to him. A second later, Richards crashes into her.

She braces herself for the worst of it, but it's still forceful enough to knock her backwards. She keeps her balance and grins at him. "Is that all you've got?"

He raises his stick, apparently stupid enough to take a blatant penalty. She dares him to hit her and is disappointed when one of his teammates hauls him back.

"She isn't worth it."

Sophie skates away, a giant smile on her face.

"You good?" Merlin asks once they're back on the bench.

"I'm not fragile. And Richards isn't as tough as he wishes he is."

"You didn't say that to him, did you?"

She will now. Coach Butler wants edge? She'll give him edge.

THEY BATTLE ON what feels like every shift. Houston's coach seems to think Richards is doing a good job shutting her down and puts him out against her at every opportunity. Coach Butler likes the match-up enough that he doesn't avoid it and it's the green light she needs.

On the next play, she initiates the contact. She shoves him up against the boards and laughs as she steals the puck. "Maybe next time." She taps his skates with her stick.

He jabs his into the back of her knee. Her knees buckle, and she hits the ice. She slides on her stomach for a few meters, but she's back on her skates by the time the official skates by her, arm up in the air.

As soon as Houston touches the puck, the official blows his whistle to signal the penalty. She skates to her bench, jubilant.

"*Dude*," Merlin says.

"Coach wanted more. I'm giving him more."

THEY WIN OVER Houston with their backup goalie in net and three call-ups from Manchester in the lineup. She can't tell if Coach Butler is pleased or not. He wore the same grimace all game, refusing to look happy with anything they did, but he didn't yell at them either.

"You and Richards had a few back-and-forths," Rossetti says to open Sophie's scrum. "It didn't look friendly."

"It was hockey."

Undeterred by Sophie's bland response, Rossetti pushes for more. "It looked like he had some things to say to you. Can you comment on any of them?"

Maybe she's still feeling the restless itch that made her poke at Richards because Sophie says, "We had a difference of opinion." She has to hold back her smile as all her reporters crowd closer as if they haven't learned by now that she never says anything interesting. "He wanted Houston to win the game and I wanted Concord to win."

Rossetti sighs but before she can continue down this dead-end path, Marty Owen jumps in. "You won without Hayes in the lineup. Is this a sign he isn't needed? Will we see a trade in the next week?"

She would love to tell them Hayes is an unnecessary part of their lineup, and she'd love even more to see him on another team. But she isn't fucking stupid. "Coach Butler wanted to send a message to the team tonight. It's safe to say we received it loud and clear."

THEY WIN THEIR next game against the Empires with everyone but Hayes back in the lineup. Marty Owen is at the front of her scrum after the game to shove his recorder in her face and demand, "Well?"

"No one on our team is talking about trades," she answers.

They play the very next night and, despite the back-to-back, Hayes stays out of the lineup in a decisive 4-1 victory before they head into the Thanksgiving break. Even Rickers asks her a question about trade rumors.

It's a relief to have the next few days off. And a couple of them are legitimate off days. Merlin is visiting Marissa's family for the holiday, and she overheard Theo inviting Kevlar to his parents'. Matty's hosting something for everyone sticking around, but breaks like this are few and far between, so Sophie makes plans of her own.

"Practice is optional?" she confirms for the third time. "Actually optional?"

Matty smiles at her for what seems like the first time since their Kansas City game. "Mandatory practice on the 25th but until then your time is yours. Have fun, be safe."

She pays way too much for a last-minute plane ticket, but it's worth it when Colby picks her up at the airport. He wraps her up in a giant hug, but he can't lift her off the ground the way he used to.

He slaps her shoulders as he steps back. "You've been hitting the weight room."

She grins, pleased. "You should've heard the trainers the first month. They tiptoed around it until I assured them I *want* to put on weight."

Colby plops a UND hat on her head. "You're going undercover. Come on, we're meeting the team for dinner."

"I'm only sitting next to you if you promise to share the breadbasket."

"Ha."

He does steal most of the bread, but it's worth it to be able to see him. They talk about his season and then a little bit about hers. And, later, when it's just the two of them and he asks her about the situation with Hayes, she can smile and tell him she hopes he'll be traded over the break or even by the end of the month.

She doesn't have to deflect or outright lie to her brother. She can tell him her frustrations with Coach Butler and how she feels as if she's finally proving her place on the team. The two-day break is exactly what she needs before the next stretch of games.

Chapter Fifteen

THEY WIN AGAINST Indianapolis coming off the break which gives them a four-game winning streak, the longest of their season so far. Sophie even notched herself a goal.

"We're going in the right direction," she tells Rossetti after the game.

"Hayes is back in the lineup," Owen says.

"His penalty killing was important tonight. We need to work on taking less penalties. We were fortunate that our PK unit and Lindy especially bailed us out."

"Did Butler play him to showcase his skills?" Owen asks. "It's hard to shop a player who's up in the press box."

Ah, more trade rumors. Exactly what I wanted to talk about.

THEY LOSE TO DC to snap their win streak, and everyone braces themselves for Coach Butler to mix up the roster again. He keeps it the same, and they all bring their best game against Atlanta, winning 5-2 over the Lancers.

They fly home to play their only match-up this season against Seattle. Coach Butler reminds them that even though Seattle is sitting last in the League, again, they can't underestimate them. With Kansas City still fresh in everyone's minds, Sophie doesn't think effort will be a problem.

It certainly won't be for her. It's her first chance to compare herself to the first pick of the draft. She puts up a goal and two assists in the game, and she stares down Carruthers after each one. He catches it once and looks bewildered. She bares her teeth in a smile and prepares for their next shift against each other.

The next day, they leave the snowy streets of Concord for the equally snowy streets of Boston. Coming off back-to-back wins, the mood is high in the locker room after morning skate. McArthur and Aronowitz tussle near her stall, and Sophie has to pay attention so she doesn't catch a stray elbow.

"Where are we going for lunch?" Merlin asks as he manages to pin Aronowitz against his side.

"I don't know. Where are you going?"

Merlin turns to stare at her. Aronowitz is equally shocked. "You're abandoning us?"

"I have a better offer." The entire locker room falls uncomfortably quiet. Sophie looks around, a little uneasy with everyone's attention on her. It's one thing to joke with her linemates. She shrugs and tries to sound casual as she says, "I have very important rival time scheduled."

"*Ivanov?*" Merlin demands. "Are you sure he isn't trying to throw you off your game?"

Sophie rolls her eyes. "As if I would let him."

SHE MEETS IVANOV at a little restaurant tucked between a tailor's and a stationery shop. The hostess doesn't recognize her, but she winks at Sophie when she brings her back to the two-person booth where Ivanov's waiting for her. Once the hostess is gone, Sophie wrinkles her nose. "She thinks we're dating."

Ivanov doesn't look up from the menu. "I'm buy today."

"Not because we're dating."

He tips his menu down in order to frown at her. "What?"

"Nothing." She waves off her earlier comment. They're not dating, and there's no one here watching them to spread that rumor. Hopefully. Maybe this was a bad idea. "What's good here? *And* trainer-approved. I have an important game tonight."

Ivanov grins. "Important game to lose."

She kicks him under the table and he kicks her right back. When the waitress stops by, they have to admit they haven't looked at the menus, and she leaves with only their drink orders. As soon as she's out of sight, Ivanov kicks her again.

"Stop that," Sophie says but she's laughing too hard to come across as stern.

THEY BEAT THE Barons in Boston, which feels good. Her assist on the opening goal feels pretty good too.

"You and Ivanov have both been mentioned in the talks for the Clayton," Marty Owen says.

"It'll go to whichever rookie has the best season. There's still a lot of hockey to be played." *I want it more than anything. If I win the Clayton, maybe people will stop doubting me.* She shakes off the niggling doubts. "It's good to have someone to push me to play better."

"I heard you two had lunch today. That doesn't seem like something rivals do."

Through years of practice, Sophie keeps her face blank. Owen wants a response, and the best thing she can do is not give him one. "We're rivals on the ice and friends off of it."

It's a bland answer, but it isn't enough. Marty Owen isn't the only one to publish an article about how she's too friendly with her competition. She "doesn't understand how the game is supposed to be played." It's bullshit but all she can do is grit her teeth and bring a better game against Denver.

THEY LOSE 1-2 in a grind of a game. Denver rolls out four big, physical lines, and Sophie doesn't have the space to breathe let alone make plays. Sinclair, their captain, runs her seemingly all night. And when she finally has a break from his line, there's Rawlings on the second line to check her and Kellman on the third.

Her body is one giant ache afterwards.

"You were weak on the puck all night," Marty Owen says.

She has a pounding headache, the bruise on her side throbs, and her shoulder twinges if she moves it the wrong way. She isn't in the mood for Owen and his needling questions. She takes a deep breath and winces because even breathing hurts right now. "It wasn't my best game."

COACH BUTLER MUST agree because when she comes to practice on the 6th, there's a yellow jersey hanging in her stall. She stares at the bright yellow—no hiding in that—and hopes it's another joke. Deep down, she knows it isn't. *Not good enough*, it accuses. *You should've scored late in the third to tie the game. You should've been harder on the puck to prevent the second goal.* She shoves down her disappointment and shame and guilt and pulls it over her head. Her campaign to prove herself to Coach Butler begins now.

Petrov is staring at her as she turns around. He flushes when he's caught and opens his mouth, then shuts it. He looks as if he wants to crawl into his stall until she forgets he's here.

"It's not your fault," she tells him.

"You're better than I am."

Coach doesn't think so. "Then I'll be back in the lineup in no time. Play your best." *It'll make our organization better and I'm a team player.*

Petrov looks like he wants to say something else, but the doors open and he re-laces his skates instead. Merlin pauses, halfway in the room, his gaze drawn to her jersey. "Are you fucking kidding me?"

"Coach thinks I need to be better." *If you're not the best, then you don't get to play.* She shoves down her bubbling panic. "And I will be."

"Sophie—"

"It's his job to wring the best out of his players. He shouldn't have to scratch me to do it, but I didn't play well last game. This is my wake-up call."

Each player who enters the locker room does the same doubletake when they see her. Some, like Merlin and Kevlar, look pissed. Matty appears shocked and Lindy shakes his head as if he can't believe it. Hayes smiles before he catches himself. It's humiliating to sit in her stall as every one of her teammates realizes she won't play in her next game, but she stays where she is. Going out to the ice would be a coward's move.

She leaves with the rest of her team, but they fall back or speed up until she and Matty are side by side.

"I don't need to be coddled," she says. She's scratched because Coach Butler doesn't think her game against Denver was tough enough. Letting her captain give her a pep talk won't do anything to change his mind.

"Don't completely change your game to make him happy."

If Coach isn't happy, then she doesn't play. She'll do anything to get back on the ice again. Matty sighs as if he knows what she's thinking.

She participates in all the drills and pushes herself to make perfect passes and score on every shot. She doesn't, that would be impossible, and it feels as if Coach Butler makes a mental note of every single one of her mistakes. She's definitely keeping a list, and she ends practice frustrated, because she knows she didn't play well enough to put herself back in the lineup.

She stays to pick up the pucks and when she reaches the locker room, there's already a crowd of reporters around her stall. Marty Owen looks gleeful as he moves aside so she can sit down. "Is this the end of the Fournier Experiment?"

Next to her, Merlin makes an outraged sound. Kevlar actually stands up before Theo puts a restraining hand on his arm. Sophie answers the question before the reporters can turn their attention to her teammates. The last thing she needs is to be labeled a distraction. "I had a bad game. This—" she tugs on the yellow jersey "—is Coach Butler's warning. I need to be better."

"So it's not the end?"

"Not if I have a say."

"Is this a prelude to you being traded?" Rossetti asks.

"I want to be a Condor for a long time."

But I don't know if they want me.

SHE PULLS INTO the Wilcoxes' driveway and realizes she doesn't want to be here right now. She doesn't want to face anyone, let alone the GM of her organization. She backs out of the driveway and drives to the elementary school.

She clears the snow off one of the swings and sits down. When she made the team, she foolishly thought she'd made it. She doesn't think she played that poorly against Denver, but she grew complacent. She forgot that for her every practice is a tryout and every game is a blank slate. She has to prove herself in that moment. Past performance means nothing.

She can only hope Coach Butler will give her a second chance.

She swings until it's too cold to stay outside. She's hungry but she can't stand the thought of sitting down to dinner with the Wilcoxes right now. Hiding out in the basement sounds even worse. Next year, if she's still with the team, she's moving out. She might not be able to room with a teammate, but she can have an apartment of her own, a place to retreat when she needs it.

She eats at a restaurant, opting for a seat at the far end of the bar because all the booths are full. It isn't ideal, but no one recognizes her as she takes her seat and no one talks to her except her waitress.

The TV above the bar is on *GSSN,* showing coverage of Coach Butler's press conference. His face is set in a scowl, making no secret of the fact that he doesn't want to be here. She stirs her ice with her straw as he answers the first question, something about if he thought such an extreme choice was necessary.

"It shouldn't be. Good players don't need me to motivate them."

It's the same thing she told Merlin earlier in the locker room, but it still stings to hear Coach say it and in front of such a large crowd.

"How many games do you plan to scratch her?" Rossetti asks.

"As many as she needs to learn what I'm teaching her," he answers. *Only one*, she promises. *You don't even need to do that. I've learned. I promise.* He can't hear her, of course, and it isn't a live press conference anyway. "But if we play well without her in the lineup then it could be longer. I'm interested in what's best for the team."

"Are you worried about sabotaging her case for the Clayton?" Rickers asks.

Coach Butler scoffs. "What do I care about the Clayton? I'm focused on the team not individual awards."

Well, at least I know what they're going to ask me about at my next scrum. She rubs her eyes as a headache builds behind them. The easiest way to put all this nonsense to rest would be to play but obviously that isn't an option right now.

"Do you want me to change the channel?" the waitress asks. She hovers on the other side of the bar.

"It's okay but thank you."

The waitress, an older woman who looks at Sophie the way her mother does before a scolding, shakes her head but leaves the TV alone. At the end of the night, she sends Sophie home with a slice of cheesecake that Sophie leaves in the upstairs fridge for Kaylee and Jessi.

THE GAME AGAINST Santa Fe begins a four-game road trip. Sophie flies with the team, and she hopes it's because Coach Butler intends to play her again and not because this is part of his lesson. She's received his message loud and clear and sitting in the press box in Santa Fe reinforces it.

She watches her team warm up without her, in their white away jerseys while she's stuck in her game day suit. Mr. Wilcox and Mr. Pauling are in the box with some of the other executives. She's been offered popcorn three times and nachos twice.

The seat is cushioned and the view of the ice is good but not as good as it would be if she were *on* the ice.

Hayes has her spot on the second line, centering Merlin and Aronowitz. She hopes they don't play well, then immediately feels guilty. She should want her team to win even if winning without her proves they don't need her. She drops her hands under the table so she can squeeze the feeling out of them.

She wishes it was as easy to squeeze the feeling out of the rest of her.

HAYES SCORES A wrister that brings the press box to their feet. The old men stop talking business and the slightly younger men stop talking about the good old days as they clap and pat each other on the back as if they were the ones to score the goal.

Sophie smiles in case there's a camera on her.

Two minutes later, Hayes turns the puck over and Santa Fe converts, tying the game at one. It's a wild back and forth after that, both teams trading chances, neither of them finding their defensive footing.

The first period ends 2-3.

The second period ends 6-5.

The game ends 6-7.

"Next game," the old men in the press box tell each other.

She heads down to the visitors' locker room to answer questions on a game she wasn't allowed to play in.

THEY FLY TO LA, arriving early in the morning on the 9th. The bus takes them straight to the hotel, and Coach Butler pushes practice back so they can sleep.

There's another yellow jersey waiting for her in her stall.

She pulls it over her head.

THE TEAM EATS lunch together, but she doesn't go out with any of them afterwards. A couple of her teammates want to go shopping. A few others just want to wander around the big city. She knows there are plans to go out tonight because they don't play until the 11th, but she doesn't want any part of that either.

She's already on Coach Butler's shit list. If word gets out she went clubbing, then he'd send her down to Manchester. She goes back to her hotel room and ignores the missed calls she has from Travis and Ivanov. She even ignores the one from Colby.

She calls her dad instead.

"Hey kiddo," he greets.

Her chest grows tight and tears prickle at the corners of her eyes. "Hey." Her dad was her first coach, first trainer. He was the first person to believe in her and the first person to push her to be better. *Why didn't you prepare me for this?* she wants to ask. It's not that she never disappointed her dad. Sometimes, she feels as if it's all she did. But at the end of the day, she knows her dad loves her.

It's different with her coach.

"Your coach is an idiot."

She laughs and wipes at her eyes. "He's won the Cup."

"He won't win it again if he keeps this up. The game last night was a mess, and he's keeping you out again?"

"They're going to try Petrov on the second line."

"I guess it'll show him he doesn't have any better options. Sophie, once he puts you back in, don't give him any excuse to take you out again. One shot at the NAHL is more than most players get, and you're being given two."

"I know." The heavy weight of *not good enough* presses down on her chest, making it harder to breathe. "I'm sorry."

Sorry doesn't fix mistakes, her father's voice echoes in her head, *practice does.*

"Sorry doesn't fix mistakes," he says.

She feels worse after the phone call than she did before it.

SHE EATS DINNER and turns on *TNSN* even though she knows better. Brindle and Sorkin are on before tonight's primetime match-up between Philadelphia and Boston. The two men sit on opposite sides of a long table as if a little bit of distance will keep things civil. The talking points on the right of the screen say they're discussing Concord trade rumors.

She should turn the TV off or, at the very least, change the channel.

She leans back against the headboard as Brindle plants his elbows on the table. "The trade rumors are nonsense. If Fournier can't cut it in Concord, then she won't cut it anywhere."

This is who I looked up to, she thinks as Brindle neatly lays out all the reasons she doesn't deserve to play in the NAHL. *I have your poster in my room. I have your* jersey. She wishes she'd broken his record earlier this season.

Sorkin rolls his eyes, mid-rant. By the time Brindle's done, he looks bored. "Fournier will play for Concord again this season. Playoffs for the Condors are always a long shot and having her out of the lineup doesn't improve their chances. Besides, if they want any fans to show up to their games she'll be in by the time they're home again."

That's still three games away. Her plan is to be back in the lineup before that.

"She's a novelty," Brindle says. "The shine will wear off."

She turns the TV off to finish her dinner. What kind of world does she live in that a *Bobcat* is defending her on national television?

AFTER DINNER, SHE'S too restless to put on a movie or even review her game tape. She changes into fresh workout clothes and heads down to the hotel gym. It isn't outfitted for her to do a serious weight lift, and it'd be stupid to do one without a spotter, but she can go for a run.

She puts her phone and her keycard in the cup holder and turns the speed on high. She doesn't put music on, preferring to listen to her feet hit the treadmill as she runs. That, combined with the sweat beading at her forehead and dripping down her back, makes her feel as if she's working hard.

She's just hit four miles when the door opens. Through the mirrors lining the walls, she sees it's Kevlar. She jabs the pause button. "You didn't go out?"

Clearly, he didn't, because he's here in mesh basketball shorts and a cut-off T-shirt. He must understand what she means, because he says, "I wasn't feeling it. You stayed in too."

She doesn't dignify that with a response.

Kevlar gestures to the punching bag in the corner of the room. It isn't a staple of most hotel gyms, and she hadn't even noticed it. "Do you want to learn?"

"I'm not allowed to fight."

"When my head's too busy, I like working with the heavy weight bag or even the speed bag sometimes. Your head ever get busy?"

"When is it not?" She jabs the stop button on the treadmill and wipes her face with her shirt. Kevlar pulls a roll of tape out of his pocket.

"Left hand," he says. She holds her hand out for him to wrap. He protects her knuckles without limiting her mobility. As he does her right hand, she bites back her comments on how she's a hockey player. She isn't *soft*.

Then he wraps his own hands, and he grins as he catches her staring. "What? Do you think I only care about *your* hands staying pretty?"

She doesn't know how to answer that so she says, "My hands aren't pretty," then scowls as he laughs.

He shows her how to make a fist so she won't break her thumb then how to throw a punch so she won't fracture her hand. "The biggest mistake players make is thinking a punch is all in the shoulder. That's a great way to fuck up your shoulder. What do you know about torque?"

"I'm a hockey player. What *don't* I know about torque?"

Kevlar grins. "The more you engage your core, the quicker and harder you can hit, and you won't tire as fast as the other guy."

"How do you know all this? I've never seen you fight."

"If I have to then I know how but..." He looks around as if to see if anyone else has appeared while they've been working. "I have to be careful. I can't drop the gloves all the time like Theo or Lenny Dernier will get on TV and say I'm too aggressive. Ten years ago, he called Devante Marcoux a thug for having two fights in a month. He'd use a different word today so he wouldn't get fired, but he'd mean the same thing."

"They won't call me that if I fight." She looks at his hands. They're wrapped with the same white tape as hers, but the backs of his hands are much darker and the palms of his hands are pinker. Her hands are white except where her veins are too close to the surface, then they look blue. "They'll accuse me of being overemotional. Or it'll open the floodgates and some fourth line grinder will try and bash my face in every game."

"Gloves stay on for us," Kevlar says. "But it's always good to know how to throw a punch. Just in case."

IT'S OBVIOUS DURING the LA game there's a hole in the lineup when she's not playing. Hayes couldn't fill it against Santa Fe, and Petrov can't fill it tonight. Coach Butler double shifts Matty to limit Petrov's ice time, but it isn't enough, and they fall to the Orcas, 1-4.

THERE'S A YELLOW jersey in Petrov's stall at their next practice.

After a decisive win over San Francisco, Coach Butler sends him back to Manchester.

Sophie has her place back, but she won't forget Coach Butler's lesson; he can take it away any time he wants.

Chapter Sixteen

THEY'RE FLYING HOME when Garfield stands up and brandishes his phone. "In fifteen minutes, we'll know which unlucky sucker isn't going on vacation over the All-Star break."

Every year that isn't a Winter Games year, the NAHL holds an All-Star weekend to showcase their best and brightest players. The League picks thirty-two players from each Conference which averages to two per team, but it never ends up that way. The host city usually gets three or four players, and some teams, like Seattle and Concord, have never had more than one representative.

She knows the players think the weekend is a joke. They'd rather spend the time with their families or go someplace warm with their buddies than be a part of a grab for money and attention. Sophie has plans to visit her parents. They're spending Christmas with Colby, she'll Skype in, but she's flying out to see them over the All-Star break. She's looking forward to it. She talks to them regularly on the phone, but it's different being with them in person. She's sure her dad already has ice time booked and drills queued up.

"I'm too old to be skating for the cameras." X stretches his legs out and makes a face as his knee cracks.

"It's an *honor*," Matty says. He laughs as he stretches his own legs. "Jenna and I are going to Bermuda. Her parents are watching the kids."

"Which mean's she's leaving your ass behind if you're picked."

"If I'm picked, then I'm going to end up with a mysterious ankle injury. But I have a feeling I'm safe this year."

Several of her teammates look over at Sophie, and she can't help but scoff. She just came off two games being scratched. If her coach doesn't think she's good enough for the Condors, why would the NAHL think she's good enough for the All-Star Game?

"You have the best shot out of all of us," Merlin says. "Sucks to be you."

"Think about how many cameras will be there," Hayes says.

And—oh. She hadn't considered that angle. It's a weekend of flash and gimmicks to draw attention to the League and what better way to do it than to trot out the League's first woman?

"I guess I should cancel my plans, then," she says. Her mom will be disappointed.

"We'll find out soon," Garfield says.

They countdown the final minute then Garfield refreshes his phone. He looks at Sophie, and she knows before he says it that she's going. She'd be more excited if the selection was for real and not just a PR stunt. But maybe this is an opportunity she can use to her advantage. She'll spend the weekend with the League's best and if she can keep up with them or even prove herself better she can prove she belongs.

"It's not that bad," Matty says, interpreting her silence as disappointment. "The draft is stupid, but it's always good to see the other guys in the League and hang out. And the competitions are fun. The game itself is kind of boring."

"It's hockey. I'm sure I'll find a way to have fun."

"You're going to rock it," Merlin says. "I can help you plan some sick shootout moves."

"Don't listen to him," Kevlar says. "You'll beat anyone there at the speed challenges."

"Oh, shit!" Garfield exclaims. "We have *two*. Congrats, Haysie."

"Two All-Star rookies?" X asks. "Our future looks so bright." He wipes fake tears from his eyes.

Sophie twists to make eye contact with Hayes. He looks as excited to spend the weekend together as she feels. At least there will be plenty of other people there for her to hang out with. She pulls up the All-Star nominations on her phone and grins when she sees Ivanov's on the list.

Maybe the weekend won't be so bad after all.

"DO YOU THINK being nominated to the All-Star weekend makes you more valuable on the trade market?" Marty Owen asks. The man has a talent for taking a good thing and twisting it into something bad. She wants to know how many people actually read his articles in *The Concord Courier*. It can't be very many.

"I still have no comment on trade rumors."

"You and Hayes were both chosen by the League out of everyone else on your team," Rossetti says, and Sophie braces herself for a *do you think you're more deserving than your captain or a veteran like Delacroix*? "Both of you have been scratched in the past two months. Is Coach Butler mismanaging his players?"

The locker room falls as silent as a graveyard. Marty Owen looks as if he wants to propose to Rossetti on the spot. Even Rickers shuffles forward, sensing a potential story.

Beyond the reporters, Matty looks poised to intervene. Mary Beth, however, doesn't even look up from her phone. She knows Sophie can handle tricky questions.

"I think it shows the opposite. It's an honor to be selected for the All-Star Game, and it means the League saw something in us. Coach Butler knows what we're capable of and when we didn't give enough, he challenged us to be better."

"So you're going to thank Butler for scratching you?" Rossetti asks, skeptical.

"Coach Butler is a tenured, successful coach in this League. I trust that he knows what he's doing."

Realizing she won't give them a story, Marty Owen changes directions. "What do you say to the accusations that your invitation is just a publicity stunt?"

"People have said that at every stage of my career. I'll do what I always do that weekend. I'll play hockey and prove them wrong."

"WE CAN CHANGE our plans," her mom says when Sophie finally calls her. "We'll fly to you for Christmas and visit Colby another time."

"Don't." Colby's always had to give up things for Sophie, first because she was younger than him and then because she was the better hockey player. She won't take this too.

"I could come out and see you and your father could see Colby."

"I'll Skype you at Christmas like we planned, and I'll see you and Dad next time you fly down for a game."

"I worry about you being on your own."

"I'm not on my own. I have an entire team. We're having a Holiday party over the Christmas break, and knowing the guys, we'll have a New Year's party too." Then, because she knows that isn't what her mom cares about, she adds, "I've already promised to build a gingerbread house with Kaylee and Jessi."

"They sound like sweet girls."

Sophie shakes her head but tells her mom about decorating the house with the Wilcoxes and stringing colored lights through the trees in the front yard. By the end of the conversation, she has a few ideas on what to buy the girls for Christmas, and her mom seems less worried about Sophie being in New Hampshire on her own for the holiday.

THEY SCRAPE OUT a win on the 23rd, blowing an early lead and barely managing to pull off an OT victory on a goal from Zhang. They leave the game behind as soon as it's done. Some of her teammates go out that night, but Sophie stays in, watching Christmas movies with Kaylee and Jessi.

The 24th starts with a Family and Friends skate. She races Kaylee around the ice and lets Jessi ride on her shoulders as she does a few lazy loops. Afterwards, she skates with Granlund's kids. Earlier this year, she signed red jerseys for them. A couple of days ago, she signed black ones for him to give them for Christmas.

After everyone's tired and hungry from skating, they pile in the team kitchen for snacks and mugs of hot chocolate. Theo disappears and comes back dressed up like Santa Claus, and he patiently listens to all the kids tell him what they hope to get tomorrow morning for Christmas.

Much later, the team meets up; no coaches, no staff, no families, just them. Garfield and Aronowitz set up a Secret Psych exchange. It's like Secret Santa only, "Inclusive for those of us who don't celebrate Christmas," Aronowitz explained when he handed out assignments.

After that, everyone returns to their families or drives to the airport to fly home. Sophie drives to the Wilcoxes, a little melancholy. Mrs. Wilcox, who has a sixth sense for these things, catches her before she can head downstairs to mope in the basement.

She holds out a red and green plaid pajama set. They're flannel and soft as she accepts them. "Um, thank you?" Sophie says.

Kaylee and Jessi poke their heads out of the living room. They're in the same pajamas and they light up when they see Sophie. "We're watching the *real* Grinch tonight," Kaylee says. "Will you watch with us?"

"Oh. I—" Overwhelmed, Sophie looks to Mrs. Wilcox for help.

"You're a part of our family," Mrs. Wilcox tells her. Then, taking pity, she ushers the girls toward the pantry. "Who's going to help me make the popcorn?"

Sophie escapes to the basement where she changes into her new pajamas and takes a few deep breaths. She only has to wipe her eyes once on the way back upstairs, which she decides to count as a win.

SHE WAKES UP early on Christmas morning and makes herself blueberry pancakes. Her mom always made them on Christmas growing up. When she was little, Sophie asked why her mom picked *blue*berries for a red and green holiday but never got a good answer. Today, she has the plate on her lap when she Skypes her family.

It's the first thing her mom notices. She bites her bottom lip and looks away as Sophie says, "Merry Christmas."

Colby, his hair sticking up in every direction as if he just rolled out of bed, musters up enough energy to glare at Sophie, his expression saying *why are you making Mom sad on Christmas?*

"Merry Christmas, sweetie," her mom says. Her voice only wavers a little. She pulls Sophie's dad into the frame beside her and Colby, all three of them squished together in a hotel room.

Colby rolls up a blueberry pancake of his own and dips it in syrup. He grunts something that might be *"Merry Christmas"* and Sophie can't help but laugh. Colby's never been a morning person unless there was a promise of hockey. Even Christmas can't make him happy about being awake.

They take turns opening their presents. Sophie discovers she has a large box filled with smaller, individually wrapped boxes. The first of those reveals a pair of thick, fluffy socks. When she was younger, she refused to wear slippers, because she thought they were too much like shoes to wear in the house. Warm socks became a staple of her Christmases.

She and Colby take turns opening their little presents until it's time for their big ones. Their parents give Colby two plane tickets so he and his girlfriend can go on a post-graduation trip. He hugs their mom and fist bumps their dad. After Sophie opens her present, it's her parents' turn.

"Is this another golf trip?" her mom asks with a smile as she picks up a plain white envelope. That was the standard present for years. Sophie and Colby would pick a resort with a golf course for their dad and a nice spa for their mom. This year, she's done something different.

She's nervous as her mom opens the envelope. She pulls the card out and a piece of paper falls out. She picks up the paper and unfolds it, her eyes moving back-and-forth as she reads. Wordlessly, she hands it to her husband.

Sophie bites her bottom lip, a bad habit of hers. Her lips are chapped and she makes a mental note to be better at putting on ChapStick. She wasn't sure whether or not she should pay off her parents' mortgage but, "You've done so much for me. I wanted to do something for you."

Their house is theirs now. After years of her parents scrimping and saving and taking out loans so Sophie and Colby could play hockey, she's found a way to thank them. She thought about waiting a year or two, until she had a bigger contract and could buy them a fancier house, but she knows they'd rather have this one. It's the house they bought after getting married and the one where they raised their kids.

"Oh honey," her mom breathes. "You didn't—thank you."

Even her dad looks a little misty eyed. He gives her a small nod. Sophie nods back. "Merry Christmas."

AFTER TALKING WITH her family, she eats her cold pancakes and heads upstairs to do Christmas with the Wilcoxes. She eats an early lunch with them and far too many cookies, then takes a nap so she can stay up late tonight to watch the first games of the 2011 U-Tourney.

They're being held in Bratislava, Slovakia this year, and the tournament opens with the U21 USA squad taking on Sweden. Alexis Engelking is the Americans' best player, a brash but talented center who has been tearing it up in the junior hockey league this season. She won't be draft eligible until 2013, but she's made it clear she aims to be the first woman drafted first overall.

Despite Engelking's dynamic style, Sophie's attention is claimed by Elsa Nyberg. Unlike Engelking, Elsa is draft eligible this year. Sophie's also played against her, back in the 2007 U-Tourney when Sophie and Team Canada beat Elsa on the way to a gold medal.

Zurich was Sophie's first international hockey tournament. She was fourteen and playing on Canada's U16 team. Everything was bigger, the ice, the pressure, her teammates, and she tended to stick close to them and the comforting accents of home. Outside of her team, everything was different and foreign.

But there was one afternoon where she was separated from them and ended up eating lunch in the cafeteria on her own. That's where she met Elsa. The older girl made a face at the squash to warn Sophie off it and Sophie made the same face back after pointing to the meatloaf.

After watching Sweden win, Sophie settles in to watch Canada play the host country. The goalie in net, Gabrielle Gagnon, posts a beauty of a shutout. She's another player draft eligible this year and when Sophie finally goes to bed, hours past when she normally would, she thinks only one thing: *maybe I won't be alone next year.*

THEY DROP BOTH their games between the Christmas and New Year's break. At their practice before their first game after the break, Coach Butler runs their lines through a blender. Sophie practices with Garfield and Zhang, but they can't recapture their preseason magic so then she plays with Matty and Garfield. She centers Thurman and Nelson, which is a disaster and she's glad when it doesn't last long.

"You and Hayes didn't play on a line together," Marty Owen says after practice. "Butler tried seemingly every other combination. Are the two of you still not getting along?"

"We're teammates," Sophie answers. "If Coach Butler wants us to play together, then we will."

"Which one of you will keep the center position?"

"Hey!" Merlin stops trying to wrestle the iPod speakers away from Aronowitz. "Are you trying to steal my center from me?" He points an accusing finger at Sophie. "You better not trade me in for a younger winger."

"Younger *and* prettier," Aronowitz says. He yelps as Merlin abandons the fight for the speakers to pelt him with tape balls. And, once Merlin starts throwing them, everyone else does too.

Media wraps up quickly after that and Merlin's waiting outside her locker room when she's done showering.

"Thanks for the save in there," she says. "I would never trade you for Hayes. Figuli is an entirely different story."

Merlin puffs up, offended, then shrugs. "Yeah, that's fair."

Mikhail Figuli single-handedly played Slovakia into the quarter-finals at the Stuttgart Winter Games. He'll be a Hall of Famer one day, and she still can't believe she's playing against him. She's been on the same ice as Figuli. She's taken shifts against him and wasn't completely embarrassed.

"Are you *blushing?*" Merlin looks freaked out.

"No."

"He just turned forty! He could be your father!"

"I like his hockey not his—" Sophie makes a face "—other stuff. You're making this weird."

"*I'm* making it weird? You're the one who's into the oldest guy in the League!"

"Like you don't get all gushy over Justin Rust."

"He's the best center in the League. I played on his wing in the All-Star Game one year. It was amazing."

Sophie arches her eyebrows. "See! You can like someone's hockey without wanting to see them naked."

"We were in a locker room together. I definitely saw him naked."

"We're so done talking about this." Thankfully, they've reached her car. "I'm going home and watching the Boston game. And if you want to go home and think about Justin Rust naked in the showers, then it's your own business."

Merlin's mouth drops. "That's not...! You! Ugh!"

She laughs and hops into her car.

THERE'S NO LAUGHTER the next day. They play a hard game against Montreal, jumping to a 1-0 lead before taking two quick penalties which put them behind 1-2. They manage to even the score, only to take another penalty. The Mammoths don't convert on that one, but they score on the shift afterwards.

Going into the third period, the score is 3-4, and they battle for twenty minutes to tie the score 4-4 in the dwindling seconds of the period. Thurman takes a terrible penalty in overtime, and Ducasse converts to win the game.

The next day Coach Butler skates them until they're doubled over and panting and then he skates them harder, over and over until Wilchinski pukes. He at least makes it to one of the buckets the trainers set up as if they knew this was going to happen. Hearing him puke sets off Aronowitz, and Sophie's feeling queasy by the time everyone's gathered in front of Coach Butler again.

"Now the real work can begin," Coach says.

Her quads are burning and her lungs ache with each breath she draws and *now* is the time for the real work to begin?

They run drill after drill, Coach barking at them to quit being lazy and play the game the way it's meant to be played.

He yells at them for being sloppy even though he's the one who wiped them all out. Sophie doesn't dare complain or even rest too much between drills. The threat of being scratched still hangs over her head.

When Coach Butler says, "Final drill," she's relieved it's almost over. Then he adds, "Once someone successfully completes it, we're done."

Her relief evaporates into the dry rink air. Any drill requiring one person to complete it will be hell. Her suspicions are confirmed as Coach Butler explains. Coach Richelieu is on the breakaway and they'll go one at a time and try to keep him from scoring. Only, they're all exhausted from a hard practice, and Coach Richelieu hasn't done anything more strenuous than raise his voice.

"Fuck," Merlin mutters. He's one spot in front of Sophie in line, and his face is pale under his red facial hair. He looks like he needs a big meal and a long nap. She could use the same.

Matty's the first up. He chases Coach Richelieu down and extends his stick when he can't skate fast enough to reach. His stick barely taps Coach's skates, but he goes down, easy. Coach Butler blows his whistle. "Tripping. Everyone take a lap."

No one dares to complain but there's more than one mutinous expression as they take their lap and return to line. They go through the entire lineup, goalies included, and they have an extra lap after all of them, because they have to skate every time they take a penalty.

"The drill ends when you keep Ritchy from scoring," Coach Butler says. Sophie hopes he brought sleeping bags, because they aren't getting out of here any time soon.

"Still love hockey?" Merlin whispers as Hayes steps up for his second turn.

"Yeah. But it doesn't always love me back."

Hayes is the first who doesn't catch up to Richelieu and their assistant coach has an easy, unbothered shot on goal.

"Shit," Kevlar says.

Coach Butler's face turns so red that Sophie's afraid his head will pop right off his shoulders. Matty takes them on three hard laps around the rink without Coach having to speak. When they get back in line, Sophie feels two seconds from floating off the ice or her legs giving out on her.

"I'm napping so hard when we're done," she says as Zhang takes his turn.

"*If* we ever get out of this," Merlin mutters.

"Pretend Rust is in the stands watching."

Merlin offers her a faint smile. "Maybe you should channel your inner Figuli." He wheezes as Zhang fails to end the drill. "Maybe we need someone younger. Try being yourself." He steps up, the next person to tackle the drill.

Richelieu scores and Merlin pauses next to Sophie on his skate of shame to the end of the line. He taps her helmet with his glove. "You've got this."

She takes a deep breath and steps up to the line. One last spark of energy, one last push, and she can end this. She's faster than Richelieu when she's fresh. She needs to be faster than him now when she's tired.

If you're not the best, then you don't get to play.

Coach Butler blows his whistle and she springs forward. She takes two big strides and her quads scream in protest. Her legs wobble, but she pushes through the discomfort and the fatigue. She spends so much time in the weight room, she has to custom order her fucking pants. She isn't about to let her assistant coach beat her on a breakaway.

The mistake everyone makes is coming at him from behind. It leads to a penalty more often than not, so she takes a different approach. Coming at him from the side means she has to be even faster, but she puts every last ounce of energy into the effort. She lifts Richelieu's stick and shoves her shoulder into him. She knocks him flat on his ass and then sends the puck hurtling down the ice for a goal of her own.

"I'll see you all for practice tomorrow," Coach Butler says before skating off the ice.

Sophie drops her stick to the ice and rests her hands on her thighs, bent over as she drags in sharp lungfuls of air. Merlin's the first of her teammates to reach her, and he bumps her shoulder, careful so he doesn't knock her over. "I've changed my mind. I'd pick you over Rust."

"Nice job, kid," Matty tells her.

Lindy pats her helmet before he skates away, muttering in Swedish.

She stands up in time for X to rest his helmet against hers. She's afraid he'll fall asleep like this. She can barely hold herself up let alone the two of them, but he leaves after a murmured, "*Merci.*"

Sophie's the last one off the ice, and she heads straight for her locker room. She wants a shower, then she wants to sleep for the rest of the afternoon. Their next game isn't for another two days. Hopefully it's enough time to recover.

She digs through her bag until she finds her emergency snacks. She shovels two handfuls of trail mix into her mouth before she tackles her pads. Punishment skates in *full gear*. She's sleeping forever and going to wake up starving. If there was only some way to eat and sleep at the same time.

She wrestles her skates off and rewards herself with more trail mix. She tastes salt and isn't sure if it's from her snack or her own sweat. She gags even as she pours another handful of trail mix. Her phone dings as she debates whether or not she has the energy to pull her Under Amour over her head.

MERLIN: *We're going to Theo and Kevlar's and gorging on takeout. You're coming. You're a fucking lifesaver.*

At the top of her needs is food and sleep but what she wants is team cuddles and to be told she did a good job. Her best memories from the Winter Games were after wins when the whole team would pile into Verreault's room with their blankets and pillows and make a giant nest on the floor. They played drinking games with Gatorade and braided each other's hair and talked up each other's play.

SOPHIE: *If you don't hear from me in thirty minutes then I drowned in the shower.*

Once she's naked, she stumbles into the shower and leans against the wall to stop herself from falling over. She wishes there was another woman on the team, someone else in the room in case her legs give out on her or at least someone to talk to her to help keep her awake.

When she finally emerges from her locker room, Theo, Kevlar, Merlin, and Aronowitz are waiting for her. She sways into Theo who obligingly catches her shoulders so she doesn't fall. She lets herself lean on him on the way out to his car. Kevlar claims shotgun which means she has the entire backseat to herself because Merlin and Aronowitz get into Merlin's car. She stretches out once her seatbelt is on, but it doesn't stop her from stiffening up on the drive. She limps into Kevlar and Theo's building. When she sees the flight of stairs, she wants to cry.

"When I have an apartment, there won't be stairs," she decides as she begins the slow, upward climb.

"When are you getting your own apartment?" Kevlar asks.

"Next year." She doesn't untie her shoelaces before she takes her shoes off in their apartment, because she's afraid that if she bends over then she won't straighten again. Instead, she toes her shoes off and flops down on the couch next to Aronowitz. She realizes her mistake as soon as she sees the cartons of Chinese food on the table, out of her reach. She makes a grabby motion for Aronowitz's carton.

"Get your own," he says.

She looks at the coffee table and back at him. Her bottom lip wobbles. He huffs, amused, and grabs her a carton off the table along with a fork. "I hope you like beef and broccoli."

"I would eat anything right now." She shoves food into her mouth, glad for the fork. Chopsticks would take too long. The beef is hot and the broccoli is crunchy, and she eats with single-minded focus. She doesn't pay attention to anything around her until her carton's empty.

She comes out of her zone to realize she isn't warm only from the food but because she's now sandwiched between Aronowitz and Kevlar. "Hi."

Kevlar's eyes crinkle as he smiles at her. "Hi. You back with us?"

She pokes her fork into his container and emerges with some kind of chicken. "This better not be spicy."

It isn't spicy, but it isn't as good as her beef and broccoli was. Besides, now she's temporarily sated her hunger, all she wants is a nap. It seems natural to list sideways, until her head rests on Kevlar's shoulder. Her eyelids drag down, and she's about to slip into sleep when she remembers she's in a room full of teammates. She jerks away, heart pounding, and jostles Aronowitz enough for him to spill rice on his lap.

"Sorry," she says. She reaches for her keys but they're in her bag and anyway they're useless because her car's at the rink and she's *trapped*. She's so tired she could cry but she can't sleep. She *can't*. What if...

"Hey," Kevlar soothes. "Nap time, okay?" He curls an arm around her shoulders, light enough that she could knock it away, even as worn out as she is. "You're safe with us."

Tears prickle at the corners of her eyes and she tucks her head against his shoulder so no one will notice. He smells like locker room soap and Chinese food. He holds her closer as she relaxes and falls asleep.

Chapter Seventeen

THEY HAVE A light practice the next day, everyone sore and tired from the day before. When it's over, Coach Butler taps Hayes and Berky, their backup goalie, to stay and clean up the pucks. Free, Sophie scoots down to the locker room. Mary Beth's waiting for her outside the doors, and Sophie pauses, her hopes for a quick exit today vanishing into thin air.

"Press conference," Mary Beth says. "No shower but you can change. I need you in ten minutes." She glances up at the other players. "Matty, I need you too."

"Uh oh," Merlin says, joking but then he grows serious as if he's worried there might be something to talk about.

"Ten minutes," Mary Beth repeats.

"We'll be there," Matty promises. He doesn't look surprised, as if he knows what's going on. Sophie wants to ask but he goes straight to his stall to change so she goes to hers. She strips out of her practice gear and pulls on a pair of Under Armour pants and a Condors T-shirt. She wipes the sweat off her face the best she can and plops a baseball cap on her head.

She and Matty head to the press room together. Her captain looks run down, as if the past three weeks haven't been restful despite having two breaks. She hopes the upcoming All-Star Weekend is what he needs to be himself again. After the break, it's a race to the end of the season. Concord isn't in a great position to push for the playoffs, but they're not out of it yet.

Maybe, the little voice in the back of her head whispers. This year, they could do something that's never happened in their franchise's history. *Yeah, and I'll win the Cup while I'm at it.* Brushing the fantasy aside, she takes her seat behind the small table. Matty sits next to her and they look out at the sea of reporters already here.

She knew when Mary Beth said press conference it would be a big deal. She just isn't sure what the fuss is over. They've talked her All-Star nomination to death already. Maybe they want to talk about the Clayton again? Or maybe they want to know about yesterday's practice.

Marty Owen looks smug, never a good sign. "Are we finally going to talk about the trade?"

Sophie's prepared to deny the trade rumors when what he said catches up to her. *The trade*, not *the trade rumors*. She looks over at Matty who stares straight ahead, his shoulders set as if he's preparing for an OT faceoff in his own zone. He's no help. She glances at Mary Beth, but the woman's on her phone, fingers flying over the screen.

"What trade?" Sophie finally asks when it's clear no one is going to say anything.

"Hayes, Berklund, and Custer to Cleveland for Cleveland's 2012 first round pick and Theodore Augereau."

Hayes was traded. She catches herself before she smiles, because this isn't the time to celebrate. Later, she'll punch her fist in the air because Concord chose *her* over Hayes, and she'll laugh because being the second overall pick wasn't worth as much as he thought it was. She's the one Concord wants to invest in. He was the expendable one. She knew it but the fact her organization agrees means more than she can say.

She adjusts the brim of her hat. "It's always tough to say goodbye to teammates, but I'm looking forward to a new one."

"Is there any truth to the rumors that Hayes is being traded because the two of you didn't get along?" asks a reporter from *TNSN*.

Matty fields this one. "Hayes is a promising young player, but he wasn't a good fit for our team. We wish him the best in Cleveland."

"You've lost your second representative to the All-Star weekend," Rossetti says. "Will you petition the League to reassign Hayes's nomination to someone else on your roster?"

The All-Star weekend. Sophie hadn't even thought about that. It's a week and a half out and in *Cleveland*, the city they just traded Hayes to. There's no way the Commissioner yanks his nomination. This will be ratings gold. And hell for her.

"Hayes earned his nomination the same as everyone else," Sophie answers. "And it's the perfect way to introduce him to his new city." Bland and boring, she repeats to herself. That's been her brand since she was a kid, and it's served her well.

By the time the press conference is over, she's ready for her post-practice nap. She's glad that after today, she'll never have to pretend to like Hayes again. She and Matty are the only ones in the locker room; they were kept so late that everyone else cleared out.

Matty claps her on the shoulder once they're inside. It's a show of support, one he couldn't give her in the press conference without sparking a whole new line of questioning.

"Management made a choice," she says because no matter how they spin it, that's what happened today. Management chose her over Hayes which means the future of this franchise is even heavier on her shoulders. "I won't let them down. I won't let you down either."

"You don't have to do it alone," Matty tells her. He squeezes her shoulder.

She looks at the team logo on the floor as she walks past it. *Concord Condor for life,* she hopes. She's a step closer to it today than she was yesterday.

THEY HAVE A late practice on the 5th so the team makes plans for a mid-morning brunch. It'll be their first chance to meet Augereau before they practice with him. Sophie finds herself on welcome duty which is how she ends up crashing his hotel room with Merlin, Kevlar, and Theo.

Augereau opens his door in loose running tights and nothing else. He leaves the door open before returning to his open suitcase to hunt for a shirt. He looks too skinny. She never understands how, in all their pads, goalies look like they're one deep breath away from filling the entire net but out of them, they're tiny. She wants to drag him to brunch early and pile his plate with food.

"How do your legs even support you?" she asks. His spandex is *loose*.

"Be nice," Merlin says. "Not everyone has tree trunks for legs."

She elbows him as Augereau finds a shirt he likes. He pulls it on backwards. "I need coffee."

"Your shirt is on backwards," Sophie tells him.

"Be patient with her," Merlin advises as Augereau fixes it. "She doesn't socialize much." He dodges another elbow and offers their new backup a smile. "Jeff McArthur, but you can call me Merlin."

"Theo Smith," Theo says.

Augereau stops fussing with his shirt. He looks Theo up and down, all six and a half feet and two hundred and fifty pounds of him. Then he crosses his arms over his chest. "I'm Theo."

"You're new. And you look like a Teddy."

"I do not." He gestures at the defenseman. "You're big and bearded. I bet you're very cuddly. You be Teddy."

Kevlar looks delighted as he leans in to stage whisper, "Did you hear that? Teddy here just told us he isn't cuddled enough."

Augereau shakes his head and takes a step back. He isn't quick enough, and Theo wraps him up in a hug and drops onto his bed. Kevlar and Merlin pile on them, laughing as they aggressively cuddle their newest teammate. Sophie takes a picture and sends it to Matty, warning him that they might be late to brunch.

WHEN THEY SHOW up to brunch, half the team looks up at Sophie then looks away. Zhang opens his mouth and closes it. Garfield, from his customary place next to Nelson, barely even glances at her. Her step falters as she realizes maybe not everyone's as excited about the trade as she is. No, that's not quite it. They're angry *she's* the one still here. It stings, but she does her best to brush the hurt aside as she takes the empty chair next to Petrov.

"I got the call-up," he says.

"Awesome. Now I have someone new to practice faceoffs with."

"Just say no!" Merlin cheerfully calls as he worms between Nelson and Garfield.

Neither man pays enough attention to stop him. Nelson keeps looking at Sophie, and her shoulders draw up tighter with each glance. Hayes lived with him, and she knows Nelson's one of the older players who wasn't thrilled to have a woman on the team in the first place. Maybe the Hayes trade was the final straw for him. It doesn't help that Coach likes to sit him whenever he plays her with Matty, but she doesn't control Coach's choices. And she won't say no to more ice time in big minutes because it hurts Nelson's pride.

Finally, Nelson hands his phone to her.

Garfield makes a grab for it, and more than one of her teammates glares at Nelson as Sophie takes it. He has an article pulled up from *The Concord Courier*. Marty Owen's slimy face stares at her as she scrolls down to the article itself. Yesterday, everyone wrote about the trade from Concord's side. Apparently, this morning is the trade from Hayes's.

I'm not surprised I was the one traded. There can't be a lot of interest in the last pick of the draft. I'm excited for a fresh start with a new team. The Cleveland Presidents...

It was strange playing with the League's first woman. I know that isn't the right answer. I'm supposed to be excited for inclusion and diversity. Maybe she's the wrong first woman, because it was hard sharing a locker room with someone so entitled. Not that we were even in the locker room together that much. She had her own...

I hope I can still go to the All-Star weekend. I know I was just traded, but it's another opportunity to play in front of my new city. I want to show my fans what I can do.

She skims all the block quotes, and when she's done, she hands the phone back to Nelson. Nothing there surprises her. Hayes has hated her since the first time she stripped the puck from him when they were freshmen. But a few jabs at her in the media isn't going to break her. When it came down to it, management chose her. This was the show of faith they didn't give her at the draft, and she'll repay that faith tenfold.

"You're going to Cleveland on your own now," Merlin realizes. He must be reading the same article. Come to think of it, that might be why everyone stared at her earlier. "It's not too late to fake an injury."

"I'm not faking an injury. The League chose me to go and I'm going. You think I've never played in front of a crowd that hated me before?"

"This will be different." It surprises her that Nelson's giving her this talk. He even softens his voice as if he thinks he's breaking difficult news. "NAHL stadiums can hold a lot of people, and Hayes is going to turn every single one of them against you."

"I'll be fine," she promises.

THEY FLY OUT to Quebec after practice. After an early dinner, Merlin and the guys decide to watch *Slap Shot* for the eighth time this season. She leaves them to it and knocks on Teddy's door. He opens it, wearing a shirt this time, and frowns when he sees her. "I don't think I'm supposed to let you into my room." Even so, he steps aside so she can come in.

She takes her shoes off and lines them up next to his. He drifts back to his bed and picks up the TV remote on the way. Sophie eyes the second bed. "Who are you rooming with?"

"Wilchinski."

She sits down next to Teddy and stretches her legs out. At his questioning look, she shrugs. "I saw him puke at practice once."

"So now you can't sit on his bed?"

She looks pointedly at the remote. "Are we watching TV or what?"

Teddy puts on a poker tournament. Sophie wrinkles her nose but leans back against the headboard to watch. Being friends with someone means pretending to share their interests, even if she'd rather bag skate than watch a bunch of dudes in sunglasses play cards.

Teddy cracks first. "What are you doing?"

"Hanging out with you."

"You don't even know me."

"Which is why we're hanging out." She thinks this is sound logic, but Teddy looks at her as if *she's* the weird one.

"Is this the part where I tell you about my life?"

She ignores the sarcasm. "If you want." She offers him a smile he doesn't return. In retrospect, she didn't think this through enough. It's her fault he was traded here. Maybe he wants nothing to do with her. "I'm sorry. I should go."

She's sliding off the bed when he stops her with a hand on her arm. "No, I'm sorry. I'm being grumpy. I had to leave my girlfriend in Cleveland. She's a teacher there. She said she'll move to Concord if they keep me, but the life of a backup goalie isn't stable. I want to offer her more than having to move cities every year."

She doesn't like the frown on his face so she nudges him as she sits back against the headboard again. "Didn't you hear? I'm *entitled*, management gives me whatever I want. You'll be here a long time."

"Sure." He doesn't sound as if he believes her, but that's okay. She's good at proving people wrong.

TEDDY PLAYS HIS first game for the Concord Condors in their final game before the All-Star break. It's a 5-2 win and Sophie's first two-goal game of her NAHL career. After the game ends, she skates straight for the goalie crease and clasps Teddy's helmet between her hands. He's taller than her and has to bend down to tap their helmets together.

"First of many wins for you here," she tells him.

His eyes crinkle as he smiles behind his mask.

MATTY INSISTS ON driving her to the airport when she flies out to Cleveland. He claims it's because he wants to save her from the parking bill, but she suspects it's so he can fuss over her one last time.

"It'll be fine," she says, unsure of how she's the one reassuring *him*. "It's hockey. I'm good at it, remember?"

He laughs, weakly, and tugs on the end of her braid. "Let me know when you get there."

"Yes, I'll make sure to text you and *my mother* when I land safely."

Honestly, it's one weekend. It'll be in a city that hates her, but she's weathered worse. She'll pose for some pictures, play some hockey, and be back home before she knows it.

A YOUNG WOMAN in a fitted dress picks her up at the airport. She's wearing heels and her hair is pulled back in a professional updo. She introduces herself as Kerry, Sophie's personal assistant for the weekend.

"My what?" Sophie repeats.

"You have a full schedule," Kerry says, moving on as if they don't have enough time to explain anything twice. "I'm here to help you manage it. I hope you brought dresses."

"You do know I'm a hockey player, right?"

Kerry sighs. "We'll make it work."

SHE DRESSES UP in a suit and tells a room full of reporters how much she loves playing in the NAHL and that she's grateful for the opportunity they gave her. She dresses down in leggings and one of her jerseys to sign things for the fans clustered outside the arena. She dresses back up to shake hands with the mayor of Cleveland. They both smile for the flashing cameras as he says he "supports women in whatever careers they choose to pursue."

She spends the whole day changing outfits and being paraded around as the first woman in the NAHL. By the time she's free to return to the hotel, her feet are sore and she's on autopilot. She steps into an open elevator and sags against the cool metal wall.

"You might want to press a floor number."

She drags her gaze from the floor, then freezes when she realizes who just spoke. She's in an elevator with *Mikhail Figuli*. She fumbles with the buttons as she looks for number three. Her face is bright red when she finally manages to push it.

"Nice job on the record earlier this season."

"Thank you. Your name's in the conversation for the Maddow again. You're having a good season."

He smiles. "Thanks, kid. I appreciate that you didn't add the qualifier. It's always *you're in the running for the Maddow Trophy, an impressive accomplishment for your age.*"

"You mean like *you're in the running for the Clayton, an impressive accomplishment for a woman*?"

Figuli's smile broadens. "I like you."

She ducks her head, glad Merlin isn't here, because he would give her shit for blushing.

AFTER AN EARLY dinner she has to change *again* but at least this time it's because the weekend is finally starting. She arrives at the Cleveland rink for the draft, the only event slated for tonight, in a black car with tinted windows. There's a red carpet leading from the road to the doors and there's a rope line to keep the fans at bay. Hundreds of them push and shove each other, some holding signs above their heads and yelling for their favorite players.

Ivanov and Hippeli are a couple of steps ahead of her, and she watches as the fans cheer even louder when they spot the exuberant Russian. He waves back at them, broad sweeping motions with his arms, and he almost elbows Hippeli in the face. He signs a fan's T-shirt and a piece of paper.

He's straightening up when he spots Sophie. His smile grows, almost blinding, and he bounds over to lift her off the ground. She pats his shoulders, unsure what to do with her arms, and hopes he doesn't wrinkle her suit too badly.

"Favorite rival!" He sets her on the ground and kisses her cheek. He pulls her over to the rope line where a little girl in a Figuli jersey holds out her sleeve for them to sign.

She watches them write their names. "Are you two friends?"

"Best friends!" Ivanov hugs her again and Sophie laughs and pushes him off her even as she agrees. Pleased with the answer and her signed jersey, the girl slips into the crowd.

It's nice to have someone to stick close to even if it's slow going because Ivanov wants to stop for every kid he makes eye contact with. Three-quarters of the way to the doors, she pauses when she sees a sign lifted high above the crowd. There's a well-drawn, and graphic, image of Sophie on the ground, her limbs bent at awkward angles as a condor pecks at her intestines.

"Stupid," Ivanov says and shuffles her along.

Inside, they meet up with some of the other players. She follows Ivanov to a table that Hippeli's already claimed. Riley Dennison, a forward for Indianapolis, joins them. They played them already this season, and he wasn't a raging asshole so Sophie figures she can sit through the draft with him. Plus, he glares at Anthony Sinclair as he passes by. Sinclair *is* a raging asshole, but he graduated from the Weston School so Sophie isn't surprised.

There are screens set up throughout the room so they can see into the rink where a stage has been set up. There's a podium in the middle and rows of chairs on either side. Once they're drafted, they'll walk out, receive their jersey, then sit on either Team Farage's or Team Rust's side of the stage. As the host city's captain, Farage has the first pick. He uses it to select Hayes, and the crowd is thunderous as Hayes struts out to receive his black jersey. From the look Farage and Rust exchange as the Minneapolis captain steps up to the podium, she figures she's in for a long wait before it's her turn.

"So," Dennison says once Rust makes his first pick. "When do you think you're going?"

Hippeli snorts. "Farage is a dick and Rust is biased towards Americans."

"That ups my odds, then."

"Unless he's holding a grudge over your last game," Sophie points out. "A 6-3 win and you had your first three-point night of the season."

Everyone at the table turns to stare at her. Ivanov grins as he bumps her shoulder with his. "Know my stats too?"

"They're worse than hers," Hippeli says. He laughs at the mock outrage on Ivanov's face. "You need to put up some assists on top of all your goals if you don't want to be smoked in the Clayton race."

"Or score more goals," Dennison says. "You only score the pretty ones. You need some dirty ones too."

"I'm score dirty." Ivanov waggles his eyebrows.

"Keep it in your pants," Hippeli says.

Dennison is the first of their table picked, Team Rust. Hippeli's next, Team Farage. When Ivanov's name is called, Sophie's left alone at the table. It's easier to sit here and listen to everyone's names called ahead of her than it was at the real draft. She's prepared for it this time around, and she knows that whatever team she plays for this weekend is temporary. When it's all over, she's going home to *her* team.

The crowd does the math and when they realize she's the last one left, they boo so loudly they drown out Rust as he steps up to the podium. She takes a deep breath and walks out on stage.

THE COMMISSIONER GIVES another speech and then the athletes are shuffled into a room full of reporters. She isn't surprised to find herself with a crowd right away.

"You went last again."

She knows they're looking for a story so she adopts her blandest tone as she says, "I'm grateful for the opportunity to play."

On a normal day, Marty Owen would poke at her soft spots, and Rossetti would push deeper for something to write about, but this isn't a normal day. Ivanov's holding court in the corner, his hands flailing and his face expressive as he regales them with a story. On the other side of the room, the Cleveland contingent is talking up their fan base. Sophie isn't interesting enough, and she's quickly abandoned.

"Impressive," Dennison says, his silver jersey matching hers as he stands next to her. "I thought you were actually that boring but it's how you get them to leave you alone."

"I am pretty boring, though."

He shrugs. "After this mess is over, we're having a party, our team only, in my room so even the babies can get drunk."

"I don't drink." She offers a self-deprecating smile. "Part of the boring thing."

He looks as if he doesn't completely believe it, but he taps her water bottle. "Fill it with juice, soda, something that isn't clear. I'll tell everyone I spiked it."

She stares, too long, but she isn't used to people outside of her team being nice to her. It's his turn to smile, a touch sad, but he doesn't say anything before leaving to talk to another Team Rust player.

FIGULI'S THE ONE who opens the door when she knocks. The party's already in full swing, music playing, people laughing and talking. He ushers her inside and taps her water bottle. "Do you need something extra in that?"

"Dennison's helping me out."

They've packed Team Rust into Dennison's room and the adjoining one, and Sophie's gaze flits around the place. Rust has a crowd of older players around him and in the far corner, Ivanov's with what looks like every Russian at the All-Star weekend this year. Her fingers curl around her water bottle, crinkling the plastic, as she wishes she had a teammate here.

"Go play nice with the other kids," Figuli tells her.

She wanders closer to Ivanov but stays on the outskirts when she realizes he's speaking Russian. He's quicker and smoother in his native tongue, far more comfortable than she's ever seen him in an interview or even talking to her. She's been envious of his media coverage this season, because they eat up how dynamic he is while she has to be controlled and *boring*. But maybe he's blunt because he doesn't have the vocabulary to talk the media in circles the way she does. He doesn't hide behind words because he can't.

Ivanov catches her staring, and he ducks out of his conversation to join her. His smile is dimmer than usual. "Different, yes?" He nods at the group of Russians who continue their conversation without him. "Not big, dumb brute."

"I don't think you are."

He shrugs as if it doesn't bother him either way. "English is hard."

"I can teach you a few soundbites," she offers. "You can tell BaronsTV you spent too much time with me and the boring rubbed off. It'll be good for a few laughs."

He frowns. "Laugh at you."

She mirrors his earlier shrug. "Okay, so, when they ask you why your power play is slumping, you tell them you need to work getting pucks on net."

"Power play is great!"

She arches her eyebrows. "You can't lie to me, I watch your games." He clutches his chest and gasps as if she's stabbed him. She laughs and shoves his face away so she doesn't have to see him pout.

THE SKILLS COMPETITION is fun. She wins the stickhandling and the obstacle course, and she smiles with too many teeth as the fans boo her. *You have no power over me*, she thinks as the Commissioner hands her an oversized check for being the best. She schools her face into something friendlier for the cameras and then skates to the bench to watch Ivanov in the shootout competition.

The next day is even better, because it's the All-Star Game, and she centers a line with Figuli on her right wing and Ivanov on her left. They're *amazing*.

There's no defense, because no one takes the weekend seriously, but it doesn't stop her line from celebrating every time they connect on a goal. It's an eight-point game for her, and she comes off the ice, grinning, and feeling as if there should be a dent in her helmet, because Ivanov's clapped her on the head so many times.

Afterwards, in the locker room, Figuli trades sticks with her. "Don't let them get you down," he tells her, far more serious than anyone has been all weekend.

"Yeah," she says, stunned. "Thank you. Good luck with the Maddow."

"I'd rather have good luck with my knees. Downside of getting old, I don't recommend it."

"But it's worth it. The stiff knees and everything. It's worth it to play."

She doesn't realize it's a question until Figuli smiles and answers. "Yeah, kid. It's all worth it."

Chapter Eighteen

SOPHIE'S ON THE bike, warming up for their game against Quebec when her phone buzzes, interrupting her music. Text after text floods in, and she stops pedaling, wondering what's happened. Colby's texts are all expletives and emojis. Her mom's are more restrained but still excited. Mary Beth cautions her to keep her focus on tonight's game but also sends her four thumbs-ups.

"Sofe?" Teddy asks. He's paused his pre-game stretches to look over at her, concerned. Once she stops staring at her phone, she realizes the rest of the team is worried, probably because she never lets herself be distracted.

But if anything could distract her from her pregame routine, then it would be this. She beams, unable to temper her smile into something dimmer. "Elsa Nyberg and Gabrielle Gagnon will be at the draft this year."

She pedals again, faster than before, until she remembers Mary Beth's warning. She slows back down to a warm-up pace, but she doesn't do anything to fight her smile.

MORE WOMEN AT the draft doesn't necessarily mean they'll be drafted. Sophie takes the ice for warm-ups with *take a chance* ringing in her ears. She doesn't want Elsa or Gabrielle to be drafted last like she was. And while she knows their draft order depends a lot on their play, it depends a little bit on hers.

For better or worse, all women looking to break into the NAHL are judged based on Sophie. If she comes across as inconsistent, then Elsa will bear that label too. If she's seen as uncoachable, then Gabrielle will have to struggle to prove she isn't. If Sophie wants more women to play with her, she has to prove drafting women is a safe bet.

She assists on Witzer's goal on their very first shift. She waits for him to celly then knocks him into the glass, laughing as she rubs her glove over his helmet and then his face. Toward the end of the period, she assists on another, Zhang's power play tally this time.

Two assists in one period, and she can't help but want more. For Elsa and Gabrielle but also for herself. Those were assists forty-seven and forty-eight on the year for her. Could she hit fifty tonight? That's the kind of milestone which will remind everyone she was the better option to keep between herself and Hayes. Maybe it'll even put her name back in the conversation for the Clayton.

Ever since Butler scratched her, she's been dismissed from the talks. Everyone acts like it's Ivanov's trophy to lose. He's showy and he scores big goals, but she's a good player too. She's *better*. She won't end the season with more games played, but she'll end it with more points. His assist total is nowhere near hers and even though she won't catch his goal count, she's on pace to have a better season points-wise. Will that be enough?

She takes a deep breath and shoves the thought of the trophy out of her mind. One game at a time. If she looks too far ahead she'll lose focus on where she is now. She has two more periods left of hockey to play and two more goals to assist on.

FIVE MINUTES INTO the second period, Concord goes on the power play again. She taps Matty's skates as they go over the boards. "Be ready to shoot. I'll find you."

He nods and skates up to the faceoff dot. He wins it back to her and she skates around the net, dodging Rotrand's stick and then Coderre's check. The defense shifts as she comes up the far end. She passes up to Faulkner and bangs her stick on the ice so he'll pass back. He fakes a pass to Zhang before he passes to her and it freezes the Bobcats long enough for her to sling a pass right in front of the net.

Matty's waiting on the other side. He shoots, the puck going top corner. Sophie throws her arms up in the air. He points to her and kicks his leg up in celebration.

Assist forty-nine.

WITH THREE MINUTES left in the third period, she loads up a shot. She doesn't normally have enough time to rocket one like this, but the puck whips past her own teammates and the Bobcat defenders and hops over Silverman's glove and lands in the back of the net.

It's the first four-point night of her career, and while she would've liked to have an assist, she won't say no to a goal. Or a win. Her goal puts them up 4-2 which means Quebec is certainly going to pull their goalie at the next opportunity.

She skates through the fist bump line, then sits on the bench and looks up at the Jumbotron. They replay her goal and she tilts her head, considering. She punches Merlin's arm as they show it again, slow motion this time. "Did the puck deflect off your elbow?"

"I don't think so—huh." It's his turn to tilt his head. "Maybe."

"That would explain the change in direction. Silverman had it, then he didn't. I think that's your goal."

It takes a long time for them to announce the goal, probably because they're trying to figure out if the puck went off Merlin or Rotrand. But when they do announce it, it's Merlin's goal with a primary assist from Sophie and a secondary assist from Theo.

She punches Merlin's arm again. "Right place, right time."

"You're not mad? I stole your goal."

"Fifty assists," she says. "Next time, I'll be pissed if you steal my goal. Today it's okay."

"THAT WAS QUITE the statement game," Rickers says during her scrum. She has her "fiftieth assist" puck, and she turns it over in her hands, smiling every time she sees her accomplishment written across it in silver Sharpie.

"What statement were you trying to make?" Marty Owen asks. "Was that a warning to other women?"

No, Sophie thinks, and something must show on her face, because a few of the reporters take a step back. She coughs and rubs her fingers over the puck. "I'm excited for Gabrielle and Elsa to be at the draft. They're both different players than I am. For one, Gabrielle's a goalie. And Elsa's more of a goal scorer. She's tearing it up in the SHL this season."

"You're keeping tabs on her?" Rickers asks.

"I watched the U-Tourneys in December, and I've caught a few of Gothenburg's games this season. I want to play with or against other women next season. After today's announcement, we're one step closer to that happening."

THE TRADE DEADLINE approaches and even though Concord's too far out of a playoff spot to have any hope, it still disappoints her when they're sellers. Their big trade is Thurman, and Coach Butler gives his A to Nelson for the rest of the season. They trade a couple of other players, and Sophie vows to herself that next year, they'll be buyers at the deadline. There won't be weeks of anxiety, wondering who will stay on the team and who won't. There won't be the continued anxiety of surviving the deadline and wondering what will happen as soon as the off-season hits.

Good teams keep their players. Bad ones trade them for picks in hopes of being good a year or two down the line. It sucks to lose pieces of their team, but it only motivates her to be better.

Right after the deadline is the Moms' Trip. Sophie thinks it's poor planning, but she isn't in charge of these decisions. It's Martin Pauling, their owner, who champions the biannual trip. It switches every year, Moms' Trip this year then Dads' Trip next one. He believes family is important, especially since most players play so far from home.

Coach Butler calls it a distraction, but he also isn't in charge, of this at least, so all their moms show up at practice to cheer on their kids. Sophie doesn't think much of it until Theo laughs and says, "No fucking way," with the kind of glee which means hell to pay for someone.

Kevlar's the next one to burst into laughter. Her gaze sweeps through the moms, gathered by the glass, but she doesn't spot anything out of the ordinary. There's Zhang's mom, between Sophie's and Kevlar's. X's mom has a 39 on both her sleeves to match her son's number. All the moms are in red Condors jerseys, and they wave when they notice the players looking.

"Yo, Merlin, how's it feel to be your mom's second favorite player?" Zhang asks.

"Fuck you, I'm *your* mom's favorite player," Merlin says, automatic. Then he looks over and groans. "Aw, fuck."

Sophie scans the crowd again until she spots the woman with curly red hair, standing near the end of the line. Her hair's the same color as Merlin's and—oh, her jersey has a 93 on the sleeve. Sophie doesn't know whose face turns redder, hers or Merlin's.

AFTER PRACTICE, EVERYONE takes a quick shower so they can meet up with their moms. Well, not everyone brought their mom, as she learns when Garfield steers her away from where her mom is still talking to Kevlar's in order to meet his grandmother.

"Your grandmother?" Sophie repeats as she stares at the woman. She doesn't look that old. Her hair is all black still—even Sophie's mom has a few grays coming in—and her face has a few deep-set wrinkles, but she doesn't carry her age the way Sophie's *mémé* does. Realizing she's being rude, Sophie flushes. "I'm sorry. It's a pleasure to meet you."

"Call me Mona. You're a sweet thing. But there must be some steel in that spine of yours if they haven't broken you already."

"Oh." Caught off guard, Sophie glances at Garfield, who looks resigned and a little bit amused. "Your grandson is a good player. I'm proud to be his teammate."

"Of course he's good. I didn't drive him two hours to practice for him to be *bad*."

"Two hours?" Sophie repeats.

"Each way." Mona nods and waves off her grandson when he groans. "Yes, you've heard this story too many

times. Go talk to someone else because I'm telling it again."
Garfield obediently wanders over to talk to Nelson, leaving
Sophie alone with Mona. "He was good at hockey. It was the
first thing he ever fell in love with, and I was going to make
sure he had it."

Sophie nods along to a familiar story. Then Mona adds,
"The nearest midget team was the Chieftains, and if you
thought I would let my grandson play for them, then you'd
be wrong. The next nearest team was shit. It took two hours
to drive him to every practice and two hours to drive him
home, but he was a Lethbridge Railer."

"And now he's a Concord Condor."

"He sure is." Mona's pride is unmistakable as her gaze
finds her grandson. "After he signed his entry level contract,
he set up a breakfast program at all the schools in town. And
after he signed his first extension, he helped build a ball
hockey arena. He's a good kid."

"Hockey is all about giving back," Sophie agrees. She
fell in love with the sport and now she wants everyone like
her to have the same opportunity.

"*Life* is about giving back," Mona says. Then, with a
discerning look, she adds, "Though, for you, I think the two
might be the same."

THEY FLY TO Cleveland for the first game on the Moms'
Trip. Sophie escapes to the bus so she doesn't have to talk to
her mom about it. But then she sits down next to Teddy and
he says, "Do you—?"

"No," she snaps. Then she sighs. "I'm sorry. No, I don't
want to talk about it." She had a preview of what it was like
to play in Cleveland at the All-Star Game, and she knows
tonight will be even worse. There were distractions then,

plenty of players to focus on. But now all the focus is on her and Hayes, the rivalry the NAHL was hoping to get out of her and Ivanov.

"We all have your back," Teddy tells her.

"I survived the All-Star Game all on my own."

Teddy, unruffled by her prickliness, says, "Yeah, so now imagine how much better it'll be with us at your side."

Some of the tension ebbs from her body. She nudges Teddy's knee with hers, a silent thank-you.

THERE ARE PEOPLE gathered outside the rink when they get off the bus for morning skate. A couple of them wave and Sophie hesitates. No one's yelling or throwing things. Maybe Concord has a couple stray fans in Cleveland. And if they do, she doesn't want to brush them off.

"Are you coming?" Zhang asks.

"In a minute."

A group of girls have noticed her, and, unless she needs to be somewhere, she never ignores girls who are excited about hockey. Part of why she wanted to play in such a well televised and marketed league was because she wanted little girls to see her on their TV screens and know they can chase their dreams too.

She can see the red of their shirts from here and what she thinks is the Condors logo. She'll pop over, say hi, then join her team in the locker room before anyone can miss her. She approaches the group, a smile on her face. It falters as she gets closer and she sees that the condor on their shirts isn't the same as the one on hers. This bird is hunched over roadkill, its beak stained red.

"Good morning," Sophie greets, her throat tight with regret. It's too late to turn around now. "Do you have tickets for the game tonight?"

The girls shake their heads. The tallest one smiles, a mean twist of her lips. "We're going to watch at my house, because I have HD. We can watch you cry on the big TV when you lose."

There's a boy standing off to the side, his phone held up to record the encounter. Sophie doesn't know what to do. Walk away? She certainly can't start a fight with a bunch of teenagers, no matter how mean spirited they are. She rocks back on her heels. "I have morning skate, but I can sign something before I go in if you want."

"Sure." The girl hands Sophie a marker and turns around to show off the 224 and LOSER stamped across the back of her shirt. Sophie's expression stays neutral and her hands don't shake as she signs all three shirts. It's a slow walk back to their rink with their laughter chasing her the whole way.

She's subdued when she reaches the locker room. Zhang lifts his eyebrows in a question, but she shakes her head. If she has to talk about it, then she might crack, and she can't afford it. She has a game to prepare for.

She changes quickly and hits the ice, hoping for a distraction.

"Where have you been?" Merlin asks.

So much for a distraction. "Signing some things." She forces her tone to stay light. "I have fans everywhere. One day, you'll be famous like me."

Merlin squawks and tries to put her in a headlock. By the time they're straight up wrestling, she's distracted them both. She has a solid morning skate, but she's still quiet, enough that Matty notices and pulls her aside.

"Cleveland has last change so you'll be up against Hayes all night. They think it'll crack you."

Because it's only her and Matty left on the ice, Sophie rolls her eyes. "It won't. I've been beating him for the past four years. I'm not about to start losing now."

Matty laughs and claps her on the back. "That's the fire we need."

They head off the ice together, but before she reaches the locker room, Mary Beth rounds the corner. Sophie knows without having to ask that it's her Mary Beth wants to see. She waves Matty into the locker room and steps to the side to hear whatever pep talk Mary Beth has for her.

Her PR manager has her phone in her hand, but she does Sophie the small kindness of not making her watch the video from the episode outside.

"Do you remember the first time we met? What did I ask you in that hotel room in Denver?"

"You asked me why I play hockey."

"What did you tell me?"

"Because I love it," she answers again, voice soft.

"Because you love it," Mary Beth repeats. "If you inspire some girls or young women along the way, then it's a bonus. First and foremost, you play for you." Mary Beth squeezes her shoulder. "Play hard tonight. Remember why you love the game."

THE STADIUM IS thunderous from the moment they take the ice for warm-ups. The stands are full of signs like *Go Home or Go Home in an Ambulance* and *Girls Get Out*. There are a few with her corpse being eaten by a condor which apparently is going to be a thing. Fans, already drunk, pound the glass and shout at her when she skates her two easy laps. As she does her stickhandling, they start up a *"Sophie sucks"* chant.

When the team comes together at the bench for one last talk, Coach Butler is positively beaming. "Tonight will be fun." She thinks he might actually mean it.

"Play smart, hard hockey," Matty tells them. "You all know where the line is, don't let them drag you over it."

THE FANS BOO every time she touches the puck and cheer every time she's knocked around. She keeps the irritation off her face and makes sure she's all smiles and reassurances when the guys look to her. She refuses to be blamed for a poor performance tonight. She's here to prove Concord was right to keep her. She's known for almost five years now that she's a better player than Hayes. It's time to show everyone why.

The crowd boos especially loudly during a TV timeout, and she looks up at the Jumbotron. The camera is on the Concord moms and they all turn so everyone can see they're wearing Fournier jerseys. It's an unexpected show of support, and Sophie meets Coach Butler's gaze, ready to take on the world and win.

He must notice because he says, "Fournier's line is out after the timeout."

She wins the faceoff, and they carry the puck into the offensive zone. Olsson leaves his coverage to lay a hit on her, but she sees him coming the whole way. She passes the puck to safety, takes the hit, then pushes off Olsson and skates to the net. Merlin shoots the puck and it dings off the crossbar.

Sophie snags the puck and fires it on net. It bounces off Strindberg's pads and back onto her stick. She lifts the puck this time, up and over his outstretched pad.

Goal.

The crowd boos so loudly she feels it, but she doesn't care. She throws her arms open and laughs as her teammates flock to her. "That's how we fucking do it," she says.

On the way back to the bench, she skates by Hayes. "Some things don't change, eh?" He snarls and gives her a two-handed shove. Reckless off the goal, she grins around her mouth guard. "Little weak there, *Haysie.*"

He grabs two fistfuls of her jersey and yanks her closer as the crowd roars, demanding her blood on the ice. "I'll show you weak."

She smiles, eyes glittering behind her visor. "You've never shown me anything else."

He draws his arm back as if he's going to hit her. She dares him to do it. She isn't supposed to start a fight, but no one can blame her for finishing one. Before he can take a swing, there are officials stepping between them. The crowd boos again.

Sophie returns to her bench, hopped up on adrenaline and the goal and wanting more. Nelson makes room for her as she sits down on the bench. "Remember Matty's speech about the line?"

Sophie knows Nelson has an A now, but he's never understood her and Hayes and, more than that, he doesn't understand *her*. She spits her mouth guard into her glove. "I played against him for four years. I know exactly where the line is."

"Shit," Garfield mutters. "Remind me never to end up on your bad side."

Sophie's smile is too full of teeth to be friendly.

SHE'S STUCK IN the box for a bullshit tripping call, made by an official who needs a new fucking glasses prescription. She fumes as her team battles for control of the puck and sucks in a breath when Cleveland gains possession. They settle into a rhythm and throw shot after shot on net. It's everything Lindy can do to keep the puck out.

Hayes drifts back door, and Sophie wants to shout a warning, but no one will hear her. They don't see him either. Farage passes down low and Lindy pushes off his post, but he's too slow. He won't make it. Hayes has an open net and—

He *misses*.

The crowd groans, disappointed.

Sophie pops her mouth guard back in and stands up as her penalty time winds down. At the far end of the ice, Strindberg taps his stick on the ice to warn his team that the power play is nearly over. As soon as the door to the box opens, she charges out of it. She catches a stretch pass from Nelson, then skates on Strindberg.

He makes the stop, but it gives her team an offensive zone faceoff and badly needed relief on the defensive end. She makes sure to skate by Hayes on her way back to the bench. "You're giving my number a bad reputation." Her gaze lingers on the 93 on his sleeve.

He puffs up, always so easy to rile. "*My* number."

"I've worn it longer."

A PARTIAL CHANGE has Sophie on the ice with Witzer and Garfield. They're pinned in the defensive zone, struggling to break the puck out. At this rate, they'll all need to change once they're free.

There's a scramble in front of the net. Farage has two good whacks at the puck and an extra jab for Kevlar. Lindy covers the puck and Farage jabs at him too. Everyone descends on the net, Cleveland looking for a fight and Concord looking to protect their goalie. It's a normal post-whistle scrum, the kind of thing which ends peacefully most of the time.

But Walker sneers something, all Sophie hears is, "The Rez." Garfield freezes, shock and disgust on his face. It's all the time Kevlar needs to jump in, his gloves on the ground. He hauls Walker away from everyone else. The officials let them fight, choosing to focus their attention on everyone else.

Farage grabs a fistful of Witzer's jersey. Hayes steps forward as if he wants to land a sucker punch. Sophie grabs him from behind and pins his arms to his sides, holding him immobile.

"I don't fucking think so," she says.

Pierre Delmonte hurries over to separate them. It takes some time, but the officials calm things down enough to send both lines back to their benches. Sophie skates with Garfield to their bench as Kevlar is escorted in the other direction to the penalty box.

Garfield hunches his shoulders as if he's bracing for Sophie to ask questions he doesn't want to answer. She's been in his position too many times to force him to relive the moment by explaining it to her. "Hockey players are shitty," she says. She doesn't need to know details. All she needs is for Garfield to know that everyone here has his back.

Surprised, Garfield looks over at her. Then he looks back at Kevlar, sitting in the penalty box with bags of ice on his knuckles. "Only some of them."

AFTER THE GAME, once the team is done with the media and their showers, their moms flood the locker room. Mrs. Faulkner heads straight for her son, and Kevlar ducks his head, somehow looking small even though he dwarfs the woman in front of him.

"I had to," he says, almost too quietly for Sophie to hear.

"I know." His mom reaches up to cup his cheek. "I'm proud of you, Kevin."

Sophie looks away, uncomfortable intruding on a private moment. Her own mom stands next to her, watching Sophie. "Is everything okay?" she asks once she has her daughter's attention.

Sophie smiles. "We won for you so yeah, I'd say things are good."

"You won for *you*. I haven't seen you play like that in years."

Sophie shrugs. "Someone reminded me I play because I love this sport. I went out there and showed it."

"You certainly did." Her mom pulls her in for a hug. Sophie would be embarrassed but most of her teammates are being hugged too.

Chapter Nineteen

THEIR GAME AGAINST Cleveland is one of the highest points of the season. Their game again Boston is the lowest. On March 18th they lose at home to the Boston Barons, and it's the final nail in the coffin of their season. They still have eleven games left to play, but they're mathematically eliminated from the playoffs. Just like that, there's a countdown to the end of Sophie's first NAHL season, and she isn't convinced they'll give her another.

She was the dark horse, the secret weapon who was supposed to spark a turnaround for the franchise. Instead, they're in the same place they always are, on the outside of the playoffs looking in. They aren't the worst team in the League—that dubious honor goes to Seattle again—but this wasn't the triumphant entry she was hoping for.

Coach Butler told her at the beginning of the season the playoffs weren't a realistic goal this season, but she didn't listen. In a tiny part of her brain, she dreamed of lifting the Maple Cup in her first season. *That* would've proved everyone wrong. Instead, she's at dinner with Dmitri Ivanov, wondering if winning the Clayton will be enough of a statement that Concord will let her play again.

Last pick of the draft, a voice in her head that sounds suspiciously like Hayes sneers. *What happens when the Fournier Experiment is a failure?*

She wishes they'd gone to a diner instead of a steakhouse, because she can't tear a cloth napkin into shreds the way she could a paper one. She can only wring her fingers as she remembers Ivanov scoring on back-to-back shifts. His team didn't even need those goals. They were already up 3-1, and goals four and five sealed the win and emptied the stadium. By the third period, the stands were nearly deserted and when the fans gave up, the team did too.

It's going to be a long slog to the end of their season.

Ivanov orders them virgin cocktails because they aren't old enough to drink. At Sophie's raised eyebrows he shrugs. "Good to have fun."

Her smile is fleeting, because there's only one thing she loves—hockey, especially *winning* at hockey—and that's been lacking this year. She drags a hand down her face and wonders, not for the first time, if she should've canceled. She made these plans last week, before the game, the humiliating loss, and the finality of the season. She's in a shitty mood, and Ivanov doesn't deserve that.

"No hockey," he tells her as if he can read her mind.

Probably, he can just see her feelings, plain as day on her face. Does he now see her panic, because they have nothing in common besides hockey, and if they don't talk about that, then what else is there to say?

He moves so they're sitting next to each other on her side of the table and pulls out his phone. He has a truly alarming number of pictures featuring at least ten different dogs. Apparently, in his free time, he visits the animal shelters around Boston, petting their dogs and donating the adoption fees for families who are looking for a pet.

"You don't have one of your own yet?" she asks. Given all the puppy selfies, she's surprised he hasn't bought an entire shelter's worth of animals.

"Blinsky says no. Have to wait for own house."

From there, it's an easy transition into talking about whether they're keeping their living arrangements or looking for something different next year. That leads into talking about their families and by the time dessert comes out, they've passed an entire meal without talking about hockey.

The waitress places a giant slice of chocolate cake between them. The rim of the plate is covered in whipped cream, and Ivanov happily grins as he hands Sophie a fork. "Remember our first cake?"

"I didn't sing to you."

"Terrible friend." He pokes his tongue out, teasing. "I'm sing for your birthday. I'm call from *Russia*."

"You won't," she says which is a mistake, because she's now guaranteed that he'll call *and* sing.

"Will. I'm best friend. Not like you. I—"

She shoves a forkful of whipped cream into his open mouth and laughs as he splutters, caught off guard.

PRACTICE IS SUBDUED the day after they're eliminated, for obvious reasons. Coach Butler is surprisingly laid back. Maybe he's giving them one day to mope, then he'll return to shouting the laziness out of them? Or is this what the rest of the season looks like—glum and miserable?

Not for her. She did some thinking after her lunch with Ivanov. She has eleven games left in her rookie season, and yes, there are no playoffs for her, but those games still matter. Eleven more opportunities for her to make her mark on this League. She can finish strong even if her team can't.

"Liney lunch?" Merlin asks after practice. Everyone's stripping down, ready for showers, then lunch and a nap.

"Dinner?" Sophie counters. She exchanges her on-ice practice clothes for her off-ice ones. "I want to hit the weight room."

Kevlar lifts his head from where it was hanging between his shoulders. "The weight room?"

"We have eleven games left. I want to be my best for them."

There are a few eye rolls and a couple of fond smiles, the *Oh, Sophie* reaction she expected. Let her teammates think it's a canned answer. They don't understand. The year of the lockout was torture for her, waking up every day and wondering *is this the day they'll decide to let me play?* She spent her senior year racking up points and records, unsure of where she'd be the year after. The NAHL? The SHL? Would she make her mom happy and go to college? And now she's here, but her place isn't guaranteed. Coach Butler showed her that when he scratched her. At any point, her dream can be snatched away from her.

She doesn't know what she can do to solidify her place in the League. Does she have to win the Clayton? The Cup? Does she need a letter on her jersey? She can do them all. She'll win the Clayton this season and the Cup the next. She'll show Coach she has the consistency and leadership to deserve not only a permanent roster spot but a letter as well. She will make herself a fixture of this city.

But she can't do those things if she doesn't put in the hard work. She ties her sneakers and tucks the bows under the laces so they won't come untied.

"Do you want a spotter?" Matty asks.

The locker room falls silent. Sophie looks over at her captain. "I won't say no to one."

"Okay, then." He grabs a clean shirt from his stall and pulls it over his bare, sweaty chest.

"Ugh," Merlin says but he changes into a fresh T-shirt too.

X wipes his face with a sweat towel and grabs a T-shirt of his own. "I'll stretch. I'm not as young as you lot."

Bewildered, Sophie watches as her teammates switch from shower-and-food mode to more-practice mode. She didn't mean to make this a thing. She tries to tell Matty that when they reach the weight room.

"We need something to motivate us," he tells her.

He doesn't sound angry or like he thinks she's trying to show them up. And he looks better than he has all day, as if he has a reason to look forward to their next game. If her team needs motivation, she'll be their motivation. She grins and loads up the bar so she can squat.

"Hey, check this out," X says. He's looking at something on his phone. "Figuli and Rust are first and second in the Maddow race."

"Tell me something I don't know," Merlin says.

A giant smile spreads across X's face. "Our Sophie's in third. She's only five points behind Figuli."

"Five points isn't that many," Zhang says.

"We have eleven games," Garfield agrees.

This isn't quite what Sophie meant when she agreed to be her team's motivation. But, as she looks around the weight room, everyone's locked in. They're ready to play out the rest of the season for *her*.

Teddy tsks as he inspects her rack. "Only one plate on each side? Weak legs won't win you a scoring title." He hefts another plate on. "You can't skip leg day," he says, serious as if he's delivering sage advice and not quoting an internet meme.

She puts another plate on the other side so she's balanced. "Let's do this, then."

THEY SET UP a board in the locker room to keep track of the scoring race. They make sure to cover it when the media's around, but they forget one time when Coach Butler enters the room. Sophie holds her breath as he notices it, afraid he'll lecture her on the importance of being a team player. He doesn't like the attention she's gotten, the way she's been singled out for being a woman, and he might think this is arrogant.

He surprises her by studying the board and saying, "We can make this happen."

The whole locker room cheers.

Coach starts double shifting her.

THEY FLY OUT to Indianapolis for their final game in March. She has a three-point night and would've had her first NAHL hat trick if she hadn't missed on the empty net at the end of the game.

"You're only three points back now," Faulkner tells her after the game is over.

She's tied with Rust for second and only three points back of being tied with Mikhail Figuli for first. Earlier this season, it might have intimidated her. She's competing for the scoring title with one of her hockey idols, a man who's already won it half a dozen times. And she has a legitimate chance at beating him.

No, she *will* beat him.

"Four more games," Matty says. "We're doing it."

SHE CONGRATULATES IVANOV when Boston clinches a playoff spot, her chest tight with envy. But he can have the playoffs. She's winning the Maddow *and* the Clayton. Then next year she's winning the Cup.

SHE'S TWO POINTS back of Figuli headed into the final game of the season. Their game against *Cleveland*.

Emotions churn as she prepares for the game. Disappointment that this will be the end of her season. Worried this could be the end of her NAHL career. Fired up to catch Figuli. So fiercely proud of her team and the way they've battled these past eleven games. It's their strongest stretch of the season and Bobby Brindle has suggested, more than once, if they'd played like this from the start of the season they might actually be in the playoffs right now.

It feels like the whole city turns out for the game. The stands are packed with people who want to witness firsthand the rivalry building between Concord and Cleveland. After the last game in Ohio, they're hoping to see blood shed on the ice.

Sophie has bigger plans than a couple of fights.

"Cleveland needs a point out of this game to clinch," she says in the locker room as they dress for the game. "We didn't make the playoffs this year, but the next best thing is to spoil someone else's chance. We're winning this game in regulation."

There's no way in *hell* Michael Hayes is playing a NAHL playoff game before she does.

The guys all look up, recognizing the steel in her voice. Matty stands. "Did you hear that, boys? We're winning in regulation."

"They're not clinching in *our* stadium," X declares.

The team cheers, everyone looking focused and ready except for Teddy. He's played the past four games for them, because Lindy twisted an ankle early in their game against Indianapolis. She has a few guesses as to why Teddy's hesitant with their game plan; a lot of it hinges on him playing well against the team that gave up on him.

She finds him on the ice as he does his goalie stretches. "You've been great for us down this stretch, and you're going to be great tonight."

"I didn't play well for them. I'm the worst backup in Cleveland's history."

"You don't play for them anymore. You play for us." Sophie rubs his helmet with her glove. "Let's show this crowd what it means to be a Concord Condor."

SHE BEGINS THE game on Matty's wing. He wins the faceoff to her and she carries the puck up the ice, all the way into the offensive zone, before she drops a pass back to him. She keeps skating until she's in front of Strindberg, blocking his view. He shoves at her and misses the puck as it whips past him into the net.

First shift, first shot, first goal.

Sophie spins around and laughs as Matty crushes her in a hug. "One down," he says. "Two more."

She can't tie with Figuli on points, because he has more goals, giving him the edge in the tie-breaker. She has to beat him outright. With the way her team is flying tonight, they can do it.

SHE SCORES LATE in the first on a wrap-around. She curls the puck around the post, then Strindberg kicks from the far post to the near one and knocks the puck into his own goal. It isn't the prettiest goal, but it's *hers*.

When she returns to the bench, Ben Granlund offers her a smile and a fist bump. "Figuli scored."

Which means she still needs two points to beat him. She catches the water bottle that Merlin tosses her and takes a swig. "I guess I better keep playing hard."

HAYES SCORES IN the dwindling minutes of the first period and stares her down as the crowd boos him. She meets his gaze evenly and wonders what, in their five years of playing against each other, makes him think he can intimidate her.

OLSSON OPENS THE second by laying a monster hit on her. He slams her into the boards and her helmet smacks into the glass, a cracking sound that echoes in her ears. She falls to the ice once he isn't pinning her anymore. With the breath knocked out of her, it takes her an extra moment to regain her bearings.

Theo appears at her side, even more enormous when she's down on the ice. He holds a hand out to her. "He's in the box for boarding. Are you okay?"

She's stunned, but all she needs it to get her breath back and she'll be fine. She nods as she clasps his hand and accepts his help. He hauls her to her skates and skates with her to the bench. Coach Butler puts the second unit on the ice, and she sits on the edge of her seat, poised to go over the boards as soon as Coach gives the okay.

She wants to be on the ice right now. She wants to set up in their zone and work their D until she scores. She wants to wring every last ounce of playoff hopes from their minds.

Coach finally sends her unit over the boards. They carry the puck back into the zone before Cleveland can swap out its tired penalty killers. *Period of the long change*, she thinks.

She, Theo, and Garfield go tic-tac-goal, Garfield scoring an absolute beauty. Theo lifts Sophie off the ice and bellows even though she isn't the one who scored.

"One more," Garfield says, as Matty joins their celebration.

PETROV TAKES A holding penalty with 4:03 left to go in the second period. Farage buries the puck, and the score is 3-2 headed into intermission.

"THIS GAME IS ours," Matty tells them, when it's just the players in the room. "We have our game plan. Keep executing. Push until we win."

When Coach Butler comes in, taking over, Matty sits down next to Petrov. Whatever he says, Petrov doesn't look as gutted afterward. She makes a note to talk to Teddy before they head up. His head was hanging after the goal even though there was nothing he could've done to stop it. He's been solid for them when they've needed him. Now, they stay disciplined, stay out of the box, and win the game.

"Milwaukee's done," Coach Vorgen says. "Figuli only had one point."

Which means Sophie is tied with him in the points race. One more point and the title is hers. She takes a deep breath and smiles. One point in twenty minutes. They can do this.

MERLIN GIVES UP a good shot attempt to pass to her, and Hayes jumps into the lane to intercept the pass and bring the puck the other way.

Two shifts later, Theo does the same thing. Once was a fluke but twice is a pattern, and she addresses it the next time she's on the bench. "I don't need a goal. I only need a point. So shoot the fucking puck."

Merlin tosses her a salute. She considers spraying him in the face with her water bottle, then decides she'd rather drink the water.

With 4:22 left in the period, Cleveland ties the game.

As soon as the goal light flashes, the excitement is sucked out of the stadium. The fans fall silent; they've seen this show before. Sophie wants to grab them and shake them. *Believe in us. It'll be different this time.* The kids by the bench stop jumping up and down. They put their signs away and sit back in their seats.

Sophie chews on her mouth guard. The next time there's a TV timeout, she's the first to talk. "I'd rather we win in regulation than get another point." She wants to breathe life and hope back into their fan base.

"We're doing both," X says, with the authority and finality of a veteran player.

With 2:21 left in the game, Matty hits the post.

With 1:47 left, Theo thinks he scores, and his arms are lifted in celebration when the official waves off the call.

With 1:02 left, Sophie picks up a rebound off Strindberg's pads and tries to stuff the puck in the net. Strindberg slaps his glove over the puck and she pokes at him as if she can just push him and the puck into his net. Olsson hauls her out of the crease.

With 0:32 left, Coach Butler uses his timeout.

"Augereau, you're on the bench," he says. "Mathers, your line is out. Fournier, you're our extra skater. I want Smith and Faulkner on the backend. Any questions?"

Kuzy looks around, then offers a hesitant, "The game is tied?"

"And if it stays tied for another thirty-two seconds then Cleveland makes the playoffs. So you better put the puck in the fucking net."

They skate out onto the ice. Farage is the first to notice that Teddy isn't in his net and his lips curve in an unfriendly smile. "Desperate?" he asks as he lines up across from Matty for the faceoff.

Matty doesn't answer. He wins the faceoff, sending the puck back to Sophie. She passes to Theo who winds up and shoots. Garfield recovers the puck and passes back to Theo.

Time slows down as Theo brings his stick back for another shot. Olsson shifts into the shooting lane, and she can see how the play will unfold—Olsson will go down and block the shot, then Farage will fling the puck down the ice at the empty net.

She starts skating before Theo makes contact. She reaches the redline before the puck hits Olsson's shin guard. He grunts, then Farage gathers the rebound and shoots. The puck skitters down the ice, slow but not slow enough. She forces her legs to move faster. If the puck reaches the net, then Cleveland's going to the playoffs.

She won't make it in time.

She *has* to.

This is like the stupid fucking drill they did with Coach Richelieu. She won the drill then and she'll win it now. She finds another gear and dives forward, sweeping her stick out to knock the puck away from her goal. Her chin slams into the ice, then she collides with the boards. Her chin throbs and her quads burn and her ankle twinges and she needs to get up.

The crowd is a roar of noise in her ears. *Get up*, they seem to shout. She hears Coach Butler's voice, then her father's. It's impossible and she wonders if she hit her head too hard. She plants her stick on the ice and struggles to her feet. She needs to get back in the play. They need to win.

Her team skates toward her. They come from Cleveland's side of the ice and they pour over the boards and that means the game is over. Did they win? They must've if they're this excited. Her legs tremble, ready to give out on her. Her knees buckle but Theo's there to catch her before she falls again. She's swept up in a current of joy and excitement and... "We won?"

"We fucking did it," Matty tells her. He leans in to tap his helmet against hers. "Listen."

The roar of the crowd solidifies into something she can understand. "So-phie! So-phie! So-phie!" They're chanting her name. They're back on their feet again, pounding the glass and cheering for this team, and tears spring into Sophie's eyes.

"You did it, kid," Matty tells her. Their helmets are still pressed together. "Secondary assist on the game-winning goal. The Maddow is yours."

Her eyes widen but before she can demand to know if he's joking or not, X elbows their captain out the way. "A hundred and one points, rookie. Not bad."

She's given head pats and helmet rubs from everyone on the team. Then they skate a few laps and raise their sticks in a salute to the fans. *We'll be better next year*, she promises.

They're going to do great things in this city. She can feel it.

Chapter Twenty

THERE'S LOCKER ROOM cleanout, a final round of interviews, and one last team get-together before they scatter for the summer. It's bittersweet leaving Concord and her team behind. She knows now she'll be back next season, the way she knows the Clayton is hers and that she'll never feel more at home anywhere than she does on a fresh sheet of ice.

Some of the teammates she parts ways with after the party at Matty's won't be her teammates come fall. They'll be traded or they'll sign somewhere else during free agency. She'll have new teammates next year, from those trades, and also called up from Manchester. Petrov was good for them this season; she wonders how much more talent they have hidden away on their farm team.

She returns to Thunder Bay and her parents' house and she hugs her mom for what feels like forever. It isn't long enough. She wants to cling to her mom's narrow shoulders and breathe in the faint hibiscus perfume that means she ran errands today.

"I'm so proud of you," her mom says. She tries to tuck Sophie's face against her neck as if Sophie's a kid again and not a full-size hockey player.

"I won't be home this early next season," Sophie says, an apology and a promise rolled into one.

Her mom laughs, a little watery, and herds Sophie toward the island. "You've been home for five minutes and you're already thinking about next season? Some things never change, I guess."

Sophie nods even as the word *home* makes her think of red and black; of a winged bird, tall and proud, and of a jersey with her name written across the back. She paid off her parents' mortgage this Christmas. This is *their* home. Hers hasn't been here for many years now.

She knows better than to say that, though. She starts to slide off the island stool, but her mom holds up a hand. "I'll get you a snack. I know you must be hungry." She eyes Sophie critically. "You look skinny. You'll need a new suit for the NAHL awards."

"It'll be worse next year when we're in the playoffs. I can never keep weight on during the post-season. But we can go shopping this week or next."

"We?"

Sophie shrugs. "Together. Mother-daughter bonding time." She's pretty sure that's what mothers and their daughters are supposed to do. She always did most of her shopping with her dad, picking out the perfect stick and thick socks to keep her warm and help guard against being cut by a skate blade. Shopping for a suit won't be the same as shopping for a prom dress, something she never did, but it's still something they can do together.

Her mom hands her a plate with a sliced apple on it then, before Sophie can ask, the jar of peanut butter. She drops a kiss to Sophie's forehead. "I'm glad you're home."

Sophie hugs her again.

HER DAD MAKES her watch the playoffs with him. He says it's a learning experience. The playoffs are full of players, and teams, who did things right and she should study their habits and their plays. She doesn't tell him how painful it is to watch all these people play hockey when she can't. He already knows and that's another lesson.

If she's not the best, then she doesn't get to play.

She texts Ivanov thumbs-up emojis when he's had a good game and sad faces when his team loses. Boston's knocked out after a brutal game seven in the first round. Her first reaction is relief because if Ivanov powered his team to a deep playoff push, then the NAHL might've awarded him the Clayton.

Guilt hits her almost immediately after. *This is why I don't do friends*, she thinks as she watches Ducasse celebrate his series-winning goal. *I'm not any good at it*. Ducasse is dogpiled by his teammates, then they skate a victory lap in front of their thunderous fans.

Sophie's *mémé* calls to crow about her team's win and how "Captain Canada put that filthy Russian in his place". Sophie has to leave after that, retreating upstairs to her bedroom. The walls are still decorated with her old hockey posters. Mikhail Figuli stares her down as she flops down on her bed. *I played with you this season. I beat you this season. Whoever would've thought?*

She pulls her phone out of her pocket and calls Ivanov. She knows he won't be checking his phone right now, but she leaves him a voicemail telling him how hard he played this season. He won't want to hear it, she certainly wouldn't, but he probably won't listen to her message when there's so many other people vying for his attention.

She brushes her teeth, changes into her pajamas, and climbs into bed. The first round of the playoffs ended tonight. There are three more, and each one will be harder to watch.

She falls asleep quickly only to be woken by her phone buzzing at her nightstand. She squints at her clock—it's 1:12 in the morning—and answers the call. "Hello?" she whispers, because everyone else in the house is asleep.

"Next year we play you." Ivanov's words slur together, and she can't help but hope he has a teammate keeping an eye on how much he's drinking.

"You don't want that," she tells him. "If we play you, then you'll lose."

He laughs, a strangled sound. How close is he to crying? "Want to win."

"I know." After their loss to Boston, her entire team sat in their stalls, saying nothing, because there was nothing to say. There were no playoffs for them. She took a forty-five-minute shower and cried during the whole thing.

"Should've done more. Hit two posts. Should've—" his voice cracks and falls quiet.

"It sucks. It's awful going home when you want to play, but your family will be there. Hug your mom a lot."

"Sophie secret?"

"Yeah," she answers, a quiet confession that she wouldn't give if it weren't so early in the morning. "My mom and I are going shopping for a suit for the awards."

"Will see you there."

"Then you better get a new suit too. I don't want to show you up."

He laughs, soft, as if he knows she's trying to cheer him up. They talk for another half hour, until his English slips into Russian and then into silence.

ONE BENEFIT TO being out of the playoffs is that she can go to Colby's graduation. She sits with her parents in uncomfortable folding chairs and watches her brother walk across a stage and receive his diploma.

"Congrats," she tells him once they find him in the crowd of graduates. There's a shadow lurking in his eyes. His hockey career is over. There's no draft for him, only a rec league or beer league if he can find one once he's settled and has a job. Sophie hugs him. "You can pick where we have dinner. Apparently, today's a big day for you or something."

"Jerk," he says, laughing. He tries to push her away but she only hugs him tighter.

HAVING COLBY HOME to watch the playoffs with her and her dad is better and worse. It means she isn't the only one being lectured at every stoppage of play, and she can tune her dad out sometimes and pretend it's Colby he's talking to.

The three of them watch Toronto and Chicago battle it out for six games in the Maple Cup Finals. At the end of it, Valentin Shishkin, Chicago's captain, lifts the Cup on home ice.

That'll be me, Sophie promises herself. *I'm going to win the Cup before I'm done.*

SHE WEARS HER new suit to the NAHL awards. It's black and fitted, and she wears a white dress shirt underneath but she tucks a red pocket square in the breast pocket. There had been a red suit at the shop she and her mom went to, but that seemed overly aggressive. In her other pockets, she's stashed her Maddow speech and her Clayton speech. She has a third piece of paper: bullet points of notes in case Ivanov wins it.

There's another rookie nominated, Victor Serov out of Indianapolis. Lenny Dernier has already lamented, loudly and several times, on *Rinkside* that there's something wrong with the state of hockey if two Russians and a girl were the nominees for the Clayton.

She sits by herself in the audience, waiting. When she's announced as the winner of the Maddow, there's light applause which is a nice change of pace. She walks down the long aisle and up the steps.

"I would like to thank my parents and my brother," she begins, voice steady as it carries through the microphone and into the crowd. "They were the ones who introduced me to the sport I love. I also want to thank my teammates, because without them, I wouldn't be standing here receiving this award."

She returns to her seat as more awards are handed out: best coach, best defenseman, best forward, best goaltender. There are videos for each nominee, then the winner is announced. She claps politely for each one as the anticipation grows inside her.

The very last award of the night is the Clayton. There are video packages here too, and she watches the highlights from Serov's season. Then they play hers. She sees her first assist and how she laughs as she's pied for breaking Sorkin's record. She sees her hard won first goal and then her four-assist night that got her to fifty. The video ends with her final game of the season, each point she put up to win the Maddow.

Ivanov's video package is flashier, full of highlight-reel-worthy goals and big celebrations. It ends with his OT game-winning goal in Game Six against the Mammoths. It was a big goal in an even bigger moment, but he must feel bittersweet watching it, knowing now what happens in the next game.

She folds her hands in her lap as the presenter steps up to the microphone. He taps it, even though it's worked all night, just to build suspense. She takes a deep breath and holds it.

"The Rookie of the Year for the 2011-2012 season, the winner of the Clayton Trophy, is Dmitri Ivanov of the Boston Barons."

Sophie claps, feeling numb, the same way she did at the draft when Concord picked Hayes second overall. This isn't the way it's supposed to go. Boston had a better season than Concord, but Sophie had a better season than Ivanov. She was the best. Didn't she prove that by winning the Maddow?

Ivanov's speech passes in a blur. She doesn't hear a single word of the Commissioner's wrap-up speech. She's still in a haze as everyone moves into the lobby for the party portion of the evening. She drifts along with the crowd, unable to believe it. Someone bumps into her and she spots a camera on the far side of the room. Remembering where she is, she pastes a smile onto her face.

She shakes hands with Serov and congratulates him on a strong season. She chats briefly with Ivanov before a reporter swoops in to steal him. She turns to leave and is surrounded by her own group of reporters.

"How does it feel to have won the Maddow?"

"What do you mean you couldn't have done it without your team? Are you saying you're not a strong enough player on your own?"

"Was it easier losing out in the Clayton race knowing you'd already won an award?"

"How did you win the Maddow and not the Clayton? Do you think you were slighted? Was it because you're a woman?"

She answers every question put to her and hopes her media training won out, because she doesn't remember a word of what she says. When she finally escapes, she takes the stairs up to her hotel room. Down the hall, Ivanov's opening the door to his room. Can she slip into her room without him noticing her? Talking to him surrounded by people was one thing. She knew the right things to say and the bystanders ensured that she said them.

If it's only the two of them...

"Friend!" Ivanov calls.

Sophie was too slow to hide but maybe she can still escape. She heads straight for her room without acknowledging him. She jams her keycard into the reader and pushes the door open. She kicks off her shoes and turns to close the door but Ivanov's there.

The smile has slipped from his face. His surprise quickly morphs as his lips curl into a scowl. "Sore loser? Think press tell lies. Maybe not."

Sophie has been smiling and *lying* for the whole fucking season. For her whole *life*. She's never allowed to tell the truth, not the full truth anyway. She has to be soft, polite, *gracious*. She doesn't feel any of those things now, and she's sick of pretending.

She grabs the sleeve of his suit jacket and yanks him into her room. She slams the door shut and turns the deadbolt. He wants to know the truth? She'll give him the damn truth. She takes a step toward him and he takes a step back deeper into her room. She presses forward, something she can't control bubbling under her skin.

"I won the Maddow," she says. "I scored more points than anyone in the League. I blew *you* out of the water, and they gave you the Clayton anyway. They said you were the best, but you weren't!"

Ivanov, puffed up and ready to fight, deflates. "You're upset."

She walks past him, knocking their shoulders against each other. On the ice, it would earn her a crosscheck, a few insults hurled her way. Ivanov just watches her, and it pisses her off even more. "You don't get it. If I'm not the best, then I don't get to play. You only have to play for you. I have to prove women are worth drafting. If I'm not the best, then *none* of us get to play."

She drops down on her bed, exhausted.

"Idiot," Ivanov says. He drops to his knees in front of her and covers her hands with his. "They cancel contract because I win trophy? No. You win Maddow. You set record. You play. We stay rivals. Stay...friends."

He's crouched on a hotel floor so he doesn't loom over her and his hands are gentle as they cradle hers. After she's yelled at him and tried to start a fight. Her eyes burn with tears she shouldn't shed in front of him. "I'm a shitty friend."

"Is tough to be Sophie Fournier, so I'm here. When tough to be Dima, you there."

"Just like that?" She pulls a hand free so she can wipe her eyes.

"Just like that."

He sounds so sure. She wants to believe him. "There are going to be times we don't like each other."

"Yes. Then we have dinner, maybe cake, become friends again."

He makes it sound so easy. "I—" her voice cracks and it reminds her of their last phone call. His team was eliminated from the playoffs and instead of drinking himself into a stupor with his team or calling home, he called *her*.

She cups his face between her hands, then slides her fingers into his hair. It's stiff with hair gel and he lets her tip his face up so they're looking at each other. "Friends?"

Dima nods, careful that he doesn't knock her hands away. "Friends."

SOPHIE MEETS WITH management the day before the draft. She's ushered into Mr. Pauling's suite and it feels like déjà vu as she notices all the familiar faces; Mr. Pauling, Mr. Wilcox, the coaching staff. Mary Beth's already here this time so not quite the same as after Sophie's draft.

"Our scouts worked hard this season," Mr. Pauling says. "We know who we want to draft, but there's one selection we wanted to run by you."

She glances around the room, catching Coach Butler's scowl and Mary Beth's small nod of support. She doesn't understand why they need her approval to draft anyone. Do they think she's difficult? She and Hayes didn't get along, but that was an exception.

"What's your opinion on Elsa Nyberg?" Mr. Pauling asks.

She's amazing. She's one of the best players I've ever watched. I only played against her once, but I'll never forget it. She was nice to me in the cafeteria.

Sophie takes a deep breath and tries to organize her jumble of thoughts into something professional. "Speed is the first thing I think of. I've never seen anyone accelerate as fast as she does. She can close gaps on the backcheck, and she can leave defenders in the dust on a breakaway. She has soft hands, some of the best I've ever seen. She—" Sophie pauses when she sees most of the room smiling. "Do you want more?"

Mr. Pauling chuckles. "Did you know Nyberg used to be a center?"

Sophie nods. There isn't much she doesn't know about Elsa Nyberg's game. She played center in Zurich. The next time Sophie saw her play, she was a left winger, but Sophie never found out why.

"She switched after the 2007 Zurich U-Tournament," Mr. Pauling says. "Apparently there was a Canadian center she wanted to play on a line with when she went pro. She's been waiting a long time to play with you. We'd like to give her the chance."

Coach Butler grunts something Sophie doesn't catch. She won't be alone next season. They're letting other women play. She'll have another woman on her *team*. She'll have *Elsa*.

"She'll be a good fit for our franchise," Mr. Pauling continues. "We won't risk anyone else snapping her up. We're selecting her with the first of our first-round picks. We'd like you to make the announcement."

Holy shit. Sophie has to take a moment to compose herself. "I would be honored to select Elsa for our team."

"I suppose this answers the question of whether you'll live with us next year," Mr. Wilcox says. "Amber and I would love for you to stay another year, but we understand if you want to live with your new teammate."

"I want to make sure Elsa feels like part of the team," Sophie says. They can live in an apartment like other rookies do. They can carpool to practice like Theo and Kevlar and wrestle over who has to cook and do the laundry. They can fight over the remote in their hotel room the way Merlin and Witzer do.

She—she won't be alone anymore.

THE ST. LOUIS crowd boos the commissioner as enthusiastically as Cleveland had at the All-Star weekend and Denver did at the draft last year. Sophie sits on her hands, nervous, because what if one of the five teams before them picks Elsa? She's the best player here, she deserves to be first, and if she ends up in Seattle, then Sophie doesn't know what she'll do.

Seattle makes their first selection.

Then Kansas City.

Neither of them pick Elsa and Sophie's torn between outrage and relief. By the time Concord has their first pick, she's sweated through the underarms of her shirt. She's glad her suit jacket hides it. She walks onstage with her management and tucks her thumbs into the pockets of her pants as Mr. Pauling steps up to the microphone.

"Thank you to the city of St. Louis for hosting us today. I would like to invite Sophie Fournier, the first woman drafted into the NAHL, to make our first selection."

Sophie takes his place in front of the microphone and, with a voice that's steadier than her heartbeat, says, "On behalf of the Concord Condors, I would like to use the fifth selection of the 2012 draft to select Elsa Nyberg."

She tracks the audience, searching for movement. There. On the far right, a woman makes her way to the aisle. She's tall, all of it leg. Or maybe she has a really good tailor, because her suit makes her legs look exceptionally long. *Good for speed*, Sophie thinks idly as Elsa walks down the aisle toward her.

Her suit jacket is well-tailored, the buttons undone to show off a truly horrific tie. It's lime green with yellow swirls, but somehow Elsa pulls it off. The Swedish woman smiles brightly as she accepts the jersey Mr. Pauling offers. She tugs it over her head and, instead of searching out the cameras, she stares right at Sophie as she settles the jersey over her suit.

Sophie steps forward to fuss with it. "Welcome to the team," she says quietly, only for the two of them.

Elsa beams and throws her arm around Sophie's shoulders before finally turning to the cameras.

ONCE THEY'RE OFF the stage, Sophie herds Elsa off their expected path. There will be cameras and reporters and endless questions, but first Sophie wants a moment alone. There are so many things she wants to tell Elsa, so many things she wants to ask, but those will have to wait for the upcoming season.

She tells Elsa the most important thing. "I'm so excited to play with you."

Elsa's taller than Sophie remembers; she has quite a few inches on Sophie, but she doesn't use them to loom. Her hair is blonder and her eyes are bluer and maybe it's because it's been five years since they last saw each other or maybe Sophie's memory didn't do the woman justice.

Sophie wants to ask if Elsa really switched to left wing in hopes of playing with her one day. And she wants to confess that she almost went to the SHL instead of the NAHL so they could be in the same league if not on the same team. It seems too personal for a first meeting.

"I'm more excited," Elsa says in accented, but understandable, English. She sticks her tongue out, teasing.

"I bet you aren't." Sophie's never met a competition she didn't want to win, and this isn't an exception. She already has apartment listings bookmarked on her computer and a list of her favorite restaurants to take Elsa to when she's here.

Elsa laughs, big and loud, and drapes an arm over Sophie's shoulders again. Sophie leans into the touch. "Come do interviews with me."

"Okay." Sophie schools her smile into something more subdued for the media. "Let's do this."

Elsa frowns and touches the corner of Sophie's mouth, a question Sophie doesn't answer. She leads them to where Rickers and *GSSN* are set up so she can ease Elsa into the process. If they're lucky, Marty Owen's plane was delayed and he didn't make it.

LATER, AFTER GABRIELLE Gagnon is drafted eleventh overall by Quebec and Sophie learns that Elsa's accent thickens when she doesn't want to answer questions, Dima finds them. Elsa's knocking back her third Gatorade of the hour which leaves Sophie unattended and unprotected. Dima wraps her up in a big hug and lifts her off her feet.

He spins her around and plants a kiss on her cheek for the cameras. Then, only for her, he says, "Two women drafted. You good enough, yes?"

He sets her down on her feet and she turns so she can hug him back. "Looks like I was."

Acknowledgements

Writing a novel is a labor of love and patience and something I could not have done without an extensive and incredible support network.

Thank you to my parents who have believed in me since the beginning.

To my sister Courtney who encouraged me to begin this series.

To my sister Casey who read every single word of every terrible first draft and kept pushing me to write more.

To my friends and fellow writers, Lis and Ray, for all their critiques, emoji reactions, and allowing me to drag them to a hockey game.

And finally, a thank you to the Steve Dangle Podcast, both for the hockey content, and because Steve, Adam, and Jesse have been a constant inspiration to find what you love in life and pursue it wholeheartedly.

About the Author

K.R. Collins went to college in Pennsylvania where she learned to write and fell in love with hockey. When she isn't working or writing, she watches hockey games and claims it's for research.

Twitter: @kcollins1394

Also Available from NineStar Press

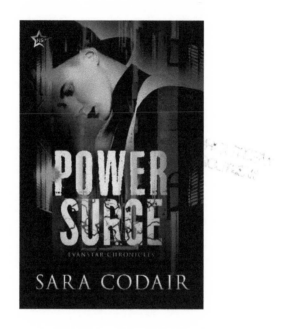

Connect with NineStar Press

www.ninestarpress.com

www.facebook.com/ninestarpress

www.facebook.com/groups/NineStarNiche

www.twitter.com/ninestarpress

www.tumblr.com/blog/ninestarpress

CPSIA information can be obtained
at www.ICGtesting.com
Printed in the USA
LVHW111202050619
620111LV00009B/34/P

9 781950 412341